International Acclaim for Bernhard Schlink's

FLIGHTS *of* LOVE

"Powerful. . . . Admirable . . . [Schlink displays] a deft handling of moral dilemmas, a tender generosity toward his characters and a sense of the past weighing heavily on the present."
—*Newsday*

"Striking. . . . Like *The Reader,* the tales have a surface smoothness that conceals a fierce moral kick." —*New York*

"Provocative. . . . Schlink is a sophisticated and conscious artist who combines questing scepticism and romantic expectation. . . . His writing . . . is grounded in unvarnished observation and often spiced with irony and wit."
—*The Times Literary Supplement*

"If there is a renaissance in the art of storytelling, this is it."
—*Der Spiegel*

"[*Flights of Love*] will delight and surprise Schlink's admirers while converting his critics. It has a humour, lightness of touch, beguiling candour and subtle irony. . . . *Flights of Love* is rich, honest and human. It is also as diverse as life itself." —*Irish Times*

BERNHARD SCHLINK

FLIGHTS *of* LOVE

Bernhard Schlink was born in Germany. He
is the author of the internationally bestselling
novel *The Reader*, as well as four prize-winning
crime novels—*The Gordian Knot, Self Deception,
Self-Administered Justice, and Self Slaughter*. He
is a professor at the Benjamin Cardozo School of
Law at Yeshiva University in New York. He lives
in Bonn and Berlin.

INTERNATIONAL

FLIGHTS

of

LOVE

S T O R I E S

———

BERNHARD SCHLINK

Translated from the German
by John E. Woods

VINTAGE INTERNATIONAL
Vintage Books
A Division of Random House, Inc.
New York

FIRST VINTAGE INTERNATIONAL OPEN-MARKET EDITION,
AUGUST 2002

The Library of Congress has cataloged the Pantheon edition as follows:
Schlink, Bernhard.
[Liebesfluchten. English]
Flights of love : stories / Bernhard Schlink ; translated from the German by
John E. Woods.
p. cm.
Contents: Girl with lizard—A little fling—The other man—Sugar peas—
The circumcision—The son—The woman at the gas station.
ISBN 0-375-42090-8
I. Woods, John E. (John Edwin). II. Title.
PT2680.L54 L5413 2001
833'.914—dc21
2001031399

Vintage Open-Market ISBN: 1-4000-3199-0

Book design by Trina Stahl

www.vintagebooks.com

Printed in the United States of America
10 9 8 7 6 5 4 3 2 1

CONTENTS

FLIGHTS

of

LOVE

GIRL WITH LIZARD

1

IT WAS A painting of a girl with a lizard. They were looking at each other and not looking at each other, the girl
gazing dreamily toward the lizard, the lizard directing its
vacant, glistening eyes toward the girl. Because the girl's
thoughts were somewhere else, she was holding so still
that even the lizard sat motionless on the moss-grown
rock, on which the girl lay half leaning, half stretched out
on her stomach. The lizard lifted its head and probed
with its tongue.

"That Jewish girl," the boy's mother said whenever
she spoke of the girl in the painting. When his parents
argued and his father got up to retreat to his study where
the painting was hung, she would call after him, "Go pay
your Jewish girl a visit!" Or she would ask, "Does the
painting of that Jewish girl have to hang there? Does
the boy have to sleep under the painting of that Jewish

girl?" The painting hung above a couch where the boy napped at noontime, while his father read the paper.

More than once he had heard his father explain to his mother that the girl was not Jewish. That the red velvet cap she wore, pressed so firmly down into her brown curls that they almost hid it, wasn't meant to suggest her religion, wasn't a folk costume but a matter of fashion. "It's what girls wore back then. Besides, it's the Jewish men who wear caps, not the women."

The girl wore a dark red skirt, and over her bright yellow blouse was a dark yellow vest, a kind of bodice loosely laced with ribbons at the back. The rock on which the girl rested her chin and plump childish arms hid much of her clothes and body. She might have been eight years old. The face was a child's face. But the eyes, the full lips, and the hair, which curled against the brow and fell to cover her back and shoulders, were not those of a child but of a woman. The shadow that her hair cast over her cheek and temple was a secret, and the darkness of the puffed sleeve into which the bare upper arm vanished, a temptation. Behind the rock and a sliver of beach, the sea stretched away to the horizon and surged into the foreground on rolling breakers; sunlight piercing the dark clouds left its luster on a patch of glistening sea and the girl's face and arms. Nature breathed passion.

Or was this ironic? The passion, the temptation, the secret, and the woman in the child? Was it the ambiguity in the painting that not only fascinated the boy, but also confused him? He was often confused. He was confused when his parents argued, when his mother asked her sarcastic questions and when his father smoked a cigar and read his paper, trying to look relaxed and superior, although the air in his study was so charged that the boy scarcely dared move or even breathe. And his mother's mocking words about the Jewish girl were confusing. The boy had no idea what a Jewish girl was.

2

FROM ONE DAY to the next, his mother stopped talking about the Jewish girl and his father put an end to the obligatory naps in the study. For a while the boy had to nap in the same room and same bed where he slept at night. Then there were no more naps at all. He was glad. He was nine and had been made to nap at noontime longer than any of his classmates or playmates.

But he missed the girl with the lizard. He would steal into his father's study to have a look at the painting and talk with the girl for a moment. He grew fast that year; at first his eyes were level with the gold frame, then with the rock, and later with the girl's eyes.

He was a strong boy, sturdily built, with large-boned limbs. As he shot up, there was nothing touching about his awkwardness; instead it was somehow threatening. His schoolmates were afraid of him, even when he was on their side in games, arguments, and fights. He was an outsider. He knew that himself, although he did not know that it was his appearance, his height, broad shoulders, and strength, that made him one. He thought it was the world inside him, with which he coexisted and in which he lived. None of his schoolmates shared it with him. But, then, he did not invite any of them in, either. Had he been a delicate child, he might have found playmates, soul mates, among other delicate children. But they especially were intimidated by him.

His inner world was populated not only with the figures from his reading or from pictures and films, but also with people from the outside world, though in ever-changing disguises. He could tell when there was a discrepancy between what seemed to be going on in the external world and whatever lay behind it. That his piano teacher was holding something back, that the friendliness of the beloved family doctor was not genuine, that a neighbor boy with whom he played was hiding something— he felt it long before the disclosure of the boy's petty thefts, of the doctor's fondness for little boys, or of the piano teacher's illness. To be sure, he was no more acute than others, or quicker to intuit exactly what it was that was not evident. Nor did he investigate it. He preferred making things up, and his inventions were always more colorful and exciting than reality.

The distance between his inner and outer world corresponded to the distance that the boy noticed between his family and other people. Certainly, his father, a judge of the municipal court, lived life to the full. The boy was aware that his father enjoyed the importance and visibility of his position, liked joining the regular table reserved for prominent citizens in the local restaurant, liked playing a role in local politics and being elected to the presbytery of his congregation. His parents took part in the town's social life. They attended the carnival ball and the summer gala, were invited out, and asked guests to dine at their home. The boy's birthdays were celebrated in proper style, with five guests at his fifth birthday, six at his sixth, and so forth. Indeed, everything was done in proper style, which meant with the obligatory formality and distance of the 1950s. It was not this formality or distance that the boy perceived as the distance between his family and other people, but something else. It had to do with the way his parents themselves seemed to be holding back, hiding something. They were on their guard. If someone told a joke they did not immediately burst out laughing, but waited until others laughed. At a concert or a play they applauded only after others applauded first. In conversations with guests they kept their own opinion to themselves until others had expressed the same thing and they could then second it. If sometimes his father could not avoid taking a position or expressing an *opinion*, *the* strain of it showed.

Or was his father merely being tactful, *trying not to* interfere or seem obtrusive? The boy asked himself that question as he grew older and began more consciously to observe his parents' caution. He also asked himself why it was that his parents insisted on their own space. He was not allowed to enter his parents' bedroom, had not been even as a small child. Granted, they did not lock their door. But the prohibition was absolutely clear, and their authority remained unchallenged—that is, until the boy was thirteen and, one day when his parents were out, he opened the door and saw two separate beds, two night stands, two chairs, one wooden and one metal wardrobe. Were his parents trying to hide the fact that they did not share a bed? Did they want to inculcate in him the meaning of privacy and a respect for it? After all, they never entered his room, either, without first knocking and waiting for him to invite them in.

3

THE BOY WAS not forbidden to enter his father's study— even though it contained a mystery, the painting of the girl with the lizard.

But when he was in the eighth grade, a teacher assigned as homework the description of a picture. The choice of pictures was left to the students. "Do I have to bring the picture I describe with me?" one student asked. The teacher waved the question aside. "Your description should be so good that just by reading *it we can see the picture.*" It was obvious to the boy that he would describe the painting of the girl with the lizard. He was looking forward to it, to examining the painting in detail, to translating the painting into words and sentences, to reading his description of the painting to his teacher and classmates. He was also looking forward to sitting in his father's study. It looked out on a narrow courtyard that muted the daylight and sounds from the street. Its walls were lined with bookcases, and the spicy, acrid odor of cigar smoke hung in the air.

His father hadn't come home for lunch, his mother had left for town immediately afterward. So the boy asked no one for permission, but sat down in his father's study, looked, and wrote. "The painting shows the sea, in front of it a beach, in front of that a rock or a dune, and on it a girl and a lizard." No, the teacher had said the description of a painting moves from the foreground to the middle distance to the background. "In the foreground of the painting are a girl and a lizard on a rock or a dune, in the middle distance is a beach, and from the middle distance to the background is the sea." Is the sea? Rolls the sea? But the sea didn't roll from the middle distance to the background, it rolled from the background toward the middle distance. Besides, middle distance sounded ugly, and foreground and background didn't sound much better. And the girl—was her being in the foreground everything there was to say about her?

The boy started over. "The painting shows a girl. She is looking at a lizard." But that still wasn't everything there was to say about the girl. The boy went on. "The girl has a pale face and pale arms, brown hair, and is dressed in a bright-colored top and a dark skirt." That didn't satisfy him either. He gave it another try. "In this painting a girl is looking at a lizard sunning itself." Was that true? Was the girl looking at the lizard? Wasn't she looking past it, through it, instead? The boy hesitated. But suddenly it made no difference. Because the next sentence followed from the first. "The girl is very beautiful." That sentence was true, and with it the description likewise began to ring true.

"The painting shows a girl looking at a lizard sunning itself. The girl is very beautiful. She has a delicate face with a smooth brow, straight nose, and a dimple in her upper lip. She has brown eyes and brown curly hair. The painting is really only of the girl's head. All the rest, comprising the lizard, the rock or dune, the beach, and the sea, is not so important."

The boy was satisfied. Now all he had to do was to place everything in the foreground, middle distance, and background. He was proud of "comprising." It sounded elegant and adult. He was proud of the girl's beauty.

When he heard his father closing the front door, he stayed seated. He heard him put down his briefcase, remove and hang up his coat, look first in the kitchen and living room, and then knock on his bedroom door.

"I'm in here," he called, squaring the scribbled pages on top of his notebook and laying his fountain pen alongside. That was how his father kept files, papers, and pens on the desk. When the door opened he immediately started to explain. "I'm sitting here because we've been assigned the description of a picture, and I'm describing this painting here."

It took his father a moment to reply. "What painting? What're you doing?"

The boy explained again. From the way his father was standing there, scowling as he looked at him and the painting, he knew that he had done something wrong. "Since you weren't here, I thought . . ."

"You thought——" his father said in a choked voice, and the boy thought the voice threatened to become a yell and flinched. But his father did not yell. He shook his head and sat down on the swivel chair between the desk and a table that he used for stacking files and on the other side of which the boy was sitting. The painting hung beside the desk, behind his father. The boy hadn't dared sit at the desk. "Would you like to read for me what you've written?"

The boy read it aloud, proud and anxious at the same time.

"It's very well written, my boy. I could see every detail of the painting. But . . . ," he hesitated, "it's not for other people. You should describe a different picture for them."

The boy was so happy that his father hadn't yelled at him, but had instead spoken to him in confidence and with affection, that he was willing to do anything. But he did not understand. "Why isn't the painting something for other people?"

"Don't you keep things just to yourself sometimes, too? Do you want us or your friends to be part of everything you do? If only because people are envious, it's best not to show them your treasures. Either it makes them sad because they don't have them, or they turn greedy and want to take them away from you."

"Is this painting a treasure?"

"You know that yourself. You just described it beautifully, the way only a beautiful treasure is described."

"I mean is it so valuable that it would make people envious?"

His father turned around and looked at the painting. "Yes, it's worth a great deal, and I don't know if I could protect it if people wanted to steal it. Wouldn't it be better if they didn't even know we have it?"

The boy nodded.

"Come, let's look at a book of paintings together. We're sure to find one you like."

4

WHEN THE BOY turned fourteen his father resigned from the bench and took a job with an insurance company. He didn't want to do it—the boy could tell that, although his father didn't complain. But neither did his father explain why he changed jobs. The boy didn't find that out until years later. One result of the change was that they had to give up their old apartment for a new one. Instead of occupying the fashionable second floor of a four-story turn-of-the-century town house, they now lived on the edge of town in a twenty-four-unit apartment house, built with subsidies from a government program, according to its norms. The four rooms were small, the ceilings low, and the sounds and smells of neighbors ever present. But at least there were four rooms; in addition to a living room and two bedrooms, there was a study for his father. Come evening, he would retreat to it, even though he no longer brought files home from work.

"You can drink in the living room just as well," the boy heard his mother say to his father one evening, "and maybe you'd drink less if you exchanged a word with me sometimes."

His parents' way of life changed too. There were no more dinners and evenings for ladies and gentlemen, when the boy would open the door for guests and take their coats. He missed the atmosphere of the dining room, the table set with white china and adorned with silver candelabra, his parents putting out glasses, pastries, cigars, and ashtrays in the living room, awaiting the first ring of the doorbell. He missed several of his parents' friends. Some would ask how he was doing in school and what interests he had, and they'd remember his answers on their next visit and keep track. A surgeon had discussed operations on teddy bears with him, and a geologist had talked about volcano eruptions, earthquakes, and shifting sand dunes. He especially missed one woman friend of his parents. Unlike his slender, nervous, volatile mother, she was a plump woman of sunny temperament. In winter when he was still small, she would sweep him in under her fur coat, into the shimmering caress of its silk lining and the overwhelming scent of her perfume. Later she had teased him about conquests he had not made, about girlfriends he did not have—leaving him both embarrassed and proud. And even in later years, when she sometimes made a game of pulling him to her and wrapping them both in her fur coat, he had enjoyed the softness of her body.

It was a long time before new guests came. These were neighbors, colleagues of his father from the insurance company, colleagues of his mother, who was now working as a police department secretary. The boy noticed that his parents seemed uncertain; they wanted to find their way into their new world without denying the old, and acted either too cool or too intimate.

The boy had to adjust as well. His parents had him transferred from his old high school, just a few steps from their old home, to one that again was not very far from their new apartment. And so his way of life changed too. The tone in his new school was coarser, and he was less of an outsider than he had been in the old one. For another year, he still took piano lessons from the teacher who lived near his old home. Then his parents said he was making such wretched progress that they ended the lessons and sold the piano. The bike rides to see his piano teacher had been precious to him, for he would pass his old apartment and a neighboring building where a girl lived that he used to walk partway to school and play with now and then. She had thick red curly hair down to her shoulders and a face full of freckles. He rode slowly past her building, hoping she would step outside and say hello, and then he would walk his bike alongside her, and they would, of course, end up seeing each other again. They wouldn't exactly make a date, but it would be clear when he would find her where and vice versa. She was far too young for a real date.

But she never came out of the building when he rode by.

5

IT IS A mistake to believe that people only make decisions about their lives once they are, or have, grown up. Children take actions and adopt attitudes with the same decisiveness as adults. They don't stay with their decisions forever, but then adults cast aside decisions about their lives too.

A year later the boy decided to be somebody in his new school and circumstances. He was strong enough to have no trouble earning respect, and since he was also clever and inventive, he soon became part of a hierarchy, which in his as in every school class was defined by an amorphous mix of strength, impudence, wit, and parental affluence. These things counted with the girls, too—not in his own school, which had no girls, but in the girls' high school a couple of blocks away.

The boy did not fall in love. He picked out a girl who was popular and provocatively attractive, quick with a smart remark, and who allowed herself to be known as having had experience with boys, but also was hard to get. He impressed her with his strength, with the respect he was shown—and the fact that there was something more. She didn't know what this "more" was, but there was something she hadn't found in other boys, and this she wanted to see and to have. He noticed, and would occasionally drop a hint that he had treasures he didn't show to just anyone, but that he might show to her if . . . if she would go steady with him? Neck with him? Sleep with him? He didn't exactly know himself. His public pursuit of her, to which she yielded increasingly, was more interesting, brought him greater rewards and prestige, than what actually happened between them. Sauntering with friends past the girls' high school, where she and her group would sometimes be leaning against the iron gate after classes, and where he would casually put his arm around her, or waving to her if her team was playing handball and getting a kiss blown in return, or crossing the grass on the way to the swimming pool with her, admired and envied—that was the thing.

When they finally did sleep together it was a disaster. She was experienced enough to have certain expectations, but not enough to deal with his awkwardness. He lacked the assurance that comes with love and makes up for the clumsiness of the first time. Once the swimming pool had closed and the guard had made his rounds, and they were together behind the bushes near the fence, it suddenly seemed all wrong to him—the kisses, the tenderness, the desire. Nothing was right. It was a betrayal of everything he loved and had loved—he thought of his mother, of her friend in the fur coat, of the neighbor girl with the red curls and freckles, and of the girl with the lizard. When it was all over—the embarrassment of dealing with the condom, his orgasm which had happened far too fast, his inept and merely irritating attempts to satisfy her with his hand—he cuddled up to her, seeking consolation for his own failure. She stood up, dressed, and left. He lay there in a huddle, staring at the trunk of the bush he was lying under, at last year's leaves, at his underwear and the mesh of the fence. It turned dark. He went on lying there even though he was cold now; as if he could somehow shiver away his being with her, pursuing her, struggling conceitedly to win her these past few months, the way you sweat out an illness. Finally he got up and swam a few laps in the main pool.

When he came home around midnight, the door to the lighted study was open. His father was lying on the couch, snoring and reeking of alcohol. A bookcase had been overturned, and the drawers of the desk were open and empty; the floor was strewn with books and papers. The boy made sure the painting hadn't been damaged, turned out the light, and closed the door.

6

WHEN SCHOOL was almost over and he was just waiting for diplomas to be handed out, he took a trip to the nearest large city. It was an hour and a half by train, a trip he could have taken at any time all those years for a concert, a play, an art exhibition, but had never done so. When he was small, his parents had once taken him along and shown him the churches, the town hall, the courthouse, and the large park in the center of the city. After their move, his parents did not travel anymore, whether with or without him, and at first it had never occurred to him to travel alone. Later he couldn't afford it. His father lost his job because of his drinking, and the boy had to work as well as go to school, handing over any money he earned. Now that he was graduating and would soon leave town, he was beginning to separate from his parents. And he now wanted to spend what he earned.

He wasn't looking for the museum of modern art, but found it by chance. He went in because the building fascinated him with its strange mixture of modern simplicity on the one hand and inhospitable, cavelike gloominess on the other, while the doors and oriels were playfully kitschy. The collection ranged from the Impressionists to the New Savages, and he looked at it all with proper attentiveness but little sympathy. Until he happened on the painting by René Dalmann.

At the Beach was the title, and it showed a rock, a sandy beach, and the sea. A girl, naked and beautiful, was doing a handstand on the rock, but one of her legs was made of wood—not a wooden leg, but a female leg of perfectly grained wood. No, he neither recognized the girl doing the handstand as the girl with the lizard nor could he say that it was the same rock, the same beach, the same sea. But it all reminded him so powerfully of the painting at home that he bought a postcard as he left and, had he had more money, would have bought a book on René Dalmann. When he compared the two at home, the differences between painting and postcard were obvious. And yet there was something that linked them—was it merely in the eye of the beholder or in the paintings themselves?

"What have you got there?" His father entered the room and reached for the postcard.

The boy stepped aside and let his father grab at thin air. "Who painted our painting?"

His father's gaze turned cautious. He'd been drinking, and it was the same caution with which he reacted to the rejection and open disdain his wife and son showed him whenever he was sloshed. They had long ago lost any fear of him. "I don't know—why?"

"Why haven't we sold the painting if it's so valuable?"

"Sold? We can't sell the painting!" His father took up a position in front of the painting as if to protect it from his son.

"Why can't we?"

"Then we wouldn't have anything. And you'd get nothing when I'm gone. It's for you that we're keeping the painting, for you." Delighted by an argument that would surely persuade his son, his father repeated it, and then again. "Mother and I are turning ourselves inside out to be sure you'll get the painting someday. And what do I get in return? Ingratitude, nothing but ingratitude."

The boy left his whining father standing there and forgot the whole incident, the picture in the museum, and René Dalmann. Besides working in the warehouse of a tractor factory, he moonlighted as a waiter until the beginning of the semester, and then left to study as far from home as possible. The city on the Baltic was ugly and its university mediocre. But nothing there reminded him of his hometown in the south. In his first weeks he realized, much to his relief, that he recognized no one in his law courses, or in the cafeteria, or in the halls. He could start all over again.

He had made one stop on his way there. He had only a few hours to walk through the city by the river. Again it was purely by chance that he found the museum. But once inside, chance was not enough, and he asked right away for pictures by René Dalmann, and found two of them. *Order Restored after War* was five by six and a half feet high and showed a woman sitting on the ground, head bent forward, legs drawn up, propping herself on her left arm. With her right hand she was pushing a drawer back into her abdomen; her breasts and belly were drawers as well, with nipples as knobs for the one and her navel as the pull for the other. The drawers at her breasts and stomach were slightly open and empty, but beneath them in the abdomen drawer lay a dead soldier, twisted and mutilated. The other painting was entitled *Self-Portrait as Woman* and showed the bust of a smiling young man with a shaved head; the outline of breasts was visible beneath his buttoned-up black jacket, and in his left hand he held up a blond, curly wig.

This time he bought a book on René Dalmann, and on the train he read about the childhood and youth of the artist, who was born in Strasbourg in 1894. Both the father, a textile merchant who had left Leipzig for Strasbourg, and his Alsatian wife, twenty years his junior, had wanted a daughter; they already had two sons, and a third child, a daughter, had died two years previously after her father had taken her for a winter ride and she had come down with pneumonia. René grew up in the shadow of his dead sister, until in 1902 the second daughter so longed for arrived—a liberation and a humiliation in one. He started drawing and painting early on, could not keep up in school, but at age sixteen applied successfully for the art academy in Karlsruhe.

Then the trip was over. He found a room, a garret with a coal stove and a little window; the toilet with a tiny sink was a half-flight down the stairs. But he was on his own. He moved his things in and put the book on René Dalmann on a bottom shelf along with other favorites. The top shelves were to be for new books, for his new life. He had left nothing he cared about at home.

7

HIS FATHER DIED during his third year at the university. As was increasingly his father's habit in the last few years, he had gone to drink at a bar. He tripped on his way home, fell down an embankment, and froze to death lying there. The funeral was his first visit home since he had left for the university. It was January, the wind piercing cold, the puddles on the path to the cemetery chapel frozen, and after having slipped and almost fallen, his mother accepted his arm, which she had previously refused to do. She didn't want to forgive him for not having visited for so long.

At home she had made little sandwiches and tea for the few neighbors who had joined them at the cemetery. When she realized that the guests were expecting alcohol to be served she stood up. "Anyone who's offended because I'm not offering beer or schnapps can leave right now. There's been enough drinking in this house."

That evening mother and son entered his father's study. "I think they're all law books. Do you want them? Can you use them? What you don't take I'll throw out." She left him alone. He examined the library his father had made such a to-do about—books long since revised, periodicals discontinued years before. The only picture was the girl with the lizard. In the old apartment it had had the entire wall above the couch to itself, but here it was hung between two bookcases—and still it dominated the room. His head almost brushed the low ceiling, so that he looked down at the girl now, but he remembered how they had once stood eye to eye. He thought of Christmas trees, how they used to be so tall and were so small now. But then he thought of how the painting had not grown smaller, had lost none of its power to enthrall him. And he thought of the little girl in the house where he had his garret, and blushed. He called her "Princess," and they flirted with each other, and when she asked him if she wouldn't like to show her his room, he had summoned all his willpower and said no. She had asked in all innocence. But because she wanted something he didn't want to give, she flirted with him so openly, her voice and glances and body language were so seductive that he all but forgot the innocence.

"I don't want Father's books. But I'll call a used-book dealer tomorrow. He'll give you several hundred or a thousand marks." He sat down at the kitchen table with his mother. "What do you plan to do with the painting?"

She folded up the newspaper she'd been reading. Her gestures were still nervous and volatile, yet with something youthful about them. She was no longer slender, but gaunt, the skin stretched tight over the bones of her face and hands. Her hair was almost white.

He was suddenly filled with sympathy and tenderness. "What do you intend to do?" he asked gently and tried to lay his hand on hers, but she drew hers away.

"I'm moving out. They've built a couple of terraced

apartments on the slope, and I bought myself a studio there. I don't need more than one room."

"Bought?"

She cast him a hostile look. "I always pooled your father's pension and my earnings, and took out the same amount for myself that he drank up. Do you have any objection?"

"No." He laughed. "Father drank up a studio apartment in just ten years?"

His mother laughed with him. "Not quite. But more than the down payment I saved up."

He hesitated. "Why did you stay with Father?"

"What a question." She shook her head. "For a while you have a choice. Do you want to do this or that, live with this person or that? But one day what it is you're doing and that person have become your life, and to ask why you stick with your life is a rather stupid question. But you asked about the painting. I don't plan to do anything with it. Take it with you or put it in the bank, if they have lockboxes that big."

"Tell me what's the story with the painting?"

"Oh, my boy . . ." She looked at him sadly. "I'd rather not. I think your father was proud of the painting, to the end." She gave him a weary smile. "He would so much have liked to visit you and see how you were doing with your law studies, but he didn't dare. You never invited us. You know, you children are no less cruel than we parents were. You're more self-righteous, that's all."

He wanted to protest, but did not know if she was right or not. "I'm sorry," he said, dodging the issue.

She stood up. "Sleep tight, my boy. I'll be out of the house by seven. Sleep as long as you want before you leave, but don't forget the painting."

8

HE HUNG the picture over his bed in the garret. The bed stood against the left wall, on the right were his wardrobe and bookcase, and at the front, under the dormer, his desk.

"I look a lot like her. Who is she?" The girl who asked was a student he had taken a liking to in his first semester. Because of her resemblance to the girl in the painting? He hadn't been aware of it.

"I don't know who she is. Or whether she's anybody, really." He wanted to add, "But in any case you're more beautiful." But then he didn't want to be unfaithful to the girl with the lizard. Can you be unfaithful to a girl in a painting?

"What do you think?"

"That you're beautiful."

She was very beautiful. He was lying on his back on the bed, she was lying on top of him, her arms across his chest and her chin propped on her arms as she gazed calmly into his eyes. Or was she looking past him, through him? Her dark eyes and hair, her high brow, the fresh blush on her cheeks, the curve of her nostrils and lips—she was, in all her beauty, attuned to him and yet peculiarly caught up in herself. Or was he just imagining this? Would the woman he loved, just because he loved her, become the painting? Attuned to him and yet unattainable at the same time?

"Who's the painter?"

"I don't know."

"He must have signed his painting." She sat up and closely examined the lower edge of the painting. Then she looked at him. "Gosh, it's an original!"

"Yes."

"Do you know what it's worth?"

"No."

"Maybe it's valuable. Where did you get it?"

He thought of the conversation he'd had with his father years before. "Come here." He spread his arms. "I don't want to know if it's valuable. If I knew it was and told you so, then you'd know that it is, and I'd have to keep asking myself if you love me because of my painting."

She fell into his arms. "Don't be silly. If it's valuable you can't keep it here. It's too hot in the summer and too cold in the winter, and besides, your stupid stove will set the roof and the whole house on fire someday, and maybe you'll be able to escape to the next roof, but the painting will burn up. A valuable painting needs the same constant temperature and humidity and who knows what all. And since you can't keep it here, you might as well sell it. You work and work and never buy anything for yourself, because you don't have any money. That doesn't make any sense."

To divert her he told her about his new job. But as she was leaving, she asked, "You know what?"

"What?"

"My brother is studying art history. He ought to have a look at the painting."

He didn't let it come to that. Before her next visit he shoved the painting under the bed and told her that his mother had wanted it back. But she still had a talk with her brother, who could think of no similar painting or painter who fit her description of it, but did make a connection to the magazine *Lézard violet*, ten issues of which had been published in Paris between 1924 and 1930, during the transition from Dadaism to Surrealism. Then she forgot about the painting.

Whenever she left, he would hang it again over his bed. At first it was a game; he took the painting down with a smile and hung it back up with a smile, saying good-bye to the girl and greeting her with some passing joke. Then he got tired of taking the painting down because the other girl was coming, then of her coming at all. After they had made love and were lying side by side again, he would wait for her to leave, so that he could rehang the picture and take up life where he had left off.

Finally she left him. "I don't know what goes on in

your head or your heart." She tapped his forehead, then his chest. "There's probably room in there for me somewhere. But it's too small."

9

It HURT more than he had expected. He felt angry at times—perhaps everything would have turned out differently and better without the painting. But his anger also bound him to the painting. He talked to the girl. How he'd be better off without her. What a mess she'd got him into. It wouldn't hurt her to look at him with a friendlier eye now. And was she proud of having successfully driven her rival from the field? She had no reason to brag.

One evening he picked up the book on René Dalmann and read some more. After completing work at the academy, the young artist lived in the house of a rich widow from Karlsruhe who set up a studio for him. In so proper a provincial capital that meant a scandal, which, according to his biographer, they both enjoyed more than they did their troubled relationship. He tried to establish himself as a portrait painter, and his first portraits were conventional enough, until, accused of leading a scandalous life, he began to paint scandalous portraits—the chief justice of the Karlsruhe High Court with his bureaucrat's skull carved out of wood, and the man's son, a dashing lieutenant, with epaulettes, shoulder braid, and a saber in the middle of his face. The chief justice filed suit, which René Dalmann evaded by departing for Brittany, where, with his parents and siblings, he had spent many a vacation in a house owned by his mother's family, most of whom had fled Alsace in 1871. He remained there until the outbreak of the war, in which he served as a volunteer in the French medical corps. These were the years of his sketches; he had neither time nor money for anything else. Besides wounded, maimed, and dying soldiers, there were also religious motifs—Adam and Eve as a bridal couple lost in a battlefield Paradise, the healing of a crippled soldier by a crippled Christ. After the war, he lived in Paris and spent a good deal of his time in the Café Certá—though he never joined the Dadaists—and with André Breton, who won him over to the Communist Party, but could not persuade him to join the Surrealists. He held himself apart, until he founded the *Lézard violet* with a few friends. René Magritte contributed an article on painting as thinking, Salvador Dali one on how they sliced the girl's eye, and, without the author's permission, the periodical printed an English translation of a short essay on collectivism that Max Beckmann had written on his honeymoon. René Dalmann himself wrote about liberating the imagination from the grip of the arbitrary and was in charge of the magazine's graphic design.

He found all this only moderately interesting. Finally he gave up reading and merely browsed. At the end of the book were a few pages of a chronology of René Dalmann's life, a bibliography, including works by him, and a list of his exhibitions. This contained an entry for an exhibition called "*Est-ce qu'il y a un surréalisme allemand?*" shown by the Galerie Colle in Paris in 1933, with a note that the catalog cover was *Lizard and Girl* by René Dalmann. Lizard and girl.

The next morning he went to the university's art history institute and looked in vain for a copy of the 1933 catalog. He cut his lectures, called in sick with the flu at the restaurant where he was supposed to wait tables at lunch time, and took a train to the city, where he saw René Dalmann's self-portrait and postwar paintings and bought the book about him. There was a university in the city as well and an art history institute, but there was no catalog here either. By now he was in a state of feverish excitement. The librarian noticed and asked him what was wrong. He explained that he was searching for René Dalmann's *Lizard and Girl* and couldn't find a catalog that had the painting on its cover. Where might the next nearest art history institute be?

"Why does it have to be the catalog cover?"

He stared in incomprehension.

"Presumably he photographed his painting himself, as did his gallerist, the press, and the museum where it hangs."

"You think it's hanging in a museum? Where?"

"We have a photo archive. Come with me."

He followed her down a long corridor to a room with a projector and boxes labeled with names. He grew calmer.

He even noticed the librarian's nice figure and light step and the way she was observing his excitement with a cheerful glance of well-intentioned mockery. She pulled a box from the shelf, studied a list pasted to the inside of the lid, selected a slide almost the size of a postcard and framed in black foil, and slipped it into the projector. "Would you get the light?"

He found the switch and darkened the room. She turned on the projector.

"My God," he said. It was his painting. The girl, the beach, the rock. But leaning into view from the left wasn't the girl, but a giant lizard, and it wasn't the lizard sunning on the rock but a tiny girl, adorable, with dark curls and pale face, bright bodice and dark skirt. She lay on one side, her head on her arm, half kittenish child, half seductive woman.

10

"WHAT MUSEUM is the painting in?"

"We'll have to look up front." The librarian turned off the projector, put the slide back in its box, and returned to the reference room. He watched her take one or two volumes from the shelf and thumb through them. "Will this at least earn me an invitation to dinner?" She went on paging. "Oh!"

"What is it?"

"The painting isn't in a museum. It's missing. Missing and maybe even destroyed. It was last seen in 1937 at the exhibition of 'Degenerate Art' in Munich." He looked blank.

"It was shown in Group Five. Here's what they said: 'Pornography needs no nakedness, and degeneration needs no distortion of the painter's craft. With perfect brush strokes, the Jew can present the German entrepreneur as a capitalist wastrel and a German maiden as a lewd harlot. Filthiness and the Marxist fondness for class warfare go hand in hand for Jews. When one realizes that German mothers and women will also attend this exhibition . . .' Should I go on?"

"Is there also a painting by René Dalmann called *Girl with Lizard*?"

She paged. "How about dinner?"

"When are you through here?"

"At four."

"But there won't be any dinner then."

"And there won't be any girl with a lizard to be had either. Are you sure that's the title?"

"No." His father and mother had called the painting that, so had he. René Dalmann might have called it something else. "But it shows a girl and a lizard, just the opposite of what we just saw."

"Interesting. Where did you see it?"

"Oh, I don't remember." He had not been paying attention, had gone too far. Had asked more than he should.

Luckily he hadn't mentioned his name. He would vanish without a trace.

She watched his mind race. "What's up with you?"

"I have to go. I'll be waiting for you at four downstairs, okay?"

He flew out of the institute, not caring how ridiculous he looked. But as he sat on a bench beside a lake in the center of town, it became clear to him just how much he didn't know and needed to learn. And so at four o'clock he was standing at the entrance to the art history institute. She came down the steps and again shot him that look of amiable mockery.

"Lizards are shy creatures."

"I think I need to explain some things. Would you like to sit in the sun by the lake?"

On the way there he began to tell her. As a law student he worked part-time for a lawyer whose specialty was wills and estates, disputes between heirs, locating heirs, evaluating heirlooms. Among the effects of a deceased American, a painting had shown up without attestation, without signature, perhaps of no value whatever, but perhaps worth a great deal, and he was to find out what he could about the painting.

"An American?"

He had spread out his jacket, and they were sitting on the lawn by the lake. "A German émigré whose heirs we're looking for in Germany."

"Do you have a reproduction of the painting."

"Not with me. I've got the painting down in my head well enough." He described it.

"Hey," she said with a sidelong glance, "you're really in love with that painting."

He blushed, turned his head away, pretending to watch a sailboat.

"It doesn't matter. If it's a Dalmann—he's amazing. Have you seen his paintings in our museum?" And she steered the conversation to the museum and the city and life in the city and to where they both came from and what they wanted from life. He made attempts to ask his questions—how you determine who painted a painting, how you follow its fate, find its true owner. She responded to his questions, but saw to it that they soon slipped from her conversation again. As the sun vanished behind buildings, it turned cool, and they took a walk around the lake.

"Do you have a boyfriend?" He couldn't imagine that she didn't. She was vivacious, clever, witty, and was not only pretty, but also had a charming way of brushing her hair from her face and wrinkling her nose.

"We separated three months ago. And you?"

He counted. "Four."

They had dinner at a restaurant. He realized he wanted to fall in love, wanted to share with her, to trust her. But he had to watch every word and be evasive when talk turned to his parents, to the girlfriend who had left him, to women who attracted him, to the way he lived.

He could not become as intimate as he would have liked. It occurred to him that if they were to meet in his town and decided to go to his place, he could not ask her up to his room. The picture was hanging there.

She walked him to the train station. She wrote down her name, address, and telephone number for him there on the platform. He hesitated, but then jotted down his real name and address for her.

"You really don't want to become a detective, do you?" She had that look of amiable mockery in her eyes again.

"Why?"

"Just asking." She put her arms around his neck and gave him a quick kiss on the lips. "As for your questions— you take the painting to Sotheby's or Christie's. Or if you've read a book about the painter, like my little detective here, you check who the author is and write him in care of his publisher. That is, if you don't have something to hide, something no one must know about."

"The train's about to pull out." The loudspeaker had announced that the train was departing and the doors were closing. He was already standing on the train.

"Hiding things is exhausting."

He could only nod. The doors had closed.

11

"A DIFFICULT fate awaits you," he said to the girl with the lizard. "The lizard just keeps growing, and you keep getting smaller, and in the end you have to flirt with it. You, a girl—with a lizard." He went on, "Or did you kiss it so that it would turn into a prince, but instead it's just grown bigger, and you've got smaller?" He looked at the girl, and suddenly what René Dalmann had done seemed to him a rotten thing to do, a sacrilege. "Are you his sister? Did he hate you? Or love and hate you?"

He went downstairs to the toilet with its tiny sink, above which he had set a tiny shelf where he kept his toothbrush, shaving gear, comb, and brush. He twisted the blade out of the razor and returned to his room. "You're not going to like this. But I have to do it." Following the edge of the frame, he cut the paper pasted across the back of the painting. He discovered that the heavy gold frame was screwed to another frame on which the canvas was stretched. The screws were small, and to remove them he used the screwdriver he had for loose electrical connections. He was afraid the outer frame would stick to the canvas. But he was able to remove it easily.

He leaned the picture against the wall beside his bed and sat on the floor in front of it. He was no longer surprised to find "Dalmann" in the lower right corner, written in a childish, lightly slanted hand, the *D* ending in a broad flourish. He would have been amazed not to find it, or some other name, there. What surprised him was the impression the painting now made with the additional inches previously hidden by the frame. The extra sky above the girl's head, her elbow, the tip of which was no longer covered up, the lizard now visible in its entirety—suddenly the painting opened up chest and head, the way a fresh wind and the scent of water let you breathe freely at the shore.

"Did my father lock you up? Or was it whoever the painting belonged to before, maybe still belongs to? And who is or was that?" He examined the frame and found the label of an art dealer in Strasbourg.

On the train trip to his hometown he finished the biography of René Dalmann. In 1930, he followed Lydia Diakonov from Paris to Berlin. She was a cabaret artist, the daughter of a Jewish doctor who had converted to Orthodoxy, a creature of supple, enigmatic beauty. She was Dalmann's lizard, his Lydie and his lizzie. He wrote her letters of undiminishing tenderness. Given his name and the fact that he spoke German free of accent, he was immediately recognized and accepted as a German artist; Ludwig Justi dedicated one of the small rooms in the Crown Prince's Palace to him. In 1933, when his series *In the Streets: Dirty Dance Macabre* was shown at an exhibition in Karlsruhe titled "Government Art, 1918–1933," René Dalmann publicly made fun of the whole affair. German government art? He had painted the series in

Paris in 1928. But then Eberhard Hanfstaengel closed the Dalmann Room in Berlin, and Lydia's cabaret was smashed to smithereens one night by the SA. In 1937, even before the opening of the Munich exhibition of "Degenerate Art," René and Lydia Dalmann, who had married by then, left Germany for Strasbourg. Despite his French citizenship he continued to be regarded as a German artist. In 1938 his work was shown in London at an exhibition of "Twentieth Century German Art." There were exhibitions in Amsterdam and Paris of paintings of his that had been seized and then released for sale by the German authorities; these were then bought by sympathetic dealers and collectors.

With the entry of the Germans into Strasbourg, every trace of René and Lydia Dalmann vanished. Had they stayed, fled to unoccupied France or to the United States by way of Portugal? The biographer faithfully listed the pros and cons of each possibility, but avoided a definitive answer. Whatever they had done, it must have been under new names. In 1946, there was an exhibition in New York by a Ron Valomme of paintings whose style anticipated the New Savages, but whose content was indebted to the thematic issues of Dadaist Surrealism. Was Ron Valomme, as some critics suggested, the same person as René Dalmann? There was no reliable trace of Ron Valomme either.

He had no key to his mother's studio apartment. He sat down on the entrance step, stared at the cobblestone path that led from the apartments to the garage, at the evergreen shrubs planted on the slope, and at the roses his mother had planted beside the front door in an effort to counter the sterile atmosphere of the place. He thought about his father. He realized that he knew nothing about him, nothing about *his* parents, who had died in an air raid during the war, about his education, about his activities before and during the war or his career afterward.

12

"WHAT DID Father do during the war?" He was sitting on the terrace with his mother. She had returned from work and made tea. Her gaze moved over the roofs and out across the countryside.

She sighed. "Here we go."

"Here we go—nothing. What would be the point of my accusing or condemning my dead father? I want to know how my father came by a painting by René Dalmann, which, though I'm not exactly sure of its value, is surely worth hundreds of thousands. I want to know why he made such a secret of the painting."

"Because he was afraid someone would dispute his ownership. He was on the military court in Strasbourg, but when he found out that the people he was quartered with were Jews with forged papers, he helped them. The painting was their way of thanking him."

"So what was Father's problem?"

"The painter and his wife had vanished by war's end, and there were rumors. Your father was worried that if he were identified in any way with the painting, it would put him in a bad light. He couldn't prove that it was a gift."

He looked at his mother. She was sitting beside him, gazing in the other direction. "Mother?"

"Yes?" She didn't turn her face toward him.

"Were you with him there in Strasbourg? Did you see it all happen, or did Father tell you about it afterward?"

"How was I supposed to be with him or him with me in Strasbourg in the middle of the war?"

"Did you believe what Father told you?"

She still didn't turn toward him. He gazed at her profile, which betrayed no irritation, no anger, no sadness. "When he was released from prison by the French in 1948 and we saw each other again, I had other things to do than worry about his stories from the war. You can't imagine all the stories people brought back from the war."

"If you believed him—why did you always used to talk about 'that Jewish girl'?"

"You remember that?"

He didn't answer her question. "Why?"

"I thought the girl was the painter's daughter, and they were Jews."

"That doesn't explain your scorn." He shook his head. "No, you didn't believe Father. You didn't buy his story about helping Jews. Or you thought it wasn't the whole story and that there was something between him and the girl. Was he blackmailing her? Did he force her to have an affair with him? You knew that she was the painter's wife, is that it?"

She said nothing.

"Why did Father lose his job as a judge?" He turned to look at her. She had thrust out her chin and pursed her lips, and he could see she was refusing to answer his question. "Would it be any better if I asked his colleagues or supervisors from those days? I'm sure I'll find someone who'll understand why, as a future lawyer, I want to know what happened."

"He served on a military court. He had to be strict. He had to be hard. Do you think you win friends that way?"

"No, but it didn't disqualify him for a judgeship after the war."

"He was accused of something that wasn't true, but sounded so awful that he didn't want to subject himself— or you or me—to it."

He looked at her.

"They said he condemned an officer to death for having helped Jews escape the police. Since you think you have to know everything—the officer was his friend and they said he turned him in himself."

"Whoever made the accusation must have found witnesses or documents or reports. Did it become a big story in the press?"

"Not locally, but in the rest of the country. Around here people made sure the whole thing quickly vanished from the headlines."

He could check newspaper files and track down the journalist who had made the accusation and have a look at his evidence. Maybe he could also find out where his father had lived in Strasbourg and who else had been living in the house at the time. Were there lists of Jews from Strasbourg who had been transported to the death camps? Were there relatives of René Dalmann who might be worth talking to?

"What did Father say to the charges?" But no sooner had he asked than he didn't want to hear any more.

"That he and the officer plus another officer had helped a lot of Jews and that the one he condemned had had to be sacrificed so that they wouldn't all end up dead, especially the Jews who were in danger. And that it was all by dumb chance that he ended up presiding over the case and having to pronounce sentence."

He laughed. "So Father did everything right? And everyone else just misunderstood?"

13

HIS MOTHER offered him the couch for the night; because of her bad back she often just slept on the floor. But he declined; he couldn't bear the idea of sleeping on the sofa where his mother usually slept, with its smell of her and the hollows her body had made.

When he woke up in the middle of the night, he could sense her presence as strongly nonetheless as if he were lying on the sofa. He could smell her and hear her breathing. In the moonlight he saw her clothes neatly arranged on the arms, seat, and back of the chair. At times she would shift to the edge of the sofa in her sleep, and then light would fall on her face, and he could see her white hair and hard features. He knew that she had been a beautiful woman; he had once seen a photograph his father had taken of her on their honeymoon, coming toward him between hedges in a park, wearing a pale dress, walking quietly, a soft, surprised, happy look on her face. But he couldn't recall ever having seen her so happy or so soft, either with him or his father. Was the war to blame? Or events in Strasbourg? Had his father done things to her or to others that she could never forgive him for? But why had she been so hard on him, too? Because he was his father's son?

Sadness overwhelmed him. He felt sorry for his mother, his father, and himself, especially himself. The presence of his mother, of her clothes, her breath, her smell, it all still felt unpleasant to him, and at the same time it hurt him that he found it unpleasant. Why did he have no childhood memories of his mother's attention and tenderness? If only he had them, then he could recognize and love the woman from back then in the body present now.

The next morning she gave him a file. His father had put it together. He had collected the newspaper articles about his case, glued them on white paper, noting the source at the top of the page and filling the right margin with exclamation points and question marks to express approval or disagreement. For the most part he rejected what was reported, sometimes he even made corrections, like editorial marks on a manuscript. He had crossed out an error concerning his age, noting the change in the margin and providing his true age. He had corrected a false statement as to the dates of his service on the military court in Strasbourg, errors as to the rank of officers involved, an inaccurate account of the submission and rejection of an appeal for clemency, and a wrong date given for the execution of the officer he had sentenced to death. There was an especially large number of corrections in a long article from a major paper. This was followed by several pages entitled "Rebuttal," which his father had typed on a machine his son knew well. "It is incorrect that my service as a judge of the military court in Strasbourg began on 1 July 1943. Rather, it is correct to say . . ." And it went on like that for page after page. "It is incorrect that I wormed my way into the confidence of the accused and abused it in regard to his attempt to prevent Jews from being arrested. Rather, it is correct to say that I provided whatever help I could to the accused in his endeavors, warned him of impending peril, and continued to attempt to protect both him and said Jews despite the threat of my violating important duties at considerable peril to myself. It is incorrect that I pronounced a sentence of death out of selfish motives and with the intent of bending the law to the detriment of the accused. Rather, it is correct to say that, in view of the evidence and the law, I had no choice but to condemn the accused to death. It is incorrect that I illegally enriched myself with the property of Jews and in particular ordered that portable items with which said Jews fled or planned to flee be consigned to me for the purpose of illegally misappropriating them. Rather, it is correct to say that I had neither authority to dispose of Jewish property nor the duty to protect Jewish property interests and therefore could neither abuse my authority nor fail to fulfill said duty. It is incorrect that I . . ."

His mother watched him read. He asked her, "This rebuttal—do you know it?"

"Yes."

"Did the paper publish it? Did Father send it to them?"

"No. His lawyer didn't want him to."

"Did you?"

"Surely you don't believe your father consulted me."

"But what did you think of what he'd written? How would you have felt if it had been published?"

"What did I think?" She shrugged. "He weighed every sentence. They couldn't have used a single word of it to lay a trap for him."

"He copied paragraphs directly from the penal code. He copied them to demonstrate that he couldn't be punished. But it makes for appalling reading. It reads as if he would be willing to acknowledge everything, but insists he did nothing punishable by law. As if you admit you poisoned someone's food, but insist that you followed every line of the recipe in *The Joy of Cooking*—that's the way it reads."

She took the file, ordered the pages from left to right, snapped them in place, and closed the cover. "He'd grown very cautious. During the war things had been topsy-turvy enough to last him a lifetime. After the war he was cautious, for your and my sake as well. He was even cautious when he drank. You know how drunks are, there's something they're not supposed to say, they try to avoid it, then blast it out anyway. Your father never did that."

It sounded as if she was proud. Proud that her husband had at least never bragged about what he had done to her and others.

"Did he ever ask your forgiveness for what he'd done to you?"

"Ask my forgiveness?" She stared, dumbfounded.

He gave up. He realized she wasn't holding anything back from him, but simply didn't know what he wanted to know, didn't understand what he was insisting upon or why. She wanted him to leave her and her husband in peace, just as she left him in peace. The spot in her soul that had been wounded had scarred over, and with it, its soft tissue, the stuff of happiness and love. Her soul was all scar tissue now. Maybe back then, when she was wounded, or soon after, the pain might have been healed. It was too late now. It had been too late for a long time. She had lived for a long time now with her scars, lies, caution.

Then suddenly the thought came to him. This wasn't the first time she was leaving him in peace. As far back as he could remember, she had left him in peace, wanted him to leave her in peace. As if she had nothing to do with him. As if he had once troubled her too strongly, too deeply. "When you conceived me, did Father rape you? Was it while he was in Strasbourg, doing awful things, and having an affair with the Jewish girl? Did he arrive one night, and you knew about this other woman and didn't want to sleep with him, and he didn't give a damn what you knew or wanted, and raped you? Is that how I came into the world? You've never forgiven me for that, have you?"

She kept shaking her head, over and over. Then he saw that she was crying. At first she sat there rigid and mute, tears rolling down her cheeks, dangling for a moment from her chin, and then dripping on her skirt. When she raised her hands to wipe the tears from her face, she began to sob.

He stood up, went over to her chair, and tried to hug her. She sat there rigid and stiff and refused his hug. He talked to her, but she refused his words. She was still silent when he said good-bye.

14

HE TOOK A train home and resumed his life. When the librarian wrote him that she would be in town on business, he met her, they took a walk, had dinner, and returned to his place. He had shoved the painting under his bed.

But it wouldn't leave him in peace. What if she happened to look under the bed and discovered the painting? What if the bed frame and mattress collapsed? The painting would be ruined, and, worse, would be visible when things were put back in order. What if he were to talk in his sleep with the girl with the lizard? He did it often during the day. "Girl with lizard," he would say, "I have to study," and he would tell her what he had to study. Or he would ask her opinion about what to wear. Or scold her in the morning because she hadn't awakened him in time. Or talk with her about the fate of René Dalmann or his father. "Did your painter give you to my father? Or did my father betray your painter to get you—when your painter was trying to escape with you? But why with you in particular?" Again and again he would ask her, "What am I going to do with you, girl with lizard?"

Should he look for Dalmann's heirs and give them the painting? But he didn't think much of the notion of inheritance. Should he cash the painting in and make his life easier with the money? Or do good with it? Did he owe anything to the people his father had treated unjustly? Because he had profited from his father's misdeeds? But how had he profited? The fact that he could look at the girl with the lizard and talk with her—was it a blessing or a curse?

"What's happened to your painting?"

They were lying in bed, gazing at one another. "I didn't get any further." He made a face intended to show that it was all a bit painful, but didn't matter. "I'm not working for the lawyer anymore."

"So somewhere in Manhattan there's a little apartment whose tenant has died, but a painting by one of the century's most renowned artists hangs there unrecognized? The tenant was poor and old, and now cockroaches are running across his dirty table, rats are gnawing at his shoes, the gangster, who broke into his apartment and has settled in, is lying on his bed, snoring, and bang! bang! one day in a shoot-out the girl gets a hole in her forehead, and the lizard loses its tail. Perhaps the old man was René Dalmann himself?" She was talking a little too much. But he liked listening to her. "You can live with that?"

"With what?"

"That it's all been left in the dark?"

"Anybody who wants to know can go to Sotheby's or Christie's or to the guys who've written books about René Dalmann."

She cuddled up to him. "You've learned something. Have you learned something?"

He didn't want to fall asleep. He didn't want to talk in his sleep. He didn't want her to wake up and decide to go to the toilet, search under the bed for her shoes, and find the painting. He didn't want . . . But then he fell asleep after all, and it was light when he woke up, she had just come back from the toilet and hopped into bed so hard that it frightened him. But the frame and mattress held.

"I've got to catch the seven-forty-four train so I can be at the institute by nine."

"I'll take you."

Before closing and locking the door, he looked back and his room bothered him. It wasn't his room. She had rummaged in his books, she was having her period and had left stains in his bed, during their walk along the shore, she had picked up a rusty old letter scale and carried it home. And the girl with the lizard wasn't hanging above his bed. After saying good-bye to the librarian at the station and still feeling a bit distracted and uneasy, he returned home and straightened up. Books back onto their shelves, new sheets on the bed, the painting back above it, the letter scale on top of the wardrobe, just behind his suitcase. "Yes, girl with lizard, now everything's back in order."

He was standing in the middle of the room and looking at this order. The order of books in the bookcase, which reminded him of the ordered books in his father's bookcase. The same shabby tidiness that his mother had summoned up to counter the family's decline. *Girl with Lizard*, no longer in its golden frame but a canvas stretched on wood, yet as dominating as it ever was in his parents' house. And just as had been the case at home, the painting was a treasure, a mystery, a window onto beauty and freedom, and at the same time a commanding, controlling power to whom sacrifices would have to be made. He thought of the life still ahead of him.

He did nothing that day. He strolled the streets a bit, passing the law school, the bar where he worked, and the house where the girl he had once loved still lived. Or had he never learned to love?

That evening he went back to his apartment for a moment to wrap the painting, its frame, and some newspaper in the sheet he had stripped from the bed. Then he took them to the beach. There were fires burning, with young people sitting around them, partying. He walked on until the last fire was behind him. Then he made one of his own. The newspapers flared up as did the sheet and the frame. He tossed the painting on the fire. Colors fused, and the girl melted and was no longer recognizable. But before she had burned entirely, the edge of the canvas curled back to reveal another painting stretched on the frame beneath *Girl with Lizard*. The giant lizard, the tiny girl—for a fraction of a second he saw the painting that René Dalmann had wanted to protect and take with him as he fled. Then the canvas blazed up.

When the fire died away, he shoved the embers around with the toe of his shoe. He didn't wait until it had all burned down to ashes. He watched the little blue and red flames for a while. Then he went home.

A LITTLE FLING

1

MY FRIENDSHIP WITH Sven and Paula was my only East-West friendship to survive the Wall. The others ended almost as soon it came down. Get-togethers were arranged less frequently, and then one day a get-together would be canceled at the last minute. There was so much to do: look for work, renovate apartments and houses, use the tax breaks, make deals, get rich, travel. It had been impossible to do things in the East before, because the state allowed nothing, and unnecessary to do things in the West because money for Berlin kept coming from Bonn in any case. There was always time.

Sven and I met over a game of chess. I had moved to Berlin in the summer of 1986, didn't know anyone, and spent weekends exploring the city, East and West. One Saturday evening, I happened on some chess players in a beer garden on Lake Müggel, watched the end of a match, and was invited by the winner to play a game.

When it got too dark and we had to break off, we made a date to continue the game the following Saturday.

With your first new acquaintances, a city begins to be home. On the ride back to West Berlin the bleakness of the East was less disheartening, its ugliness less inhospitable. Lighted windows, gaudy with curtains or blue from television, side by side in prefabricated apartments or lonely in firewalls, dimly lit old factories, wide empty streets, occasional places to eat—I watched and imagined Sven living here or there, working in this factory, driving along that street. I even saw myself going in or out of that door, driving along this street, eating in that pub.

My second new acquaintance in Berlin was a little boy with a schoolbag. One morning as I was about to cross the wide boulevard in front of my building, there he stood beside me. "Will you walk me across the street?" he asked, taking my hand. After that he showed up many mornings as I waited on the curb for the stoplight a few hundred yards on to turn red and bring traffic to a halt. Later, right after the Wall had come down, Sven and Paula took trips like crazy—to Munich, Cologne, Rome, Paris, Brussels, London, always by bus or train and always by night both ways, so that for a two-day stay they would have to pay for only one night's lodging. When they took trips they left their daughter Julia with me, and she and the little boy became friends. She was still in kindergarten and full of admiration for the first grader. He was a bit embarrassed by the company of the little girl, but also flattered by her admiration. His name was

Hans, and he lived a couple of buildings away, where his parents ran a newspaper and tobacco shop.

2

THE NEXT Saturday it rained. I took the train through East Berlin, which was grayer and emptier than usual. I walked from the station in Rahnsdorf to the lake; the rain was relentless, it was cold, and the hand I held my umbrella in was numb. From a distance I saw that the beer garden was closed. Then I saw Sven. He was wearing the same blue bib overalls as on the previous Saturday and the same leather cap, and with his round glasses and chubby-cheeked face he had the look of a childlike, naive revolutionary. He was standing in the open door of a shed, chessboard and box of chessmen between his feet. He waved, shrugged, and spread his arms wide in an apologetic gesture that embraced the skies, the rain, the puddles, and the closed beer garden.

He had come in his car, and he drove me back to his place. His wife and daughter were with the grandparents, would be back this evening, and until then we could play chess without interruption. Then he would have to put his daughter to bed and read her a story for half an hour, as he did every evening. But I could do that too, read her the story, and he would fix us a little something to eat.

Did I have children, too? I said I didn't, and he shook his head and sighed at the misfortune of my childlessness.

We didn't finish the game that second Saturday, either. Sven brooded and brooded over each move. I let my eyes wander. There was a homemade bookcase of blond wood, a massive dark china cabinet that matched four dark chairs and a table, its floor-length white cloth embroidered with flowers, the small bamboo table at which we sat in pale wickerwork chairs with black metal frames, and a blackish brown coal stove. On one wall was a blue-and-white tapestry of a dove, with an olive branch in its beak, and a print of van Gogh's sunflowers. The window, wet with dripping rain, looked out on a large old brick building, a school, according to Sven's mumbled confirmation of my question. Sometimes a car rattled along the cobblestone street, and at regular intervals a tram squealed around a curve. Otherwise it was silent.

Later, I got bored with Sven's long brooding, and we agreed to play by the clock, four-hour games or even blitz matches of seven minutes. And then chess began to bore us in general, and we preferred to take walks with Paula and Julia or meet with friends or play the new games I brought with me—sometimes only on the second try, if the border guards had caught me with them the first time around and turned me back. Or we just talked; we were both thirty-six, interested in theater and films and curious about people and relationships. Sometimes when we had joined other friends, our eyes would meet because some remark, some exchange of words or gestures, caught the attention of us both the same way.

The room where Sven and I played chess never looked quite the same again as on that first Saturday. It was always a hopeless mess—Julia's toys and Sven's and Paula's papers from work lay strewn about, plus teapots and cups, gnawed apples and open packets of chocolate, often racks hung with drying laundry. The whole of daily life was played out in this one room. The apartment had one tiny bedroom for the parents, an even tinier cubicle for Julia, and a narrow kitchen half its original size, its other half separated off and turned into an equally narrow bath. That first Saturday Sven had tidied up the room. He had also bought pastries. But engrossed in chess, he had forgotten about the pastries and tea; it wasn't until he heard Paula and Julia at the door that he remembered he was going to offer them to me. He stood up and said, "Oh Lord, I was going to . . . ," and spread his arms again in a gesture of regret and futility.

3

FOR JULIA and me it was love at first sight. She was two years old, cheerful, fidgety, talkative, and when occupied with her own activities she would hum to herself. Sometimes she would turn thoughtful and serious, as if she wanted to understand everything, and could. Sometimes she would look, or hold herself or move, in a way that already revealed the woman she would someday be. It was no wonder she enchanted me. The joy of it was the way she greeted me so happily that first evening, as if there was a space free in her heart and I had arrived just in time.

Paula and I had a difficult time with one another. She was serious and stern with Sven, Julia, and me, as if she disapproved of the fun we had with silliness like building a tower out of chessmen or having Julia's teddy bears perform a striptease or playing with soap bubbles—with the saucer-sized ring and soap powder that I brought one Saturday and with which we created quite a stir in Treptow Park. She also disapproved of my attempts to charm her. She saw it as flirting, and when I tried being equally serious and stern, though friendly of course, she saw it as merely another variation on flirting. Whenever she could, she ignored me.

Our relationship improved when we discovered that we both loved Greek. Paula taught it at an Evangelical seminary, and I had learned it in high school and had read texts in Greek ever since—a hobby, the way other people play the sax or buy a telescope to gaze at stars. One day I noticed from the books lying around that Paula was involved with Greek, I asked about it, and she realized that I really was interested and knew something about it. From then on she would strike up a conversation with me, at first only about questions of Greek grammar and syntax, but then about Julia as well, or something that had happened in the course she taught or a book that she was reading.

It wasn't until the summer of 1987, when we all went on vacation together to Bulgaria, that she said something about our relationship. How she had considered me too happy-go-lucky and had been afraid I would disappoint Sven's trust in me. "He was so happy about meeting you that day and making a date for the next Saturday, but was afraid you wouldn't come, too. He was like that for a long time, happy and afraid. You have no idea what it means to get to know one of you, to know you better and well. It opens up another world, intellectually and—let's admit it—materially, too, and then there's the desire to show you off and brag about you and at the same time keep a jealous eye on you. And we're constantly afraid the exotic charm we have for you will wear off, get used up, and you'll move on to other things, other people."

I could have responded that they opened up another world for me as well. Not an exotic world of middling importance and short-lived charm, but the other half of our world, separated by a wall and an iron curtain. Thanks to them I was at home in all Berlin, almost in all of Germany, almost in the whole world. Instead, I contradicted her. I sad I couldn't handle the idea that their world and my world were so different and that we were exchanging entry into one world for entry into others.

Our relationship should be a friendship, not a cultural exchange. I didn't want to be the guy from the West, and they shouldn't be the couple from the East. We should simply be human beings.

"But you can't behave as if there were no Wall. As if our friendship were like your friendships over there or ours here."

We were walking along the beach. Paula and I liked to get up early, early enough to watch the sunrise over the sea. We lived in different hotels—they in one for Eastern tourists, I in one for Westerners, and when it began to grow bright, we would meet at the harbor and walk until it was time to turn around and go back for breakfast. We were barefoot.

"Look," she said, setting her foot in wet sand that had just been washed by a wave, and then stepping back, "two, three more waves, and you'll no longer be able to see it."

"And?"

"Nothing."

4

WE DIDN'T TALK about politics for a long time. In the latter half of the eighties the world had settled down. The East was still the East, but it had grown old, tireder, and wiser, and the West, which no longer had anything to fear or prove, was happy and well fed. What was there to say about politics?

After my exams I had spent three years as an aide for one of the parties in the state legislature in Stuttgart—was at first excited by politics, but soon grew disappointed. In Berlin my political interest went no further than daily, superficial newspaper reading. Insofar as politics was relevant to my job as a judge in welfare court, I got that from periodicals in my field or contacts with colleagues. I knew that Sven and Paula listened to a comprehensive news report every day on West German radio; they didn't subscribe to a newspaper, and since Julia was supposed to grow up without television, they didn't have a TV. They weren't interested in politics, either, I thought, nor did I find that surprising either for her, a teacher of Greek, or him, a translator from the Czech and Bulgarian.

In the fall of 1987, I noticed that this was not the case. I was skeptical the first time they asked me to pass on a cryptic telephone message to someone in the West and told me a complicated story about friends who were expecting a visitor from the West, whom they wanted to ask for a favor, but because of some mix-up couldn't get hold of. And when they asked me to do it the second time, I knew the story was fabricated, and they knew that I knew. If that second time had ended the matter, I wouldn't have said anything. But then came a third request, and I called them on it. I was outraged, not because I was afraid that carrying out these assignments would put me in any danger, but because I expected them to trust me.

Paula had insisted that I should know nothing. For my own protection, she said. But before she had become a Christian and got involved with the church, she had been active in the Free German Youth and the Communist Party, and the zeal with which she had thrown herself into the cause of the Environmental Library established by the congregation of Zion Church, and her willingness to use me for the cause, both struck me as a heritage from her political past. "The end justifies the means, is that it?"

"That's unfair. I'm open about my past in the party, and you use it against me."

"I'm not using anything against you. If I'm not allowed to respond to what you tell me, then give me the rules for censorship: This is for the ears of comrades and this is for naive people like me and this . . ."

"Oh cut the self-righteousness and self-pity. Yes, we should have talked with you right off. But we're talking with you now. And trust isn't all that easy in this country."

She was leaning against the china cabinet, staring at me, her face flushed, her eyes flashing. I had never seen her look so beautiful. Why, I thought, does she always wear her hair in a bun instead of letting it down?

The request to pass on another message became a request to establish permanent contact with a journalist.

Until the fall of 1989, I reported to him about repressive measures taken against the Environmental Library, about searches and arrests among sympathizers, about the activities of Paula and her friends, who were determined to exploit the law to the full, but not to overstep its bounds. I wondered if the State Security didn't suspect me, if I was being watched. But I wasn't searched or interrogated any more often or thoroughly at the border. I never carried written matter with me in any case.

Once, in the spring of 1988, Paula and Sven took me along to Zion Church. The topics of peace, ecology, and human rights were addressed, but otherwise it seemed to me a church service like any other. But Paula insisted that I had been noticed and should stay clear of her political activities. "And you'd best do the same."

"What?" Sven stared at her, flabbergasted.

"You're there only because of me. If something were ever to happen to me, nothing should happen to you, too. Think of Julia."

"Nothing's going to happen to you."

"You can't know that for sure, can you?" She challenged him with a look, and he gave in.

5

THEN CAME the big change. Paula spoke at demonstrations in Alexander Platz, joined the Social Democrats, became involved in preparations for a new constitution, and was almost elected a member of the GDR's last Volkskammer. Sven was a member of a group that concerned itself with the files of the Ministry for State Security and published the first book about its organization, activities, and collaborators. They were both drunk on politics for a few months.

Paula woke up even before reunification, rousing Sven out of his dream of founding a political party and a publishing house, and they set about reshaping their lives. He applied successfully for a position as a lecturer at the Free University, and she was hired as an instructor at Humboldt University. They could afford to move from Schneller Strasse to Prenzlauer Berg. Their new, large apartment, their new jobs, and getting Julia started in school all made for a full life for them both. They had no nostalgic memories of the defunct GDR. "The change was good to us," they said in amazement now and then, as if they actually ought to have ended up like so many who saw themselves deprived of the fruits of their accommodation or resistance, first by the changes and then by the reunification that followed the destruction of the Wall.

For a while Sven was overwhelmed by his opportunities as a consumer. He bought a big car, wore Armani suits, and dressed Julia up like a princess. Paula disapproved of his extravagance. "Our wanting-to-have was never any better than your having, and it stinks just as much now." But she changed as well, in less obvious

ways. She continued to wear her gray or brown dresses
and suits, but they became more elegant, her shoes had
higher heels, and new glasses with thin frames gave her
face an almost haughty look. Her voice changed too,
became more powerful and self-assured. Sven tried to get
her to wear her hair down. That disappointed her—as if
her hair were a secret she shared only with him and that
he had now betrayed to fashion.

Even when Sven's and Paula's delight in short trips
had passed, Julia sometimes came to stay overnight with
me. After school she would get on the subway just around
the corner and get off just around the corner from me,
meet Hans there, and phone me from his parents' shop to
say she was staying with me and would wait for me there.
She had become quite an independent little girl.

In the spring of 1992 we took another vacation together, traveling this time by way of Tuscany and Umbria
to the beach at Ancona. Once again, Paula and I would
get up early and take our dawn walk by the sea. I told her
I no longer saw anything of their old friends, who had
become mine as well.

"We still see only two or three of them ourselves. Too
many things are too different."

"Is that because of the Gauck Authority and the
files?"

She shrugged. "We decided not to worry about our
files. We agreed that we all knew one another and didn't
want to start with all that—no mistrust, no faith in files."

"Who agreed?"

"Hans and Ute, Dirk and Tatjana, the Thiessens and the four from the orchestra. When we were all together one last time on October third, 1990. Don't be angry that we didn't ask you. We had the feeling that it's our problem, not yours."

I was angry. I had expected my friends not to define and separate things into their problems and my problems without at least asking me.

She noticed, without my having said a word. "You're right, we should've discussed it with you. It's your problem, too. All I can say is that the subject came up and we talked till everyone was hot under the collar. In the end we had the feeling that we couldn't just leave it at talk. We wanted to do something with consequences, and that's how we came to our decision."

"Unanimous?"

"No, Hans and Tatjana were against it, and Tatjana also refused to be bound by the decision. She wanted to see her files."

"Did she?"

"I don't know. We've lost contact."

I had asked myself more than once if any of our friends might have been unofficial collaborators. Now I wanted to know. I was still angry. "I want to see my files, too."

6

THAT FALL Sven got a tenured contract. He had been hoping for it for so long that he'd finally given up. Now the head of his department unexpectedly handed him the papers.

He called me at my office at court. "Join us this evening. We're celebrating."

I drove over that evening with champagne and flowers. Sven was cooking. He had opened a bottle of white wine and already drunk half of it. I had never seen him in such high spirits.

"Did your boss say what took so long for the contract?"

"Not a word. Just that he was happy that he could finally offer it. And that I was the first East German to be offered a tenured contract for an academic position at the Free University." He was beaming. "You know sometimes I'm sad that I'm just small potatoes. A lecturer in Czech and Bulgarian—what is that really? Someday you'll be a federal judge and wear a red robe. Someday Paula will pull out the thesis she started years ago and then put aside. She'll finish it and end up as a Frau Professor. But it's all us small potatoes who feed the world and make it cozy. Paula doesn't have a tenured contract, and if they no longer want her or if she's had enough because she wants to write her thesis and become a Frau Professor, then it's a good thing that I'm small potatoes."

Paula and Julia arrived. Paula had picked her up after school and treated her to some ice cream. Julia was being silly and loud. She and Sven whirled through the kitchen and the large front room. I leaned against the china cabinet and drank white wine and got caught up in Sven's and Julia's good mood. It took a while before I noticed how quiet Paula was. She smiled at Julia's clever ideas or caressed her hair. But she was distracted. When Sven put on a waltz and wanted to dance with her in the kitchen and hallway, she said no. I thought maybe she was upset that Sven was drinking so much, but she was downing one glass after another herself.

Sven noticed that something wasn't right with Paula, and went out of his way for her. He turned attentive, affectionate, tender, all with a touching tipsy clumsiness. It earned him repeated rebuffs; she dodged him whenever he got near, and pulled away when he tried to put his arm around her and cuddle his head against her. Julia began to stare in confusion from father to mother.

I felt helpless. When we sat down at the dining table in the front room, Julia and I on one side, Sven and Paula on the other, it reminded me of my own childhood and of my despair when something was smoldering between my parents and I didn't know what it was, except that I was afraid that it would burst into flames, destroying everything that formed the basis of my trust in the world. That memory was the hallmark of countless evening meals, with me sitting there at the table with my parents and trying to duck out of sight so that parental tension wouldn't ignite on my account. Julia kept a low profile, too.

I asked myself how much I really knew about Sven's and Paula's marriage. I had always thought of it as harmonious, but had wanted to think of it that way, too. Sometimes Sven had started talking about Paula and himself, and I just let him talk into the void. Like a child with his parents, I didn't want to hear about any troubles in their marriage. And I didn't want to know about their happiness, either.

I put Julia to bed. We didn't talk about Sven and Paula. I read her a fairy tale, and she fell asleep in the middle, exhausted by her day or by the evening and her parents. I went on sitting there and read the fairy tale to the end. When I tried to say my good-byes, Sven and Paula urged me to stay. The evening hadn't gone all that well, but we could finally watch those two videos we'd been wanting to see for so long, but that we'd put off playing because it seemed a shame to interrupt more successful evenings. They laid an emphasis on my staying that would have been better applied to their talking about what was wrong between them.

We watched the two films. I would have liked to have got lost in them, but I didn't dare. I could sense the tension between Sven and Paula and had the silly feeling that something awful would happen if I got caught up in the movie and didn't keep a close eye on them. We had drunk so much wine that they easily persuaded me not to drive home but to spend the night with them.

7

I SLEPT IN the big room, which had doors at each end and a window onto the courtyard. I was lying on a mattress on the floor, gazing through the open window at a dark wall and dark roof with dark chimneys set against the bright sky of a city night, and listening to a rustling that rose and fell evenly and sounded as if all the buildings around the courtyard were breathing heavily in and out in the heat of the summer night. A church clock struck once, and as I waited for it to strike again I fell asleep.

It was like a dream, and later I sometimes wished that it really had been just a dream.

She was sitting on the edge of the mattress. I wanted to ask, "What's wrong?," but when I started to, she said, "Shhhh," and touched my lips with her fingers. I looked at her, but couldn't read her face in the darkness. A hint of light fell on it from the left, illuminating her cheek and glinting in one eye. She was wearing her hair down, and it fell forward over her right shoulder, leaving the left side of her neck bare. With her left hand she clasped her bathrobe at her breast, and with her right she warned my lips not to speak.

I wondered if she could tell what was going on inside me. Paula, the wife of my friend Sven—the wives of friends are not to be desired or touched, and flirting with them is like flirting with your little sister or an old lady, a game that never turns serious. Not that Paula and I had never touched, hugged, shared a laugh or those moments of rapport and confidence in which I could imagine I loved her. There were many moments in which I could imagine that I loved her better, could make her happier than Sven ever could, and could sense her asking herself how life might be with me. But those were ideas from another world, in which Sven was my friend all the same and happy with his wife and in which I perhaps did not even love her, but rather someone just like her—instead of women who were too young and with whom I had all-too-brief affairs. No, there was no suppressed desire that would ultimately have to be lived out. We both knew that, and had we spoken we would have discussed it and set a seal upon our agreement.

But we did not speak. When her fingers no longer forbade me to speak but wandered over my face, tracing eyebrows, temples, cheekbones, and lips, I no longer wanted to speak. I closed my eyes, and the image of her stayed with me, strange and beautiful, with hair let down in promise of a different Paula from the one I knew. I felt not only her fingers on my face, but also the nearness and warmth of her body. I did not touch her, I breathed her in. When I opened my eyes again, she took my head in both hands, bent down over me and kissed me. Her hair fell around our heads, enveloping us.

We made love as calmly as if this were not the first time, as if we had all the time in the world. As if we had easy consciences. I didn't, and thought of Sven and of how he was sleeping only a couple of doors away, of what would happen if he woke up and found us, or how I would greet him in the morning. But my bad conscience was powerless, and seemed to be going through the motions, with little real interest in what I was doing. I even took malicious joy in noting that nothing and no one was stopping Paula and me. I felt free. And I felt powerful, discovering once and for all that I only had to reach out for my desires to have them. I was proud of her orgasm and of my own, the way you're proud of bodies moving in synch when you're dancing, of the woman's grace and your lightness of foot.

Afterward we lay side by side. It was the right mix of cuddling and giving each other space, and we had found it with no difficulty, as a matter of course. Now I wanted to speak, not to ask her if it had been good—I knew that—but what was to become of us. She went "Shhhh" and put her fingers to my lips again. At first, silence had bound us together, now it separated us. Then I saw tears glistening on her face. I wanted to sit up and kiss away, wipe away her tears. Maybe she thought I wanted to shake her fingers from my lips and speak after all, because she sat up, slipped into her robe, clasping it together at her breast with her left hand, bent her head forward, and seized her hair in her right hand, pushing it back over her shoulders. For a moment she sat there on the edge of the mattress in a repetition of her original pose. Before I could decide whether to speak or hold her back, she had left the room.

8

WHEN I AWOKE again it was still dark. This time I heard the door open and the sound of feet on hardwood floor. It was Julia.

"What is it?"

"I woke up and can't go back to sleep. My parents are arguing."

She was standing in her nightshirt beside my bed, waiting. I invited her to sit down and hoped that it wouldn't smell too much of lovemaking and that Julia wouldn't find the odor too strange. She crept under my blanket.

"They're arguing so loud, louder than they've ever done before."

"Parents argue, and sometimes it's louder, sometimes it's softer."

"But . . ."

I realized she would have liked to hear about the things in life that parents can argue about without threatening the order of the world, but I didn't want to patch over her parents' argument, since I didn't know how dangerous it really was. "Do you know the story about the sheep?"

"The one with the fence? That they jump over, and you count till you fall asleep?"

"No, a different story. It has a fence too, but the gate is open, and you don't have to count the sheep if you don't want to. Should I tell you the story?"

She nodded so eagerly that I saw it even in the dark. Now I could hear Sven and Paula quarreling too, despite a long hallway that first turned a corner and ended at their and Julia's bedrooms. I heard their voices, far off and weak, but enough for me to wonder if I should get up, slip away, and never show myself again. I was angry at Sven and Paula for not being able to manage their own marriage, at Paula for dragging me into it and then dropping me, at Julia for demanding my attention, as if I didn't have problems enough of my own. I was angry at myself, for making a mess of things between Sven and me, and at having let Paula get so close to me.

"Aren't you going to tell it?"

"Sure. Somewhere there's a land with very high mountains. When you're at the top there's snow and ice, and when you start down, first there are boulders and pebbles, then grass, and then dense forests. In front of the highest mountains are others that are not so high, and the last, lowest mountains are covered with grass, too, the same brown grass that grows on the plain that begins where the mountains end and that stretches beyond the horizon, farther than the eye can see. Are you listening?"

"Yes, but I can hear my parents arguing, too."

"So can I. Should I go on? It's not an exciting story. But exciting stories make it hard to go to sleep."

"Go on."

"At the foot of the mountain is a sheep pen. A large sheep pen with lots of sheep."

"What's a sheep pen?"

"A sheep pen is like a barn, but without a roof and with sides made of just two planks of wood. Can you see the sheep pen?"

"Yes."

"This morning you were in the mountains, at the very top. Then you started—"

"How did I get to the top of the highest mountains?"

"I don't know. Maybe you were born there?"

"Uh-huh."

"At any rate you've started down from the high mountains. It took a long time; you plodded through snow and slid over ice, sometimes you had to climb over boulders, and you had trouble scrambling across the fields of pebbles. Sometimes you had to go over a pass, first climbing up one side, so you could go down the other. You walked for a long, long time through a dense forest. Then, just as the sun is setting, you come out of the forest, and up ahead, you see the last, low mountains and the wide plain."

"And the sheep pen."

"Yes, you also see the sheep pen up ahead. It's already in the shade, because the sun is setting behind the highest mountains. But the plain is still lighted by the sun, a warm sun, and in its light the brown grass of the plain shines like gold. Someone has pushed aside the wooden planks that form the gate of the pen. You can't tell who did it, there isn't another person to be seen anywhere. But you can see that some of the hundreds and hundreds of sheep in the pen have wandered off and are grazing outside, at first only a few, then more and more, right up close to the pen, then moving farther and farther away. You sit down. You're tired from the long day and glad to sit down. You're tired, but you watch anyway."

"Uh-huh." She turned on her side.

I patted her head and tucked the blanket around her. "You watch and watch as the sheep leave the pen. Some of them take their time, nibbling at the grass. Others are restless, moving every which way. But they all want to get out onto the wide plain. The fastest of them are already way in the distance, while others remain in the shade of the mountains. Then the sun sets and the plain is all in shadows, strewn with bright dots moving slowly but steadily away from you. The pen is empty. Sometimes you hear a sheep bleat. And the bright dots keep moving farther away, farther and farther away. Can you see them?"

Julia had fallen asleep.

9

I HAD HEARD Paula's and Sven's voices rising several times. But they had faded again, and I had hoped the argument was over. But it was still going on. I remembered agonizing fights with my wife years before; we had argued to the point of exhaustion, but exhaustion didn't bring peace, we just needed a break so we could continue with the same ferocity.

I got up, pulled on my pants and sweater and tiptoed across the creaking floor. I softly opened the door, slipped into the hall, and closed the door behind me. I stole my way to the door of Paula's and Sven's bedroom.

"How often do I have to say it? I had no idea you'd carry on like this." He spoke slowly, with exaggerated precision.

"Then why didn't you say anything?"

"Because those were the rules. Not to talk about it."

"Those were their rules, not ours. We promised that we'd tell each other and tell them that we had told each other."

"That was when we still thought we wouldn't play their game. But when I started playing their game, that no longer worked."

"You should never have played without talking to me and without my agreeing. What we promised each other wasn't subject to some condition you could treat as you pleased."

"Would you have agreed to do it?"

"No, I wouldn't, no matter how many times you ask. I—"

"I'm really not asking to get you to agree after the fact, I'm trying to make you understand that I couldn't count on you, and the only person I could depend on was myself. I had to—"

"You didn't have to do anything. Don't tell me you had to. You wanted to. And for hours now I've been begging you to finally tell me why that was."

"Stop acting as if it was for my own enjoyment, as if I'd done it for my enjoyment. I did it for you."

"For me? Without so much as asking? Behind my back? How can you presume to treat me—"

"I know, I know. I have no right to know better than you what's good for you. But can't you get it into your skull that I have a duty to know what's good for our child? Our child doesn't need a heroine or a martyr, she needs a mother. I saw to it that she would keep her mother."

"And for that you betrayed everything that was important to me. Important to us. You turned it into something cheap and sleazy."

It sounded as if they were not saying all this for the first time. They spoke in worn-out voices; his tone of anguished reason had grown tired, and there was desperation in her attempt to make him realize both his betrayal and her dismay. I didn't want to listen to any more of it. But just as I was about to steal away, Sven flung the door open.

"Spying on me? A spy knows when he's being spied on. You're right, Paula, I must be a spy. And our friend here, with his ear to the door and his eye to the keyhole, knows it now too. Come right in and join the excommunication." He made an ironic bow and swept out one arm in an inviting gesture. I entered, he closed the door and stood in front of it, as if to prevent Paula or me from leaving the room. She was standing at the window with her back to us.

I took a couple of steps into the room, but didn't know where to go, where I should stand or sit. I just stood there, Sven on my left, Paula on my right. "Julia came to me because she couldn't sleep with you two arguing. And once I was awake I couldn't help overhearing you any longer, either."

"So then you wanted to know the details. Pure curiosity? A power trip? Knowledge is power, and to know something about friends is to have power over them. Or was it friendly empathy that drove you? The friend who stands by his friends in a crisis while crouched at the keyhole?"

"I didn't know what was up and if I should knock or ask. I was about to walk away."

"Walk? Or slink, did you want to slink away on tippy-toes, so we wouldn't notice that you'd been eavesdropping?" Sven's voice was heavy with mockery. He emphasized every "you" by pointing at me.

"Enough, Sven." Paula spoke without turning around. I could see her face in the window. "You betrayed him, too, him and all the others."

"That wasn't necessary."

"They'll learn about it anyway."

"From you?"

She turned around. "No, Sven, not from me. Helga has an appointment to see her files next week, and you know that she won't keep it to herself."

"Ah, Helga's a chatterbox. Nobody takes her seriously."

"Sven, wake up. You're going to lose everything, your job, your friends, and your wife. And someday Julia will ask you what you did, and what are you going to tell her?"

Sven was silent. He stared at Paula, eyes and mouth wide—a dull, obtuse, uncomprehending look. "Why do you want to leave me? You're behaving as if I had been unfaithful to you. But even a little fling is no big deal anymore. The Thiessens managed to get past both their affairs, and we, we . . . I've never been unfaithful to you, Paula, I couldn't be. I've always loved only you and I will always love only you."

"I know." She walked to the door. "Let me out. I need to get something that I want to show you."

He grabbed her arm. "You're coming back?"

"Yes, I said I would."

10

HE LOOKED at me, just as chubby-cheeked and childlike as on our first chess date, and waved his arms in that familiar gesture of regret and futility. "A bit of a mess. Any ideas?"

"No." I shrugged. I would gladly have taken him in my arms to comfort him, but couldn't.

"Maybe I should tell you . . . I mean, before you hear it from Helga or maybe even read it . . . Not that there's a whole lot to say . . ." He winced. "I showed off with you a little for the Stasi. Saying you'd be an important man someday and that I could get to important information through you, not right now, but later. Actually I didn't say anything about you and your affairs, just held out the prospect that maybe someday I'd . . . that maybe someday you'd . . ."

"Either don't say anything, or say what actually happened." Paula was standing at the door.

"What happened, what happened . . . Okay, I said that he was disappointed by the political system in the Federal Republic and that I might be able to get him to work for us. That political disappointments had left him looking for somewhere to fit in, for something he could commit to." Sven turned from Paula to me. "I'm sorry, I'm sorry. I thought no one would get hurt and it might help a lot of people—you, Paula, and if Paula, then Julia and me, too. I didn't betray you. I didn't betray anyone. I just—"

Paula handed him a bundle of papers. "Read this!"

He let the hand holding the papers drop to his side and looked from her to me and back to her. He was searching for words—as if there were words that would spare him from having to read the papers. As if he could bury the truth in them and leave it hidden there. But finding no words, he sighed and began to read.

"No," he said after a while, "that's not how it was."

"You didn't talk with him about our marriage? Just wait, you'll soon get to the details. Things he can know only from you." She was standing by the window again, arms crossed, her eyes fixed on him.

He went on reading. Then he lowered the arm with the papers. "He wasn't a dislikable guy. And we sort of worked together. No, we weren't colleagues, but we were like colleagues somehow, and colleagues talk about their wives and girlfriends. Come on, Paula, I didn't say anything bad about you. I was even showing off with you."

"You talked about us in bed—with that creature from the Stasi. You betrayed us, us and you and me. You weren't talking to a friend or a colleague, you were talking to them. Yes, you showed off with me, with me in bed, and as for all the rest, I was harmless, a humanist, an idealist, just led astray by religion. 'You shouldn't take what my wife says at meetings all that seriously. She lets herself be influenced and involved by others.' That's what you told him, and you sold Heinz down the river. You made him the ringleader, the one pulling the strings, the—"

"But only to save you. I only did it so that you wouldn't . . . After all that had happened, they had to have somebody, and if they hadn't grabbed Heinz, they might very well have grabbed you. And Heinz got deported to the West after a couple of months, that's all that happened to him."

"You don't get it." She was so agitated she was shaking now. "You didn't save me, not the me I am, but the me that pleased them. Apparently that's how I please you, too—as a harmless woman, good in bed, but otherwise don't take her too seriously. That's how you saved me—but who I really am doesn't matter to you at all. That I'd let myself be arrested, would prefer to be arrested, for my beliefs, rather than betray them, and that my daughter would be better off with a mother in Bautzen prison than with a mother who's a traitor—I have a right to that, it's my life, my faith, it's who I am as the mother of my daughter. You took that away from me, behind my back, like a gutless coward. And don't say you did it out of love. That isn't love."

"But . . ." Sven was ashen. He stared at Paula in bewilderment.

"No, it isn't love. Whatever it is, I don't want it. And don't start in again about how a little fling is no big deal. You didn't just have a little affair. You pulled the rug right out from under my life. Our life. I'm leaving you. I can't stay with you."

Sven pulled away from the wall. He walked unsteadily to the door, opened it, and went out into the hall. We heard the bathroom door open. Then we heard him retching.

11

WHEN WATER started running and the door closed, Paula and I looked at one another. "What happened with Heinz?" I wanted to ask something else.

"Oh, he and I organized a pacifist protest in Alexander Platz. By the world clock. On January 1, 1988, we pasted signs on the globe showing the number of casualties from all the wars and civil wars in 1987. That wasn't allowed, of course. For them war wasn't war and civil war wasn't civil war. How could we throw wars of liberation for exploited peoples into the same pot with imperialist and capitalist wars of repression? We were arrested, I was interrogated for three days, given a warning, and let go. Heinz sat in jail for seven months and was then expelled to the West. In my case, thanks to Sven, it was just a foolish girl's prank, in his it was the continuation and aggravation of subversive agitation and propaganda controlled by the West and incubated in the church. Even though we'd been working together for years, and he didn't do anything different from what I did."

"Does Heinz know?"

"We're no longer in contact. He never sent word from the West, not even after the Wall came down. Maybe he thinks I betrayed him back then, to save my own skin."

"Did Sven tell the Stasi everything he knew?"

She nodded. "And talked with his operations officer as if he were an old friend—about himself, about me, about Julia."

"For how long?"

"It was starting when we all first got to know one another, the summer or fall of 1986."

"Was he given anything for it?"

"A couple of hundred marks here, a couple of hundred there. I wondered sometimes about the presents he gave Julia and me, but I never asked. No, he wasn't greedy. But then who was in the GDR?"

"Did you ever suspect?"

"Because I told him back then to stay out of my political stuff?" She shrugged. "I don't know. I don't think I suspected anything. I know that I didn't want to suspect anything."

"Paula?"

"Yes?" She smiled, tired and sad, as if she already knew where the conversation was headed and that it wouldn't get us anywhere.

"Why did you sleep with me?"

She didn't answer.

"Paula!"

She sighed and turned around. I saw her face in the window again.

"Did you do it because he'd betrayed you and you wanted to see if you might not be able to make up with him again if you had a little fling of your own?"

She said nothing, didn't even nod, and I couldn't make out the expression on her face in the reflection.

"Did you want me to feel guilty dealing with Sven, so I'd have no hard feelings about his having betrayed me?"

Again, she said nothing.

"Say something, Paula. You weren't concerned for me, not really. Were you concerned for yourself, did you want me to comfort you? But you didn't leave me any time to do that." I waited for her to say something so that I could have a sense that it was about me, not as a great love of hers, but as someone close and to be trusted.

She was as silent as before.

"Then you must have been concerned for Sven, in one way or another. Then you'll have to admit that to yourself and stay with him. I don't know whether that's awful or wonderful—he betrays you, and you love him all the same."

I waited, and was already assuming she wouldn't respond again. But then she asked her own reflection, "Can you love someone you don't respect?"

"Why did he even start as an unofficial informer?"

"He went to them on his own. He'd been afraid for me for a long time, especially after my first arrest in 1985. When he got to know you he thought he could report about you in exchange for leniency for me. But there was nothing to report," she said with a smile, "except the little bit of stuff he came up with on his own, and once they had him in their clutches, he was easy game."

Sven was standing in the room. I hadn't heard him come in. He must have intentionally avoided making a sound. How long had he been standing outside the door, listening?

Paula whirled around. "You want to keep on doing it? Slinking around and spying? If you want to know something, ask me. But don't come slinking up from behind, not ever again, and—" She was shouting at him, but suddenly broke off. "Oh, do whatever you want." She made for the door.

"Don't go, Paula. I wasn't slinking. I was just being quiet because Julia's asleep. And I thought, if I know what you two are talking about, then I'll know what I still need to say. But I wasn't spying on you."

They were standing face to face. He lifted his arms and dropped them again in regret. There were tears in his eyes and his voice. "I've been so afraid, so afraid all these years. For you, for us, and after the Wall, afraid you'd find out all about it. You never wanted to hear about my fear, I mean my fear for you and us. It was driving me crazy, and you never helped. I'm not as strong as you. I was never as strong as you. I tried to talk with you about my fear and whether you needed to go so far, and you would never deal with any of it." He was crying. "Why didn't you leave me then, when you realized I was weaker than you, more afraid, that I didn't approve of what you were doing? Because you needed me then? In bed? For Julia, because you didn't have time for her? For the housework?" He wiped his hands across his eyes and nose. "Now you don't need me anymore. You're leaving me because you don't need me anymore."

"No, I might need you. But you're no longer the man who—"

"I'm the same man." Now he was shouting. "The same man, do you hear? Maybe I'm no longer good enough for you, maybe you want a better man or already have a better one. But then be honest and say so."

"You don't have to shout, Sven. I'll say what I have to say."

"Yes, once you've decided what you have to say." He turned to me and looked me up and down. "And you? Have you got nothing to say?" He waited, and when I didn't reply, he sat down on the bed and stared at his feet. Paula made for the door, but didn't leave the room. She leaned against the wall where Sven had been leaning.

12

We waited. For what I didn't know. For one of us to say something that hadn't been said yet? For one of us to do something? For Paula to take her things from the wardrobe, pack her bag, and leave? For Sven to leave?

I wanted to leave. But I couldn't. I couldn't leave without a word, and yet didn't know what to say. So I stood there, paralyzed, because words failed me. When I looked over at Paula and she noticed my glance, she gave me a weary and sad smile. Sometimes Sven would lift his gaze from his feet to scrutinize Paula and me.

Then it turned light outside. The sky was gray at first, then white, then pale blue. Before the sun reached the roof next door, its light fell on the massive globe of the television tower, and it glinted our way. What a lot of birds there are in a big city, I thought. They were setting up a racket in the old chestnut tree in the courtyard. I went to the window, opened it, and let air stream in. City air, with a morning freshness only because it still bore the cool of night. From the courtyard came the stench of a row of garbage cans and a compost heap that the eco-commune on the ground floor had started. The church clock struck six.

Suddenly Julia was at the door. She looked around in sleepy surprise. "I've got to be at school by a quarter after seven. We're having rehearsals. Am I going to get breakfast?" She turned around and headed for the bathroom.

Sven got up and went to the kitchen. I heard the refrigerator door close, the oven door, the rattle of dishes, and after a while the whistle of the tea kettle. When Julia came back from the bathroom and pattered down the hall, Paula moved away from the wall and followed her. I heard the closet door in Julia's room open, drawers being opened and shut again, and mother and daughter talking about the rehearsal, what to wear, and the day's schedule. After they had both gone to the kitchen, Sven called out my name.

On the table were four cups and four plates with warmed hard rolls. "You'll have coffee, won't you?" Sven poured. I sat down. Julia talked about the play her theater group was rehearsing, about how rehearsals were going and the technical preparations for the opening. Paula and Sven would make an occasional remark, express admiration, ask a question.

"I'll take you." When Julia stood up, Sven stood up with her.

Paula nodded. "I'm coming along. I'll just go from there to the institute."

Sven closed the apartment door behind us. Julia held my hand on the stairs. Outside she pulled on the school-bag she had been carrying, and took the hands of her parents. The sidewalk was empty, and Paula motioned me to her side and took my arm.

That's how we walked to school. There was hardly any traffic. Only the bakeries were open this early, serving their first customers. As we neared the school we met other children heading for rehearsal. Julia called out to greet them, but did not let go of her parents' hands.

13

AFTER THAT I broke off all contact. I didn't want to see Sven, didn't want to run into him, either. Wouldn't I have to confess to him? Could I confess without compromising Paula? Did I have to compromise both Paula and myself? At times I was afraid his informer's report about the welfare judge with GDR sympathies would become known. Even if it didn't endanger my job, I would have to listen to the stupid remarks of colleagues and attorneys. The very thought made me furious. But above all I was furious when, in my own mind, I heard the cases of Paula against Sven, me against Paula, Sven against me, and me against Sven. I didn't come off all that well, and the better Sven did, the worse I fared. Sven had used me, spied on me, betrayed me. But he had been afraid. He had wanted to save Paula, and had saved her. What was a little spying compared to saving his wife? But then what he'd done to Heinz and Paula was more than just a little spying. But how much more? How was I to measure it? And how would that exonerate me? Paula hadn't wanted to exonerate me; she'd actually tried to draw me in and get me tangled up in it.

I saw her once at a concert. She was in an orchestra seat, I was in the balcony. I was furious at the relaxed way she sat there, stood up at intermission, moved up the rows of seats to the lobby, and returned to her place after the gong. I was infuriated as well by the fact that she was wearing her hair down and by that gesture with which she brushed a strand back behind her ear.

From Julia I learned that Sven and Paula were still living together. She acted as if nothing was wrong. When she visited Hans she would put her head in, sometimes with him, sometimes without, and if it got too late, she would spend the night at my place.

My anger was not good anger. Good anger is directed at others. It requires a clear state of affairs, not a muddle like the one we had managed. When things are in a muddle, your anger is directed not only against others but also against yourself. I was wounded by my own anger. And time and again, I simply felt sad. I missed Sven's childlike, confiding nature, his comments on movies and plays we saw together; I missed Paula's serious way of carrying on a conversation, her flushed face and flashing eyes when she was excited.

All East-West stories were love stories, with corresponding expectations and disappointments. They lived on the curiosity each had about the strangeness of the other, about what he or she had that you didn't have yourself, and what you had but he or she lacked—the things that made one interesting without any effort. And there were so many! Enough to turn the winter when the Wall came down into a spring of curious love for both East and West Germans. But then, what was once strange and different and far away, was suddenly near, commonplace, and bothersome. Like those black hairs of your girlfriend in your bathroom sink, or her big dog that you liked on your walks together, but that got on your nerves in the apartment you now shared. At most the only abiding object of curiosity was how you managed to live together in the midst of the muddle you'd created—that is if you still cared about being together.

Julia invited me to her tenth birthday party. Her parents let her invite whomever she pleased, and it seemed to her the right thing to do was to celebrate not just with friends of her own age, but with older friends as well. Her first pair of glasses, the switch over to middle school, and the crisis in her parents' marriage had made her quite precocious.

Hans and I went together. It was a beautiful day, and when we emerged from the subway near Sven and Paula's place, the sun shone on freshly painted, newly stuccoed façades that had been gray and crumbling on my last visit. There were new sidewalks and bike paths, a new copy shop, a new travel agency, and a new Tunisian restaurant around the corner. The children's playground across the street had new equipment, new benches, new green grass. The past had been dismissed.

We climbed the stairs and rang. Sven opened the door and spread his arms in what looked like a hug but became the gesture of regret and futility I knew so well. "Coffee's all gone. Do you like hot chocolate?"

The table had been extended and set for guests in the living room. Sven's parents were there, Julia's favorite teacher from her old school, a neighbor with his two children, plus friends from school, both boys and girls. From the West, besides Hans and me, was a specialist in Slavic studies, who had worked with Sven at the Free University. The children stormed noisily through the living room, hallway, and Julia's room. We adults stood out on the balcony and didn't know what to talk about. The Slavic studies specialist was outraged by both East and West, everything was going either too fast or too slow for him, demanding too many or too few sacrifices. But no one wanted to argue. We preferred to praise how much Julia had grown, how well she was turning out—athletic, sensible, and always ready to help.

Once everyone was seated around the table, Julia stood up. Sven cast Paula a questioning look, but she just shrugged. Julia gave a speech. She thanked us all for her gifts and for having come, both young friends and old, from both East and West. Unfortunately we didn't see each other as often as we used to, people used to have more time for each other. Now I cast Paula a questioning look as well. It was so easy to lose sight of each other, Julia went on. "Unless," she said with a serious, determined look, "we women hold everything together."

Paula pressed her lips together and her eyes danced. Sven kept his head down. Julia finished her speech, someone began to clap, the others joined in, and Hans was so pleased with Julia that he started laughing, and then Sven could lift his head and join the laughter, and then Paula laughed, too, and we then all laughed at each other.

THE OTHER MAN

───

1

A FEW MONTHS after he retired, his wife died. She had cancer, inoperable and untreatable cancer, and he had taken care of her at home. When she died and he no longer had to worry about her meals, her waste, her emaciated body, her bed sores, he had to worry about the funeral, the bills, the insurance, and that the children received what she had intended them to have. He had to see to it that her clothes were cleaned, her lingerie washed, her shoes polished, and that it was all packed into boxes. Her best friend, who owned a secondhand store, picked up the boxes; she had promised his wife that her elegant wardrobe would be worn by beautiful women.

Even though these were unfamiliar chores for him, he had grown so used to keeping busy around the house when there wasn't a sound to be heard from her sickroom that he constantly had the feeling he had only to climb the stairs and open the door, and he'd be sitting down beside her bed to exchange a word, share some news, ask a question. Then, like a sudden blow, would come the realization that she was dead. It often happened when he was on the telephone, too. He would be leaning against the wall between the kitchen and living room, where the telephone was, everything perfectly normal, talking about normal things, feeling normal, and then it would come to him that she was dead, and he'd have to stop talking and hang up.

Then one day the work was done. He felt as if the line had been cut, the ballast tossed overboard, and he was drifting over the land with the wind. He saw no one and missed no one. Both his daughter and his son had invited him to spend time with them and their families, but although he felt he loved his children and grandchildren, the idea of living with them was unbearable. He didn't want to live in any world of normality that wasn't his old normality.

He didn't sleep well, woke up early, drank tea, played the piano a little, sat staring at some chess problem or other, read and jotted down notes for an article on an issue that he had encountered in his last years on the job and that had stayed with him ever since, without ever really occupying him. By late afternoon, he would begin to drink. He would take a glass of champagne with him to the piano or the chessboard; at his evening meal, a bowl of canned soup or a small sandwich or two, he would finish the champagne and open a bottle of red wine, which he would empty as he jotted his notes or read.

He went for walks through the city streets, in the often snow-covered woods or along the river, frozen at its banks sometimes. He would set out at night as well, at first a bit unsteady on his feet, stumbling now and then, scraping against a fence or wall, but soon with a clear head and firm stride. He would have liked to walk by the seashore, hour after hour. But he couldn't bring himself to forsake the house, this husk of his life.

2

HIS WIFE HAD not been especially vain. At least she had never seemed especially vain to him. Beautiful, yes, he had thought her beautiful and had shown her the delight her beauty gave him. She in turn had shown him that she delighted in his delight—with a glance, a gesture, a smile. There had been a charm in those glances and gestures, and in the way she would eye herself in the mirror. But not vanity.

And yet she died of her vanity. When her doctor discovered a lump in her right breast and advised an operation, she had stopped going to him, out of fear of the mutilation. All the same, she had never boasted of her high, full, firm breasts, nor had she complained as she wasted away during those last months before her death and her breasts hung like empty pants pockets turned inside out to show there's nothing in them. He had always had the impression that she had a perfectly natural relationship with her body, for good or ill. Only after her death, when he learned from a casual remark the doctor made that she had avoided the operation, did he ask himself whether what he had thought was a natural relationship had not in fact been one of self-indulgence and, ultimately, resignation.

He blamed himself for having noticed nothing back then as the operation loomed before her, for her having not wanted to talk with him, to share her fears and arrive at some decision. Back then—he had no spontaneous memories of the period when she must have heard the news about the lump and the need for an operation. He fitted memories together piece by piece, but found nothing remarkable. They had been as close as ever, he had been under no special pressure at work or traveling any more than usual, and she had gone about her job as always, too. She was a violinist in the city's orchestra, coprincipal, first desk, and also gave lessons. He recalled that for the first time in years, after only talking about it, they had actually made music together again, the sonata *La folia*, by Corelli.

His self-reproach fell silent before such memories and made room for an uneasiness as to the closeness between them. Had he deluded himself about that? Had they not been so close? But what could have been lacking? Had they not had a good life together? And they had made love until the last stages of her illness, and talked right up until her death.

The uneasiness also vanished. He often had a feeling of emptiness, though he couldn't say himself what was missing. Even though he could never imagine putting the question to the test, he would ask himself if it was really his wife he missed or not simply a warm body in bed and someone to exchange a few words with, who found what he said fairly interesting and to whom in return he could listen with a fair amount of interest. He also asked himself whether the longing to return to work that he occasionally felt was really about his work and not about a social context of some sort, and some role that he could play well. He knew that he was slow, slow to perceive and to process things, slow as well to involve himself, slow to cut free.

Sometimes he felt as if he had fallen out of his life, was still falling, but would soon hit bottom and could then start all over again—tiny, but from scratch.

3

ONE DAY A letter came for his wife, from someone whose name he didn't recognize. There was always mail for her—printed matter, bills for magazines and club memberships, a letter from some friend he hadn't included when sending the death announcements, but immediately recalled just by looking at her letter, the death announcement of some former colleague, or an invitation to a gallery opening.

The letter was brief, written with a fountain pen in an easy hand.

Dear Lisa,

You think I shouldn't have made things so difficult for you back then, I know. I don't agree, not even now. And yet, as I didn't know then but know now, I have myself to blame. But you're to blame as well. How lovelessly we treated our love back then. We suffocated it. You with your worry and I with my demands, when we could have let it grow and blossom.

There are sins of an unlived life, of an unloved love. Did you know that a shared sin binds the two sinners for life?

I saw you a few years ago, when your orchestra was here doing a guest performance. You've grown older. I could see your wrinkles and the weariness of your body, and I thought of your voice, how it could turn shrill with worry and defensiveness. But none of that helped; if the situation had offered itself, I would have simply got into the car or boarded the train with you and gone off, to spend nights and days in bed together again.

You can't deal with my thoughts? But with whom should I share them if not with you!

Rolf

The return address was a large city in the south of Germany. When he had read the letter, he got out a map of the city, searched for the street, and found it near a park. He pictured the man writing the letter at a desk with a view into the park. He himself looked out at the treetops along the street in front of his house. They were still bare.

He had never known his wife's voice to be shrill. He had never spent nights and days in bed with her. He had never simply got into a car or boarded a train with her and taken off. At first he was merely amazed, then he felt cheated and robbed; his wife had cheated him out of something that belonged to him, or at least was due to him, and the other man had robbed him. He grew jealous.

His jealousy was not restricted to things his wife had shared with the other man and he knew nothing about. How was he to know if she was one person with him and a different person with the other man? Maybe the person she had been with him was the same person she was with the other man. When Lisa and he were at a concert and their hands found one another because they both liked the piece, when he watched as she put on her morning makeup and she tossed him a little glance and a little smile before returning to concentrating on herself in the mirror, when she woke up in the morning and snuggled up to him and stretched, when he told her about a problem at work and she seemed scarcely to listen, only to surprise him hours or days later with a remark that showed how attentive and considerate she was—the intimacy of their life together had been revealed to him in such situations. He had found it self-evident that theirs was an exclusive intimacy. But now nothing was self-evident any longer. Why shouldn't she and the other man have been just as intimate with one another? Why shouldn't she have also sat hand in hand with the other man at a concert, winked and smiled at him while putting on her makeup, stretched and snuggled up to him in his bed?

4

SPRING CAME, and in the morning he would be awakened by chirping birds. It was the same every morning. He would wake up happy to hear the birds and see the sun shining into his room, and for a moment the world seemed in order. But then it would come to him again: the death of his wife, the letter from the other man, their affair, and how in that affair his wife had been a totally different woman from the woman so familiar to him, and yet at the same time must have been exactly the same woman he knew. Affair—that's what he had begun to call what the letter had revealed, and as for the question of whether there were two reasons for his jealousy, he had come to the conclusion that that was the case. Sometimes he asked himself which was worse: that the person you love is another person with someone else or is in fact the person you know so well. Or is one just as bad as the other? Because you're robbed either way—

robbed of what belongs to you and of what should belong to you?

It was like an illness. A sick person likewise wakes up in bed and needs a moment to recall that he's ill. And just as illness passes, so mourning and jealousy pass as well. That much he knew, and he waited to get better.

With the onset of spring his walks became longer. Now they had destinations. He no longer just headed off, but crossed fields to arrive at the locks in the river that angled across the plain, or walked through woodlands to the castle above, or through blossoming orchards at the foot of the mountains to reach a neighboring town, where he stopped for dinner and then took the train home. More and more often he would take his usual late-afternoon bottle of champagne from the fridge, only to put it back. More and more often he also found himself thinking of things that had nothing to do with his wife, her death, the other man, and their affair.

One Saturday he walked into town. He had had no reason to do so for the last few months. There was a bakery and a grocery where he lived, and he hadn't needed anything more. As he neared the center, as traffic grew heavier, and the shoving throngs of people ever larger, as he passed store upon store and the air became filled with voices, the hum of traffic, the melodies of street musicians, the cries of peddlers—he became frightened. He felt the busy, noisy crowd pressing in on him. He went into a bookstore, but it was also full of people jammed between the shelves, at the tables and cash register. He stood for a while near the door, unable to decide whether to stay inside or leave, blocking the way as people bumped into him and muttered annoyed apologies. He wanted to go home, but did not have the energy to step out on the street and walk home, to board a tram or look for a taxi. He had thought he was stronger. Like a convalescent patient who overtaxes himself and suffers a setback, he would have to start healing all over again.

When he finally managed to get himself onto the tram, a young woman stood up and offered him her seat. "Aren't you feeling well? The way you were standing there in the bookstore had me worried." He did not remember having seen her in the bookstore. He thanked her and sat down. His anxiety didn't let go. To start healing all over again—did that mean that he had hit bottom? He would have gladly believed it, but had a sense that he was falling ever deeper.

At home, he lay down on his bed in broad daylight. He fell asleep and woke up a few hours later. It was still bright, and the anxiety was gone.

He sat down at his desk, took out a sheet of paper, and wrote, without date or salutation:

Your letter arrived. But it could no longer reach the woman you wrote. The Lisa you knew and loved is dead.
B

For a long time his wife and friends had called him BB, until at some point it became simply B. He had signed memoranda and directives at the office with a *B* for Benner. He had made a habit of signing personal mail with a *B* for Bengt as well, even notes to his children, who called him "baba," not "papa," slipping affectionately into the soft regional dialect. He liked the idea that B was right for so many different roles.

He put the sheet of paper in an envelope, addressed it, added a stamp, and tossed it in the mailbox a few blocks away.

5

THREE DAYS later he received a reply.

> *Dear Bay!*
>
> *You no longer want to be the Lisa that I loved? She is supposed to be dead to me?*
>
> *How well I understand your wish to forget the past when it reaches so painfully into the present. But it can only reach into the present if it is still alive. The past we shared is still as alive for you as it is for me—how good that feels! And how good, too, that, although you never answered my letters back then, you have written me now. And that you have remained my Bay, even when you hide it in an abbreviation.*
>
> *Your letter has made me happy.*
>
> *Rolf*

Bay? Yes, she had had brown eyes and reddish-brown curls, fine brown hair on her arms and legs, bleaching to blond in summer when she tanned, and a lot of brown moles. Out of admiration he had sometimes called her my brown beauty. My Bay—that was something else. It was curt, overbearing, possessive. Bay—that was a mare whose muzzle you stroked, whose flank you patted before swinging up onto her and exerting the pressure of your thighs.

He went to his wife's writing desk, a Biedermeier piece. He knew that it had a secret compartment. But when he had gone through her things after her death, he had been reluctant to search for it. He emptied out all the compartments, pulled out all the drawers, found the wall where the secret compartment had to be, and, after a while, the piece of molding that he had to push to turn the wall into a cube that rotated on its axis till it revealed a door. It was locked; he forced it open.

A packet of letters with a red ribbon—from the postmark he could tell that they were the letters of the young love his wife had told him about. A poetry or photo album with leather straps and a lock. He recognized the handwriting of her parents on another packet with a green ribbon. He also recognized the handwriting of the other man. Four letters were held together by a large paper clip. He took them over to a chair by the window, a wing chair with a sewing table, both Biedermeier pieces like the desk, all bought together with Lisa before their marriage. He sat down and read.

Lisa,

Things have turned out differently than you imagined at the beginning and they're more difficult. I know that it sometimes frightens you and that you'd like to run away. But you mustn't. Nor do you have too. I'm with you, even when I'm not beside you.

Do you doubt my love because I don't make things easier for you? That's not within my power. Yes, I would like it better, too, if things were easier for us, if we could be together, live for one another, and nothing else mattered. But the world isn't like that. And yet it's a wonderful world, for it allowed us to find and love each other.

I cannot leave you, Lisa.

Rolf

No, Lisa, not again. We tried a year ago, and six months ago, and you know that I cannot leave you. I cannot be without you, any more than you can be without me. Not without my love, not without the passion I give to you. If you leave me and I crash I'll drag you down with me. Don't let it come to that. Be mine, just I shall always be your

Rolf

You never came. I waited for you, hour after hour, and you never came. Ah well, she's not going to make it on time, I thought at first, and then got worried and telephoned around, to be told by your cleaning lady that you couldn't come to the phone. By your cleaning lady! You didn't just not come, you had your cleaning lady make excuses for you.

I am full of anger, forgive me. I have no right to be angry with you. It was all too much for you, things couldn't go on like this, they had to change, and you could only show me that by not coming. And that's the only way I could possibly have understood this.

I have understood it, Lisa. Let's forget everything for a while that's weighing down on us. You'll be in Kiel with your orchestra next week, add an extra day or two to the trip for us. And let me hear from you soon.

    Rolf

The cleaning lady! The cleaning lady! Is she there every day? At least she's there every time I call. Or your husband— he's soon going to start to wonder about the man who calls in the evening and then always hangs up when he answers. Oh, Lisa. There's something absurd, comical, about my failed phone calls. Let's put an end to the absurdity, let's laugh at the comedy, laugh together, laugh in bed, cuddle and laugh and cuddle again and laugh again and . . .

I'll be here all next week. I'm waiting for you, not just on our day and at our usual time, I wait for you every day and every night and every hour.

    Rolf

The writer had not dated any of the four letters. The postmark on the first letter lay twelve years in the past, eleven for the other three, mailed within a few weeks of each other.

What happened after that last letter? Had Lisa given

in? Had the other man given up? Simply given up without another letter?

6

HE COULD remember the period the letters came from quite well. There had been an election eleven years ago, and although the same coalition remained in power, the cabinet secretary for his department had changed. The new secretary had sent him into temporary retirement, replacing him, as an independent, with a member of one of the governing parties. Granted, within a year he had been reassigned to a position in a state-funded foundation, an interesting job as it turned out. But he no longer had the kind of power he had had and enjoyed for a few years in the cabinet department.

Yes, during those last years in the department he had been under a lot of pressure, had had to travel a lot and work on his files on the weekends, if not at the office then at home. All the same, he had thought everything was fine with his marriage and family; he had also believed that he had made sure of it by periodic but adequate interactions with his wife and children. But had he really? It seemed to him now as if he had not only been fooling himself, but had done so knowingly. He recalled situations when Lisa had seemed distracted, cold. "What's wrong?" he would ask. "Nothing," she replied. "Something's not right." "No, everything's fine. I'm just tired," or "It's that time of the month," or "My mind's just on the orchestra" or "on a student of mine." He had not probed any further.

And then, when he had lost his department post, soon after that last letter? To his shame he realized he had even fewer memories of his marriage and family from his year of temporary furlough. He had felt he had been treated unjustly, had felt hurt, had licked his wounds and waited for someone—the world at large, the government, the cabinet secretary, his friends, his wife, his children— to right the wrong. He had been so busy watching what he got or didn't get from others that he had never even noticed how things stood with them. He remembered his campaign against his noisy children and their friends. In his mind their happy racket had been a failure to respect his need for peace and quiet.

He found nothing in his memories that could answer the question of whether the affair between Lisa and the other man had continued after that last letter. There had been occasions during that difficult year when Lisa would approach him, and he, as children do, would push her away, so that she would love him in spite of it, really love him. He remembered that much, but nothing else of what went on between them. He couldn't imagine that she could have spent a great deal of time outside the house, except with the orchestra, without his noticing, since he had been at home the entire time. But what had he noticed for that whole year?

He wrote:

Your letters now are like your letters back then; they're pushing me. You're pushing me. If that doesn't change, or better, if you don't change, you'll never hear another word from me. Don't make the same mistake again.
B

It left him feeling uneasy. But he found it didn't matter. He would have felt as uneasy if he hadn't written the letter. Or written a different one. Lisa had pulled away from the other man, and if that is how things had stayed, he wanted to come to terms with that. And if it had not lasted long. And if it had not gone too deep.

7

Lisa, my Bay,
Be fair. I was desperate back then. I had made a mess of my life, despite all your help and my own efforts to fight back, and then you tossed me out of your life as well, the way you would throw a stray dog out of your apartment, and then close all the doors and windows. I didn't know what to do. I wasn't trying to push you. I only wanted to reach you, see you, talk to you. I don't remember precisely what I wrote in those letters to you back then. But I can't imagine that what you call my being pushy doesn't show my desperation, my fear of losing you or

*having already lost you. And then when I finally got you on the
telephone and met you in the rain, just around the corner, and
you told me that it was over, for good, that you no longer could
or would see me—didn't I leave you in peace?*

Or maybe you don't mean just the end. Do you mean the
beginning? When you ran away from me and I ran after you
and caught up with you there beside the church wall? Yes, but if
I hadn't pushed my hands against it, one on either side of you,
and trapped you inside my arms, I couldn't have told you what
I had to say. But I didn't touch you, until you put your arms
around my neck. And our first night, you put your arms around
me then, too—don't you remember? It was cold, so cold you
didn't want to come out from under the blanket, and so I sat up
and leaned across you and turned out the light on your side, and
then you finally brought your arms out from under the blanket,
and took me to you.

I know you kept asking me later if I hadn't been plotting
our first meeting for a long time, whether I hadn't set you up.
Back then I was unwilling—still am—to say that we met by
chance. It was a gift from heaven.

Do you still have the pictures? Only you have prints of that
first set. A colleague of yours took them, and I can still see you
in one: the restaurant in Milan, all those musicians sitting
around a big table, and me beside you, after the oboist saw me
sitting alone at a table and invited me over to join your party.
The next set of pictures are from Lake Como—I still have the
negatives. We had the little boy from the fruit stand snap one of
them, and we look confused but in love, happy and determined.
And another shows that big old white hotel where we spent our

first night; the mountains still have snow on them, and you're leaning against our rental car and have a scarf wrapped around your head the way Caterina Valente did in the fifties. You took only one of me, without my noticing; I had stepped out on the balcony, my coat on, ready to leave, and I'm looking down at the lake where there's not a single boat or ship in sight because it's still cold. And the one of you in the early morning light, the one you gave me in a silver frame.

If you felt that I was pushing you—at the beginning, at the end, whenever—I'm sorry. I thought we both were suffering under the pressure of the situation, that neither of us was as free as we would have liked to be. Each of us was trapped in a different way, and perhaps you found your conflicts harder to bear than I did mine. But I didn't have it easy, either, and the hardest part was that I constantly had to ask you for help.

I don't dare ask to see you again. But you should know that I would like that very much.

Rolf

He had put the album back in the secret compartment where he had found it. He took it out now, cut the leather strap, and opened it. The album also began with the pictures of the table in the Milan restaurant: eyes blinded by the flash, gestures animated by alcohol, empty bowls and plates, full and empty carafes, bottles, and glasses. He recognized several of Lisa's colleagues. She was sitting beside a man he had never seen before. In every picture he was smiling at his neighbor, at Lisa, at the camera, raising a glass in his left hand, his right arm around Lisa's shoulder. Then came the pictures from Lake Como: Lisa and the other man beside a fruit stand, Lisa with a car in the driveway of a turn-of-the-century hotel, Lisa beside a palm tree at the shore, Lisa in a café, a cup of espresso and a glass of water on the table in front of her, Lisa with a black cat in her arms. He also found the other man on the balcony overlooking the lake. And he found Lisa in bed. She was lying on her side, arms and legs wrapped around the quilt, and her sleepy, contented face turned toward the camera.

There were other pictures too. In some he recognized the buildings, streets, squares, the castle or a church in the city where he lived. Some might have been taken in the other man's city. No pictures suggested any more trips. The last one showed the other man in a swimsuit coming across a lawn and carrying a towel. Tall, slender, with good posture and a confident stride, a full head of hair and a gentle smile—he was a good-looking man.

8

HE EXAMINED himself in the mirror. The white hair on his chest, the liver spots and moles all over his body, the fat at his hips, his thin legs and arms. His head with its sparse hair, the wrinkles in his forehead, the deep creases etched between his eyebrows and running from his nostrils to the corners of his mouth, the thin lips, the sagging skin under his chin. He did not find pain or sadness or anger in his face, only vexation.

Vexation was eating away at him, consuming his past life in little bites. Whatever had kept his marriage afloat—love, intimacy, habit, Lisa's cleverness and solicitude, her body, her role as the mother of his children—it had kept his life outside their marriage afloat, too. It had even kept him afloat during his occasional fantasies of another life and other women.

He slipped on his robe and called his daughter. Could he come tomorrow? Not for long, just a few days. No, he was still managing on his own. He wanted to talk with her.

She told him to come. He could hear the hesitation in her voice.

Before he left the next morning he wrote a reply. He still couldn't bring himself to address the other man directly. Once again the letter began right in:

You're so good at self-deception! Yes, we each were dealing with a different situation—but what was it we had in common? And why should it have been so hard for you to have to ask me for help? I gave it. Wasn't that harder? Making things prettier than they are—you did it back then, and you're doing it now. Yes, I still have the pictures. But when I look at them, they don't bring back happy memories. There were too many lies.

You want to see me. We're not that far along yet—if we ever will be.

B

He hadn't used his car in months. He had to call a mechanic to help get it started. Driving again felt strange, but not unpleasant. He turned on the radio, opened the sun deck, and let the spring air in.

The last time he had driven this route was with his wife. She had already been very ill and had weighed next to nothing; he had wrapped her in a blanket and carried her down the stairs and across the street to the car. He had loved doing that—tucking her in, lifting her up, and carrying her. Before they went anywhere she would let him wash and comb her, and put on a little eau de cologne; she had stopped wearing makeup. He carried her, and she was fragrant and sighed and smiled.

The memory was unclouded. He noticed that his memories of the last years, the years of illness and dying, were untouched by his latest discoveries. As if the Lisa whom he had wooed, with whom he had had a family and won a place in life, and the other Lisa who had slowly ebbed away were two different people. As if sickness and dying had canceled out everything his jealousy tried to grasp.

The road led through small towns, fields, and forests, through an ordered world of white stucco and red bricks, and a well-ordered nature, too, flaunting its brilliant green and rioting colors. The streets in the towns were deserted; the children were in school and the adults at work. Between towns he met an occasional car, a tractor, a truck. He loved this rolling landscape between mountains and plain. It was part of his and Lisa's home and they had remained faithful to it even when his career had taken him to a high-level job in the capital. They had kept their house here, the children had remained in their school, and he had commuted to work sometimes only for a day, or several days, or even a whole week. The children loved this landscape as well; even when they left home they didn't go far—an hour by car to his daughter's, two to his son's. And at high speeds on the autobahn it took half that. But he wasn't in any hurry now.

He tried to plan the conversation he wanted to have with his daughter. What should he tell her about Lisa and himself and the other man? How could he ask if Lisa had spoken to her about him and the other man? He thought he knew that Lisa and his daughter had been close. But he wasn't sure. His memories of Lisa and his daughter arm in arm, of his daughter coming home and calling for her mother, or of Lisa on vacation with him, but spending hours on the phone because their daughter needed to talk with her—that all came from a time when his daughter was still a teenager.

9

"WHAT DID you want to talk with me about?"

His daughter was making up the couch in the living room for the night. He had offered to help, but she had said no, and he stood there now with his hands in his pockets. Her voice as she asked was defensive.

"Let's talk about it tomorrow."

She smoothed out the blanket and stood up. "Since mother died we've invited you again and again, and I thought it would do both of us good to get closer, since we're both . . . since you've lost your wife and I've lost my mother, and Georg and the children would have been delighted, too. You turned us down and that hurt a lot. Now here you are and want to talk. It's just like it used to be, when for months you didn't pay any attention to us and then suddenly one Sunday morning wanted to take a long walk with us and talk. We couldn't think of anything to say, and you got angry—I'd rather put all that behind me."

"Was it so bad?"

"Yes."

He stared at his shoes. "I'm sorry. I lost contact with you when I had so much to do all those years. That left me with a bad conscience, but I didn't know what to ask you. I was more desperate than angry."

"Desperate?" his daughter asked ironically.

He nodded. "Yes, really desperate." He wanted to explain to his daughter what his life was like back then and that he had been aware that he had lost his children's trust and how it had hurt him. But he could already see rejection of what he wanted to say in his daughter's face. She had become stern and bitter. Behind it all, he could still recognize the open, happy, trusting girl she had once been, but he could no longer speak to her or draw her out. Nor could he ask how that happy girl could become such a bitter woman. All the same, he could ask the question he had brought with him, even if she did snub him again. "Did your mother ever talk with you about our marriage?"

" 'Your mother'—can't you simply say 'Mother' or 'my wife' like other husbands, or 'Lisa'? You make a point of saying she's my mother, as if . . . as if . . ."

"Did your . . . did Mother ever say that she didn't like it if I spoke of her that way?"

"No, she never said she didn't like anything you did."

"Do you remember a time, about eleven years ago? You had just finished high school, and that summer . . ."

"You don't need to tell me what I did then. I know myself. That summer, to celebrate my graduation, Mother and I spent a week together in Venice. Why?"

"Did she talk about me on the trip? About our marriage? Maybe about another man?"

"No, she didn't. And you should be ashamed to ask questions like that about Mother. Ashamed." She went briefly into the hall and came back with two towels. "Here. The bathroom is yours. Breakfast is at seven-thirty, and I'll wake you at seven. Good night."

He wanted to take her in his arms, but as he stepped toward her, she just gave him a little good-night wave and slipped out of the room. Or was it a wave of dismissal?

He didn't use the bathroom. He was afraid. The trip down the hall to the bath demanded more courage than he had. What if he opened the wrong door and suddenly found himself standing in his daughter's and her husband's room? Or in the children's room. Or in the stairwell, with the apartment door closed behind him? He would ring the bell, curse himself, and have to apologize. He decided not to visit his son, either. And he wouldn't visit Lisa's best friend to ask her about Rolf.

10

HE LEFT the next morning, when the house was empty, when his daughter and her husband were at work and the children in school. He said his good-byes in a note.

The trip took four hours. He didn't know the city well, but found the street, the house on the park, and a room in a nearby hotel. He hung up his clothes in the wardrobe and went for a walk. His hotel was on a little street that crossed a wide avenue with wide sidewalks and ended on a little square. From a bench in the square he could see down the street where the other man lived. His house was an art nouveau building that had been divided into apartments, and like neighboring buildings it looked out on a brook and the park to the rear.

Over the next few days, whenever he walked to the bench, he found it empty. The warm weather certainly was inviting, but it was only a few steps farther to the benches in the park, where it was much nicer to sit. He stayed here for the time it took him to read his paper, no more, no less, then walked past the other man's building, and crossed the brook into the park. He made his rounds a bit later each day. And all the while he forged his plan— to investigate the other man, to encircle him, to research his habits and likes, to win his trust, to find his weak point. Then—he didn't know what would happen then, what he would do next. Somehow he would erase the other man from his and Lisa's life.

Around noon on Tuesday of his second week, he was sitting on the bench when the other man came out of his building. He wore a suit with a vest, had on a tie, and had pushed a matching handkerchief into his breast pocket. A dandy! He was heavier than in the photographs, but cut a stately figure as he strode swiftly along the sidewalk. When he reached the square he turned down the small street, then again on to the wide avenue. After a few hundred yards he took a seat on the terrace of a café. Without his even ordering, the waiter brought him coffee, two croissants, and a chessboard. He then took a book from his inside breast pocket, set up the chessmen, and played out a game from his book.

The next day, when the other man arrived, he was already sitting at his own chessboard, playing a game of Keres versus Euwe.

"The Indian gambit?" the other man asked, stopping to watch.

"Yes." He took a black pawn with a white rook.

"Black is going to have to sacrifice his queen."

"That's how Keres saw it too." He took the white rook with the black queen, and then took her with the white queen. He stood up. "Allow me to introduce myself, my name is Riemann."

"Mine's Feil," the other man responded. They shook hands.

"Would you care to join me?"

They drank coffee together, ate croissants, and played the game out. Then they played a game of their own.

"Oh Lord, it's three o'clock, I've got to go." The other man hastily said good-bye. "Will I see you here tomorrow?"

"Certainly. I'm staying in town for a while."

They made a date for the next day, then the next, and then they no longer needed to make a date. They would meet at 12:30, have a late breakfast, and play a game of chess. Then they would talk. Sometimes they strolled through the park.

"No, I was never married. I wasn't made for marriage. I was made for the ladies, and the ladies for me.

But marriage—occasionally I had to make a run for it if things got sticky, but I was always fast enough." He laughed.

"You never met a woman you would have liked to live with?"

"There were plenty of women who wanted to live with me. But when I'd had enough, I'd had enough. You know Sepp Herberger, the soccer coach: 'The game ends, the game begins.' "

Or they spoke about their professions.

"You see, for someone who had international responsibilities for so many years—New York one day and Hong Kong the next—my job was a bit different from going to the same office and doing the same thing day after day."

"What did you do?"

"Let's call it troubleshooting. I put things back together when other people messed them up. Rebels kidnap the wife of the German ambassador or the daughter of the representative of Mannesmann, a thief offers to sell a stolen painting back to the National Gallery, the successors to the Communist party park all their money with the Mafia—you get what I mean?"

"You negotiated with the rebels, the thief, or the Mafia?"

"Somebody has to." The other man looked important and humble.

Or they talked about their hobbies.

"For years I couldn't imagine life without polo. You

play golf, don't you? No? Well, polo is to golf as riding is
to walking."

"You don't say."

"You don't ride either? How can I explain to you? It's
the fastest, hardest, and most chivalrous game there is.
Unfortunately I had to give it up after taking my last fall."

Or they talked about dogs.

"So, you had a dog for a long time, did you? What
kind of dog?"

"A mutt. He was part German shepherd, part rott-
weiler, and part something else. We got him when he was
a year or two old, he'd been kicked around and beaten, so
he definitely had a hangdog look. And stayed that way.
But he was as happy as he knew how to be, and would've
let himself be ripped to shreds for the family. That's if he
hadn't crept under a chair first to hide."

"A loser. Something else I simply can't bear. Losers.
I once had a prize-winning Doberman, won prize after
prize. A fantastic animal."

11

A SHOWOFF, he thought, a dandy and a showoff. What
did Lisa see in him?

He called his cleaning lady and asked her to send his
mail to the hotel.

No, my Bay, it wasn't all that hard to help me. We both thought it would be a success. Besides, you enjoyed my needing you. For me the hard part was not being able to manage on my own.

It taught me a lesson. My life is different now. And it's not true that I make things prettier than they are. I see in them something pretty that others don't see. I showed you pretty things as well, things you had never seen, and I made you happy along the way.

Let me open your eyes and make you happy again!

Rolf

For fear of giving himself away he had not told the other man the name of his hometown. That was being unnecessarily cautious and deprived him of topics for conversation, little fishhooks that the other man could swallow and that he could use to reel him in. So he mentioned the city's name, saying he had lived there for a while at one time.

"I once had a place there myself. Do you know the area along the river, between the new bridge and the other one, even newer, I forget the name? That's where it was."

"We had a house in the same area, but on the meadow behind the school." He named the street, his street.

The other man frowned. "Do you remember any of your neighbors?"

"One or two."

"Do you remember the woman who lived at number thirty-eight?"

"Brown hair, brown eyes, a violinist, two children, husband was a civil servant? Do you mean her? Did you know her?"

The other man shook his head. "What a coincidence. What a coincidence. Yes, we knew one another at one point. I mean, we had . . ." He looked at his hands. "She's a fine woman."

His wife was a fine woman? Although the other man had said it respectfully, to him it sounded condescending and arrogant. It annoyed him.

It also annoyed him if he lost a game to the other man. It didn't happen often; the other man played recklessly, had his eyes on the street or on a woman or a dog at a nearby table, talked a lot, praised his own moves, huffily reneged on the bad ones, and if he lost declared, at great length, why he actually should have won. If he won, he gloated like a happy child. How cleverly he had exchanged his rook for that knight or sacrificed a pawn, how slyly he had strengthened his center by weakening his queen's flank—the other man interpreted and presented every move in the game as proof of his superior ability.

By the second week, the other man hit him up for money. Could he pay for him? He'd forgotten his wallet. The next morning he hit him up again. He hadn't left his wallet at home as he'd thought. He must have left it in the trousers he'd sent to the cleaners and he wouldn't be able to pick them up until after the weekend. Which is why he wanted to ask for a larger sum to tide him over the weekend. Four hundred marks would surely be too much, but how about three hundred?

He gave him the money. He was annoyed by the other man's request. He was also annoyed by the man's expression when he asked him for money and took it. As if his asking and taking were a favor.

He was annoyed that he didn't know what his next step should be. Go on playing chess with the other man, lending him money, and listening to his swaggering stories, including, someday, the story of the man's affair with his wife? He had to move in closer.

He wrote his cleaning lady, enclosing a letter for the other man and asking her to drop it in the mail for him.

Yes, maybe we should see each other again. In a few weeks I'll be visiting your city and we could meet. Your life looks different now—so show it to me. Show me your work, your friends, and the woman in your life, if there is one. We can't simply pick up at the point where we left off. But perhaps there is room for me in your life and for you in mine—in the center, and not just along the edges.

B

He paid the other man a visit. Uninvited and unannounced, he rang his doorbell. The plate with names, bells, and an intercom—all in shiny brass and nicely matching the art nouveau façade and doorway of the well-tended building—listed the other man's name last. The entrance door was open, and when he didn't find the man's name on either of the apartment doors on the ground floor, he started down the stairs—the treads of the same marble as the entrance hall and a railing of the same carved oak as the stairs leading to the upper floors. These led to the basement, and at their foot on the right was a metal door labeled "Cellar." But on the left was an apartment door with the other man's name. He rang.

The other man called out, "Frau Walter?" and after a while, "I'm coming." After another while he opened the door. He was standing there in baggy sweatpants and a soiled undershirt. Visible beyond the door were a window on a level with the rear garden, an unmade bed, a table full of dishes, newspapers, and bottles, two chairs, a wardrobe, and, through another open door, a toilet and a shower. "Oh," the other man said, stepping out into the hall and closing the door behind him, "this is a surprise."

"I thought I'd just . . ."

"Tremendous, really tremendous. I'm sorry I can't receive you in proper fashion. Quarters are too cramped down here, and it's been so long since I've even bothered with things upstairs. I've been camping here in the cellar for two months now because I'm taking care of the turtles. Do you like turtles?"

"I've never . . ."

"You've never dealt with turtles? Even people who keep them as pets don't really know them. And how can they like them if they don't know them? Come with me." He led him through the metal door and down a hallway leading to the furnace room. "They'll be on their own soon, but I tell myself, better safe than sorry. That almost never happens around here, that turtles bear young. When the old one started digging by the bushes last fall, I thought of everything except that she might be burying eggs. Three eggs, I put them down here in the furnace room, and little turtles hatched from two of them."

There was only a dim light in the furnace room. Before his own eyes could grow used to it, the other man took his left hand and placed a tiny turtle on the palm. He could feel the clumsily rowing legs, a gentle scratch and tickle. Then he saw it, its shell like that of a large turtle, with the same wrinkled skin at the neck, that same slow blinking of old, wise eyes. At the same time it was poignantly small, and when he rubbed it with the fingers of his right hand, he could feel how soft the shell still was.

The other man was watching him. How ridiculous the other man looked—that fat belly hanging over his sweatpants, those arms pitifully white and thin, and that face with its blatant fervent longing for praise and admiration.

Was it true? Or had the other man bought the little turtles? Could you buy turtles that small? Did he usually wear a corset to keep in his fat belly? Was he living in this dump of a cellar so that he could claim a fancy address and emerge from a fancy building every morning in his fancy suit?

The little turtle in his hand brought him almost to tears. So young and already so old, so defenseless and awkward and already so wise. At the same time, the other man annoyed him. His slovenly appearance, his shabby apartment, his braggadocio, his need for approval—and Lisa had preferred this loser to him?

12

A FEW DAYS later the other man pulled an envelope from his jacket pocket and laid it on the table. "I've just received important news." He smoothed the envelope with one hand. "A famous violinist will be visiting me— I know you'll understand that I can't tell you her name. I'm going to give a reception for her. Are you staying in town? May I invite you?"

But the man was less concerned about the invitation than about winning a financial backer. "You can come? Wonderful! Then may I also ask you to help me out of a momentary difficulty? One of the real estate deals I'm involved in at the moment has tied me up longer than I want. With the result that I'm having a little cash-flow problem—but that shouldn't be allowed to spoil my reception, should it?"

"How much money do you need?" He looked at the other man, who once again cut a neatly dressed figure in suit, vest, tie, and matching pocket handkerchief. The ties and handkerchiefs changed frequently, there were two suits, and always the same pair of black wing-tip shoes with Budapest broguing and a spotless shine. He hadn't realized all this until now. Nor had he realized until now that on their walks through the park the other man insisted they use asphalt or gravel paths that would protect his shoes. So he had something to do with real estate and was tied up in a property longer than he wanted to be. Was he the caretaker for the art nouveau villa? He would give him the money. The reception would be an opportunity for him to meet the other man's friends and acquaintances. Find an opportunity to expose him in front of them.

"Are you familiar with the Trattoria Vittorio Emanuele two blocks down on the left? It's one of the best Italian restaurants I know, and there's a back room, opening onto the courtyard, that you can rent for private parties. I know the owner. He wouldn't ask more than three thousand marks for a dinner for twenty people."

"A dinner? I thought you wanted to have a reception?"

"That's my idea of a reception. Can you help me with the costs?"

Even as he nodded, the other man began making his plans—what was to be on the menu, how the aperitif could be served in the courtyard if the weather was good, how there should be speeches, which people he would invite.

The people he would invite—that was the topic at every breakfast from now on. From the list of possible guests, whom he named and described, his own life began to take shape. He talked about the theater he had once owned, and about people from the theater and film—not famous people, or at least famous no longer, but a name or two sounded familiar all the same. He mentioned a former chief of police, a canon of the cathedral, a professor, and a bank director; he had once done them favors, and he was sure they'd be happy to come. What sort of favors? He'd been able to give the chief of police a clue during a hostage episode, without his help the professor and the bank director would not have realized in time that their adolescent children were having drug problems, and the cathedral canon had had difficulty with the matter of celibacy. He also wanted to invite the top two men of his chess team, in which he was number three. Among the real estate agents with whom he was dealing at present, only a few were people of quality, but he could invite one or two. "As for my international contacts, I unfortunately have to keep hands off. Secrecy is everything to them."

After the other man had run through the same names over and over again, he said, "And my son."

"You have a son?"

"I've had hardly any contact with him. You know how it used to be with illegitimate children. As the out-of-wedlock father, you were allowed to pay child support but there were no visits, no days and vacations together. At any rate my son knows that I'm his father." He shook his head. "I fear that as far as I'm concerned, he's somewhat prejudiced. But for that very reason it would be a good idea for him to see me in my world, don't you agree?"

After days of happy planning, he grew anxious. He

had received a second letter, with the date of the visit. "Two weeks from Saturday. The trattoria is available; but I'll have to hurry with the invitations. And what if no one comes?"

"Why don't you include an R.S.V.P.?"

"R.S.V.P.—of course. But the answers could be either refusals or acceptances. Do I write: 'In honor of the violinist . . . I have the pleasure of inviting you to dinner at the Trattoria Vittorio Emanuele,' or do I write: 'The violinist . . . is paying our city a visit, and for the occasion I have the pleasure of . . . ,' or do I leave the name out and write: 'An old friend and famous violinist is visiting our city. I have the pleasure of inviting you to dine with her . . . ,' or do I switch the beginning around, 'A famous violinist and an old friend . . .'?"

"I would leave the name out. I like brief invitations the best."

The other man left the name out, but was not to be deprived of his "famous violinist and old friend." The invitations were in the hands of their recipients two weeks before the date. Now began the wait for acceptances and refusals.

It was with mixed feelings that he observed the other man's preparations, hopes, and worries. If revenge was his goal, the invitation provided the opportunity, even if he did not yet know what form it would take. And along with the other man, he hoped for acceptances. And so he helped out with money and advice. At the same time, however, he begrudged him everything, including the acceptances. The other man was a dandy, phony, babbler, loser. He had invaded his marriage. He had presumably invaded other marriages. Presumably he wasn't the only one he had hit up, he had probably swindled other people out of their money as well.

One evening they went together to the Trattoria Vittorio Emanuele to check out the space and the menu. Paté tricolore, lamb with polenta and contorni, torta di ricotta, accompanied by pinot grigio and barbera. The food was excellent, but the other man continued to worry about every detail—wasn't the paté too firm? Was there enough rosemary on the lamb? Shouldn't there be a different selection of contorni? He worried whether people would come, if his son would come, wondered if his speech would go all right and if he could do anything else to make a success of the visit by the famous violinist and old friend. He confided that the lady was a woman who had once been very dear to him, and vice versa. Then it occurred to him that he was sitting across from one of the lady's ex-neighbors. "We spoke about her recently—do you remember? She's a fine woman, and you shouldn't jump to any conclusions."

13

MOST PEOPLE turned him down. Acceptances came from a few of the people in the theater and film, the canon of the cathedral, the second man on the chess team, and his son. Others were invited to replace those who had declined. But the other man was not really convinced about these added invitations. He scarcely knew the people he now invited, or found that they really weren't much to boast of.

As the difficulties of making a successful event of the dinner increased, he grew more subdued. "You see, I've kept my social life to a minimum of late. You know how it is. Sometimes a man focuses more on the outside world, sometimes more on his inner life. I had hoped that with the reception I could get back to a social life. It's a good thing you'll be coming. I can depend on that, can't I?"

One day on the way back from the toilet at the café terrace where they ate breakfast and played chess, he passed the telephone, where he overheard the other man saying something about his friend, a former state secretary in the Department of the Interior. He asked him about it. "Who's your friend, the former state secretary?"

"Why you. Didn't you say that you'd worked in the Department of the Interior? And a man of your stature—well, I know what's what, even if I'm not told directly."

Before whom, then, was he to expose the other man at dinner? Before guests who were as much losers as the other man himself? He had occasionally imagined how he would say that the famous violinist was unfortunately unable to come, but had responded to a letter that he, as an ex-neighbor, had written her in expectation of seeing her again. She had asked him to read her letter at the dinner. In the letter he would hold the other man up to ridicule and disdain—not crudely, not heavy-handedly, but in a seemingly most genial way: "I am happy to see your hopes finally fulfilled. I would have so much enjoyed sharing your success with you and your friends. I'm proud of you, and of myself as well. Do you see? Back then, when no one believed in you, I did and I'm so glad I had the money to help. And you've finally shown the whole world."

He was fairly certain that the nature of Lisa's help had been financial. It had been easy to discover that the other man's theater had gone bankrupt eleven years previously. He had only to speak with its current owner. He had not inquired at Lisa's bank. But nothing of the inheritance she had received shortly after their marriage had been left at her death. That had surprised him when he closed out her bank accounts, for if she had spent the money or given it to the children, he would have known. In the first years of marriage the money could have made life easier, but they had resolved not to touch it unless there was no other choice. But things went well, and soon they were earning more than they spent. So he had been surprised. But to investigate as to when and where those fifty thousand marks had gone—he had not been in the mood for that after her death.

He did not write the letter that would expose the other man. He wrote a few paragraphs of it in his head, but whenever he sat down to put the rough draft to paper, he had no energy for it. At first, the dinner was still a long way off. Then, in view of the guests to be expected for the event, the whole idea became dubious.

But it wasn't just that he didn't have the energy. His jealousy and anger had lost their power as well. Yes, he had been cheated and robbed. But hadn't Lisa done penance enough? And in those final years had she not belonged to him in ways about which the other man hadn't the least notion? But then what sort of notions did the other man have? He was a loser, a dazzler, and if things had not been so bad for Lisa at the time, he wouldn't have had a chance. He was too tawdry to be jealous or angry about.

He decided to leave. At first he was going to visit the other man in the cellar where he holed up and say good-bye to him there. Then he postponed it till their next breakfast.

"I'm leaving today."

"When are you coming back? It's only three days away."

"I won't be coming back. I don't want my money back either. Have dinner with whoever comes. Lisa won't be coming."

"Lisa?"

"Lisa, your Bay, my wife. She died last fall. You haven't been corresponding with her, but with me."

The other man's head sank. He took his hands from the table, laid them in his lap, his head and shoulders drooped. The newspaper vendor came by, laid a paper down, and then took it away again without a word. The waitress asked, "Will there be anything else?" and got no answer. A convertible pulled up to the curb and stopped in a no parking zone; two women got out, came laughing down the sidewalk and sat down at the next table, still laughing. A terrier sniffed from table to table and at the other man's legs.

"What did she die of?"

"Cancer."

"Was it bad?"

"She got very thin, so thin that I could carry her in one arm. The pain wasn't bad, not even at the end. They know how to deal with that nowadays."

The other man nodded. Then he looked up. "You read my letter to Lisa?"

"Yes."

"Then you wanted to find out what I was to Lisa? Who I am? You wanted to take your revenge on me?"

"More or less."

"So do you know now?" When he got no answer, he went on. "The revenge took care of itself because I'm a loser in any case. Right? A showoff, who brags about the old days, as if they were fine and golden, not tinsel and bankruptcy and prison. Is that it? Oh, you didn't know that bit? Well, now you do."

"Why?"

"Your wife paid my debts and paid for my lawyer at the second trial, but the court revoked my probation from the first one. I had tried to save my theater."

"But you don't—"

"—land in prison for that? Yes, you do, if you act as if everything is better than it is, as if there were money when there is none, and contracts when there's not an investor in sight for miles, and promises from actors you've never seen and never spoken with. But you know all that. Didn't you write me that I make things prettier than they are? Yes, I make them pretty. I make them prettier than they would otherwise be. I can do that because I see something pretty in them that you don't see."

The other man straightened up. "I can't say how sorry I am about Lisa." He cast him a defiant look. "But I'm not sorry for you. Because I have something else to say to you. Lisa stayed with you because she loved you, even more in bad times than she loved me in good times. Don't ask me why. But she was happy with me. And I'll tell you why that was. Because I'm a braggart, a blowhard, a loser. Because I'm not the monster of efficiency, righteousness, and peevishness that you are. Because I make the world pretty. You see only what it presents to you on the surface, and not what's hidden underneath." He stood up. "I should have noticed. Those letters sounded so peevish, as peevish as you are. I read them for prettier than they were." He laughed. "Good luck."

14

HE DROVE HOME. Inside the front door were the letters that the mailman had pushed through the slot and notices of packages waiting for him at the post office. The cleaning lady had not come again after he had asked her to send his mail to him. She had also left the garbage that he had gathered from the kitchen before he left, standing in the entryway. The entry and the stairway stank. The flowers that Lisa loved and that he had tended in her memory were gray withered things, shriveled tendrils on cracked earth.

He set to work at once. He removed the garbage and the dead flowers, cleaned the kitchen, defrosted the refrigerator and wiped it clean, vacuumed the living and bed rooms, changed the bedding, and did the laundry. He fetched the packages from the post office—those that hadn't been sent back—did some shopping, and looked around the garden, checking for what he would have to take care of in the next days and weeks.

He was finished by evening. It was late—by the time the last load of laundry was done and hung up to dry, it was midnight. He was content. He had put an end to an unpleasant episode. He had put his house in order. Tomorrow morning he would begin to live his life again.

But he woke up the next morning just as he had woken up before setting out on his journey. The sun was shining, the birds chirping, a gentle breeze came through the window, and the sheets smelled fresh. He was happy, until it all came to him: the letters, the affair, his jealousy and anger, his disgust. No, he hadn't put an end to things. He had arrived nowhere, hadn't hit bottom so that he could begin all over again, nor was he in the middle of his old life or a new one. His old life had been a life with Lisa, even after her death, even after he had discovered the affair and had turned jealous. He had lost Lisa in the course of his war against the other man. She had become a stranger to him, the way the other man was a stranger, an entry in the ledger of love, jealousy, reconnoitering, and revenge—and all of it disgusted him now. Here she had lain beside him and here, after her death, he had kept the memory of her so alive that it had sometimes seemed to him that he needed only to reach out his arm to be able to touch her. Beside him now was just an empty bed.

He went to work in the garden. He mowed, pruned, hacked, weeded, bought and set out new plants, and noticed that the flagstones by the bench under the birch had to be replaced and the fence to the street needed painting. He spent two days in the garden and realized that he could spend another three, four, or five. But by the second day of hoeing, raking, and pruning, he no longer believed that by putting flower beds or roses or boxwood back in order, he was putting his life back in order as well.

He no longer believed in falling and hitting bottom, so that he could start all over again. He had loved that image, had imagined the fall and the impact as painless, weightless. But falling could be something quite different. If he fell, then maybe it would be a crash landing, leaving him lying there with broken limbs and a shattered skull.

The third day he stopped working. It was close to noon; he put the paint and brushes away, and hung a Fresh Paint sign on the half-finished fence. He checked a schedule for trains to the city in the south. He would have to hurry. The reception was to begin at seven; the other man had told him the time often enough, and it had also been in the last letter to Lisa that had been in the waiting mail.

Once on the train, he asked himself whether he shouldn't get out at the next stop and go back, and when he arrived, whether he shouldn't go to his hotel, spend a day or two in the city, and finally simply enjoy its beauties. But the address he gave the cabdriver was the address of the Trattoria Vittorio Emanuele, and he got out there, went inside, and crossed the private room toward the back. The doors to the courtyard were open, and guests were standing outside in groups of two or three, holding glasses and little plates, and the other man was moving from group to group. Dark silk suit, dark shirt, matching tie and handkerchief, the familiar black shoes with Budapest broguing, a full head of black hair, an animated face, demeanor and movements easy and assured—he was the star. Had he borrowed the suit? Had he dyed his hair? Was he wearing a corset, or just doing a good job of holding his stomach in? As he asked himself that last question and tried to tuck in his own, the other man spotted him and approached.

"How wonderful that you've come!"

The other man led him around and introduced him as a retired state secretary. If I'm a retired state secretary, who might that be hiding behind the canon of the cathedral or these actors? Who was that behind the embarrassed smile of the colleague from the real estate business, or the loud women from the world of fashion? The second member of the chess team was genuine—a retired truck driver, who described his success at the chessboard with the same broad motions he must have used to steer his truck around curves. The son was genuine, too, a television technician, about thirty years old, who watched his father and the guests in curious, casual astonishment.

The other man was a perfect host. If a glass or plate was empty, a guest left standing alone, a conversation faltering—he missed nothing, and nudged the waiter, pulled the lonely soul into the conversation, and kept regrouping his guests, until they had all discovered that they enjoyed talking with one another. After half an hour the courtyard was filled with the buzz of voices.

As it grew dark, the other man invited his guests inside. Small tables had been assembled into one large banquet table. The other man led each guest to his or her seat, sat the retired state secretary at the upper end of the table on his right and the cathedral canon on his left, and beside each, one of the two ladies from the world of high fashion. When everyone was seated, he remained standing. His guests noticed and grew silent.

"I invited you because I wished to celebrate with you a visit from an old friend. She is not coming. She is dead. A dinner of welcome and return has become a farewell dinner.

"That doesn't mean we can't be happy. For my part I am happy you have come—friends, my son, Lisa's husband." The other man laid a hand on his shoulder. "And so I need not say farewell alone. I need not take a sad farewell from Lisa, who was a happy woman."

Was my wife a happy woman? He felt a wave of jealousy pass over him. He didn't want her to have been happy with the other man and not with him, didn't want her to have been happier with the other man than with him. With him—he tried to remember Lisa, laughing, happy, radiant, smiling at him, laughing with him, trying to infect him with her own delight in her children or a piece of music or her garden. They were rare memories. A happy woman?

The other man talked about Lisa's violin playing and the rich variety of her repertoire and interpretations, and, to make things prettier, moved her from coprincipal first desk to soloist. But then he talked about how in Milan he had heard her play the first variation of the adagio from Haydn's string quartet, opus 76, no. 3. He talked as if he could hear her violin dancing its steps with playful and yet controlled grace around the gentle rise and fall with which the melody begins. Hear how she accompanied the melody in its fall with a sob or two, before encouraging it with a little flurry to rise up again full of anticipation. Hear the melody take a new running start, begin its gentle rise and fall again, then make a defiant ascent, linger proudly on one chord as if standing on a terrace, move to a broad flight of stairs down into a beautiful garden, full of happy dignity, before saying goodbye with one grateful and gracious nod. And then the reprise: once more the violin dancing up the scale and down and then stamping several times, hard and heavy, to emphasize its defiance, before riding the turbulence of the variation to pay homage to the melody as it lingered proudly on the terrace and then in dignity descended stairs. And how, in recapitulation, she leapt boldly ahead to the terrace chord before the melody arrived—as if in protest.

The other man paused. Had he heard her playing the piece the evening before they first met? On longer tours, there was always an appearance by the orchestra's string quartet—made up of the orchestra's concertmaster, Lisa, violist, and cellist. Had he seen her play and fallen in love with her? Fallen in love because this delicate woman had played with such power, clarity, and passion that he felt he had to share in some of it? That was how she played. They had not known each other very long before he had seen it too. Later, he had no longer paid attention. Later, Lisa was his wife, the coprincipal, first desk violinist, who was often not there for him in the evenings, although he had need of her and she didn't even earn all that much.

The other man had not made Lisa prettier as a soloist. He had truly seen what a wonderful violinist she was. Whether as a soloist, as concertmaster or co-principal, whether more or less successful, more or less famous—that was unimportant to him. He did not make things prettier, he found them beautiful, found beauty where others failed to recognize it, and he applied the attributes that others used to express their wonder, to express his own. If a wonderful violinist was usually described as a famous one, he would say "famous" when he meant "wonderful." In much the same way he probably saw in himself the stuff it took to be a troubleshooter, a polo player, and an owner of a prize Doberman. Maybe he had what it took. For the beauty he praised contained within it not only a higher truth, but a robust one. He did not speak of Lisa's appearances as a soloist, even if his praise and adulation might have sounded that way to his guests, none of whom would have been disturbed had he done so; he simply described a piece in which, by way of exception, she played the decisive, definitive, dazzling role.

And Lisa's happiness was real as well. It was not that Lisa had been happy with the other man while being unhappy with him, nor had she been happier with the other man than with him. Lisa had shared her happiness in a variety of ways, had both happily received and happily given to others. The happiness she had given him was not a lesser one, it was exactly the happiness to which his ponderous and peevish heart could open. She had held nothing back from him. She had given everything he had been capable of taking.

The other man had finished his speech and now raised his glass. His son stood up, everyone stood up, and they drank to Lisa. Later the son gave a little speech in honor of his father. The canon of the cathedral spoke as well; he spoke about Saint Elizabeth of Hungary and Saint Elizabeth of Portugal, who had reconciled her husband and her son. He had drunk too much too quickly and was confused. An actress began by talking about women and the arts and after a few words about music and the theater, turned the topic to herself. The second man of the chess team stood up, tapped his glass with his fork and, with a thick tongue, asked for attention. He was not a man of grand words, he said, but once he had completed the queen's pawn opening he had been working on for several years now, he would call it the Lisa gambit.

They celebrated long into the night. After he had said good-bye to everyone, he walked through deserted streets to the train station. There he waited on the platform until he could board the first train home. As the train left the city behind, dawn was breaking. He thought of his next morning at home. He would wake up, see the sun, hear the birds, feel the breeze, and it would all come back to him, and it would be all right.

SUGAR PEAS

1

WHEN THOMAS saw that the revolution wasn't about to happen, he remembered that once upon a time before 1968 he had studied architecture, picked up his studies where he had left off, and graduated. He specialized in creating rooftop apartments, searched for suitable roofs, found clients, and took care of plans, permits, and supervision. Rooftop apartments were in fashion, and Thomas was good at what he did. After a few years he had more roofs and clients than he could handle. But they bored him. Roofs—was that all there was?

One day he ran across an invitation to a prize competition for a bridge across the Spree. Even as a boy he had been impressed by the dignity with which the old bridge in Rastatt braces its massive piers in the bed of the Murg, the pride with which the iron bridge in Cologne bears trains across the Rhine, arch by arch, and the grace with which the Golden Gate Bridge sways above the sea, making great ships look very small. The book on bridges that he had been given at his confirmation and read over and over again was still in his office library. He designed a bridge that looked so fragile that pedestrians would necessarily approach it with trepidation and drivers would instinctively cross slowly and cautiously. For he did not regard it as a matter of course that people should cross heedlessly from one shore to the other, and therefore those using his bridge should not treat it as a matter of course either.

To his and everyone else's surprise he was the runner-up. And then he was asked to take part in a competition for a bridge over the Weser. Designing this and entering still more competitions, all without giving up his roof business—it was too much. He named as his partner Jutta, a woman who had trained with his firm for a year and had just received her diploma. She remodeled roofs, he built bridges. When he learned that she was carrying his child, they married. At the same time they moved into the most beautiful rooftop apartment his firm had ever built; the original client had fallen ill and backed out of the deal. The view from the terrace extended from the Spree and the Tiergarten to the Reichstag and the Brandenburg Gate. They could watch sunsets from their terrace garden.

Then bridges no longer really satisfied him either. Success, gross sales, company, and family were all on the increase, and yet he felt something was missing. At first he didn't know what; he thought he needed a greater professional challenge, and worked all the harder. But his discontent only grew. He realized that what had been missing was painting. It wasn't until their vacation in Italy that summer, when instead of designing bridges, he began painting bridges that caught his eye. He had painted all through high school and university, until he decided that the delight he took in it could be fulfilled in architectural design. And the fulfillment had been real for a while. But without even realizing it, he had missed painting.

Suddenly the world was right again. Because architecture was no longer everything to him, he could treat it more playfully. Because he had already been successful as an architect, he no longer had to prove himself by being successful as an artist. He paid no attention to fads and trends, but simply painted what he would have liked to see in paintings: bridges, water, women, and views through windows.

2

BY CHANCE he met a woman from Hamburg, a gallerist who first promoted his paintings. They were sitting next to each other on a flight from Leipzig to Hamburg—she was on her way home from a branch gallery, he was commuting between construction sites. He told her about his paintings, dropped by with a few of them a couple of weeks later, painted one or two she suggested he try, and one day to his astonishment and delight discovered that she was showing his paintings. She had invited him to Hamburg on the pretext that she wanted him to advise her about remodeling her gallery. But when he arrived he found his paintings in all the rooms and everything set up for a vernissage. He came at four o'clock, at five the first guests had arrived, and by eight the first paintings had been sold. By nine, Veronika and Thomas were so drunk on champagne, success, and one another that they didn't wait for the showing to end, but drove to her place. By morning he knew that he had found the woman of his life.

As he sat sleepy-eyed but happy on the train to Berlin, he prepared for his conversation with Jutta. It would not be easy. They had been married for twelve years, had had good days and bad, had coped with caring for three children, including a difficult pregnancy with their daughter, with the struggle for professional success, and with her one minor affair and his two. He felt as if they had become intertwined, she a part of him and he a part of her. They had always been open with one another and also open to a world in constant motion, where things are always changing, including relationships between people. And it wouldn't be easy, either, to confront his children with separation and divorce and the new woman in his life. But Jutta would be fair, and

Veronika would find the right approach, the right tone, with the children. She was simply wonderful.

In Berlin, all hell broke loose. That night there had been a fire on a roof they were remodeling on Ansbacher Strasse. And their daughter was ill. And the woman who looked after the house and the children was visiting her family in Poland for two weeks. By ten o'clock, as they sat down to pizza in the kitchen, both Thomas and Jutta were exhausted.

"I have something to tell you." He pulled her back as she got up from the table and started toward the bedroom.

"Yes?"

"I've met a woman. I mean, I've fallen in love with a woman."

She looked at him. Her face was inscrutable. Or was it just exhaustion? Then she smiled and gave him a quick kiss. "Yes, my dear. And it's been four years since the last time." She counted. "And eight since the time before that." She stood there for a moment and stared at the floor. He didn't know if she wanted to say something else or was waiting for him to say something. She said, "Will you close the window in Regula's room?"

He nodded. His daughter still had a fever. He tucked her in and watched her sleep for a while. Jutta was already in bed. Suddenly it seemed childish for him to sleep on the couch in the living room as he had intended. He undressed and lay down on his side of the bed. Already half asleep, Jutta cuddled up to him.

"Is she dark-haired like me?"

"Yes."

"Tell me about her tomorrow."

3

VERONIKA DIDN'T PUSH. She understood that as long as Regula was ill, it wasn't the right moment for a discussion with Jutta, for separating from her. Not as long as their cleaning lady and baby-sitter was in Poland. Not as long as Jutta still had more than her hands full with the aftermath of the fire and training two new employees. Not as long as he was working on his design for a bridge across the Hudson. After all, with her gallery in Hamburg and the two branches in Leipzig and Brussels, Veronika was up to her ears, too. And in any case she wasn't the sort of woman who constantly had to have a man around. Wasn't it enough that his marriage was an empty shell, encrusted with his firm and children, and that he was living his real life elsewhere with her, every free minute of it?

He divided up his vacations. After a week of skiing with Jutta and the children, he flew from Munich to Florida for a week, where Veronika had a condo. In summer he joined his two sons on a ten-day bike ride, before joining Veronika for a two-week hike through the Peloponnese. During the holidays, he spent Christmas Eve and Christmas Day at home, but the days following and

New Year's Eve in Hamburg. Veronika had set up a studio for him in her large Hamburg apartment, and he painted there. His family understood that he needed to be off by himself when he painted and wanted to tell no one where he was.

Yes, suddenly, with spring, summer, fall, and winter, the year had come round. On January 15, the anniversary of the vernissage, Veronika opened a second show of his paintings. The next morning he again took the train to Berlin, not quite so sleepy-eyed as a year ago, and not quite so happy either. But he was happy. Granted, he didn't think his double life was the right thing. A man really shouldn't live this way. A man shouldn't treat women this way. A man couldn't be a father this way, there for his children only half the time and always on the go. And what would happen if Veronika were to have a child? She hadn't mentioned it, but he had noticed that she was no longer taking precautions. He firmly resolved that he would speak with Jutta. But everything at home was the same as always and there was no reason to talk about separation and divorce just now. As they sat around the dinner table, he knew that he didn't want to lose his family. His two sons, a little wild but great kids, straightforward and always ready to help; his daughter, his blond angel; and Jutta, affectionate, generous, efficient, and attractive as ever—he loved her. Why should he give her up?

The next year Veronika gave birth to a daughter. He was there for the birth, visited her as often as he was allowed, and spent the days in her apartment, painting and waiting until he could bring her and Klara home from the hospital. He had taken leave of his home in Berlin for two weeks, and when the two weeks were over, the apartment in Hamburg had become his home. His second home—his apartment in Berlin had not stopped being home as well. But life here was no longer life at home while life there was just time spent with another woman.

Everything became more stressful. Veronika needed him. She took a petulant tone with him that dripped with patience and drove him crazy, and she treated him as a not totally loveless, but not sufficiently dependable and ultimately egotistical bystander to what was happening— which offended him. "I don't know how I can deal with it all," she shouted at him one day. "On top of everything else, how can I prove that things are better and nicer with me than with your wife?" Later she wept. "I'm being difficult right now, I know. I wouldn't be if we could finally be really together. I've never pushed you, but I'm pushing you now. For my sake and Klara's. She needs you especially during these first years. Your kids in Berlin are long past that stage."

At home in Berlin, Jutta was getting pushy. They had never stopped sleeping together, and in the months before and after Klara's birth, Thomas had once again been as attentive and passionate as in the old days. They would lie side by side, exhausted and content, and Jutta would expand on the New York project. Didn't he want to build the bridge across the Hudson himself? Be in charge of building a bridge for once in his life? Shouldn't they all move to New York together for the two or three years it would take to build it? Send the children to school there? Move into one of those lovely apartments on the park, like the ones they'd seen on their last visit? There was nothing demanding about the way Jutta presented it all, but she had had enough of their current situation and was pressing for it to end. He noticed it, which added to his stress.

By fall it had all become too much. He set out with an old friend from high school and college to hike the Vosges for a few days. The leaves were colorful, the sun still warm, and after a week of rain, the earth now smelled rich and spicy. The hiking path followed the old German-French border along a mountain ridge. Each evening they would find a country inn or descend to a village in the valley. Their second evening, they met two girls from Germany—one a student of art history, the other of dentistry. The third evening they met again by chance. Dinner together was relaxed, cheerful, easy, and after his friend took the art historian to the room the men shared, it went without saying that the evening would end as it had to end, with him and the dentist in the girls' room. Helga was blond, with none of the delicate-limbed, delicate-nerved elegance and energy that Jutta and Veronika had in common; instead, she had a more generous substantiality and was so certain of her own delight in him and his in her, so feminine and inviting, that all the stress, all his worries, all his decisions seemed immaterial.

The next day the four of them hiked together. When on the following day the girls had to leave for home in Kassel, it turned out that they would be spending their winter semester in Berlin. Helga gave him her address. "You'll call, won't you?" He nodded. When by November everything had become too much for him and he couldn't take any more, couldn't take Jutta's proposals and Veronika's reproaches, had had enough of the sweetish odor of baby in Hamburg and the noise of his pubescent sons in Berlin, had too much to do at the office and too little time for painting in his studio, and was feeling distressed by life in general, unable to go on—he picked up the phone to call Helga.

When he was with her, and she couldn't help noticing that he made two phone calls, each one saying that he had urgent business in Leipzig, she laughed and asked, "Do you have two wives?"

4

WITHOUT HELGA he wouldn't have made it through the winter. She didn't ask many questions, didn't say much of anything, but was beautiful, soft, took pleasure in him in bed, enjoyed their drives and dinners together, his presents. He was so happy in the relationship that he spoiled her. She was there for him when he could no longer cope.

Until time came for exams. She needed a patient, asked him, and he didn't want to refuse her request. He assumed he was letting himself in for especially painful shots, especially agonizing drilling, bad fillings, and lopsided crowns, but was willing to accept it all for her sake. In fact he let himself in for something else. Nothing went wrong, there was no pain or agony. On the contrary, every move Helga made was first checked by a dental assistant and then, if he had any doubts or the procedure was especially important or difficult, by the head dentist. It all went smoothly. Waiting for the assistant or the dentist wasn't unpleasant, either. Helga and another student, who would lend her a hand and vice versa, talked and joked with him, and when Helga bent down over him she let her breasts brush against his face. But it took an eternity. He spent hour after hour, half a day after half a day at the clinic. If his appointment was for nine o'clock, the rest of his morning schedule was shot, and if he came at two, he would still be sitting there at five—no meetings held, no construction sites visited, no red tape unraveled. He had to reschedule meetings for the evening and take more work home on the weekends, and his elaborate structure of hours and days in Berlin and Hamburg began to totter.

He realized what a mess he, or Helga, had got him into and wanted to take his half-filled root canals, his half-finished fillings and crowns to his own dentist and be done with it all in two hours. When he told Helga, she reacted with cold rage. He needn't show his face to her again if he deserted her now. She didn't know how she would pay him back for the damage he'd done to her prospects for her exam, but she'd come up with something he'd never forget. He certainly didn't want to jeopardize her exams, he simply hadn't realized that cutting the procedure short would put her in jeopardy, and immediately agreed to let her go on treating him. The heavy artillery she had pulled into position wouldn't have been necessary. But it taught him that there were both determination and an inflexible will beneath her inviting femininity.

Once she had passed her exams with flying colors, she laid out her project of a private dental clinic. She would start the preparatory phase while serving her assistantship. Would he like to be a part of it? Plan and build it with her as the architect? Help shape and enjoy the financial success as a silent partner?

"Who needs a private dental clinic?"

"Who needs apartments? Or your bridges? Or your paintings?" There was a defiant look in her eyes, as if she were asking: Who needs you?

At first he was taken aback, then he laughed. What a fighter Helga was! When the architectural and business contracts were drawn up, he'd have to be make sure he didn't end up with the short end of the stick.

She realized that his question hadn't been meant as a

fundamental objection, and patiently explained to him the advantages of a dental clinic over a simple dentist's practice. "You're thinking that while your doctor often sends you to a clinic, your dentist hasn't ever sent you to a dental clinic. But you're getting older, you can bet on it, and even if your dentist takes care of the whole thing, one way or the other, you can be sure you'll be better off with specialists in exodontics, prosthetics, and periodontics."

First it was who needs you, then you're getting older—Thomas felt that when it came to the give-and-take of their relationship, she owed him somewhat more tender care.

She saw it in his face. She told him what a fine thing it was that he was in her life. How she admired him, as an architect and as an artist. What a man he was. How much she felt like a woman in his presence.

Then she didn't have to say any more.

5

THE SUMMER was full of energy. The city jabbed its cranes into the sky, dug holes in the earth, made buildings grow. The energy of the weather was released in countless thunderstorms. The days were hot, with clouds building up around noon. By late afternoon the sky turned dark, the wind came up, and to booming thunder and the zigzag of lightning the first heavy raindrops fell. It poured for twenty minutes or half or three-quarters of an hour. Then the city smelled of dust and rain and was silent, until the people the thunderstorm had driven inside came out on the streets for the evening. For a little while it turned bright again with late sunshine, a clear twilight between the dark of the thunderstorm and the dark of night.

Thomas had energy, bounce, lightness. He did it all: planned the bridge across the Hudson, finished a series of paintings, developed the private dental clinic project, managed the firm's ongoing business. Together with Jutta he planned two or three years in New York; with Veronika, a life together after his divorce from Jutta; and with Helga, what she called the fashioning and enjoyment of her success. He loved the high of a juggler who keeps adding more and more rings to his act, and it works—one more, and then one more.

And what about the juggler's fear? Does that grow, too, with each added ring? Does he know that his game can't go on forever, has to end in confusion, muddle, and collapse? Doesn't he know? Doesn't he care? In the ease of that summer, Thomas saw his game ending with ease as well—just carefully lay aside one ring after the other. Tell Helga in a friendly way that it was over, that he would gladly remain her friend and help her as a friend, but that there would be no silent partnership, no shared construction of a clinic. With Veronika he would calmly discuss what would happen once it was over. Child support, his contact with Klara, her representation of his work—she knew how to negotiate, was a business woman, as interested in her lucrative sales of his paintings as he was in staying in contact with his daughter. He would explain to Jutta that fifteen years were enough, they could remain partners for the children and partners in the firm, but as for the rest, she needed to let go. What was so hard about taking the rings away again? Or at least one or two of them?

It was his forty-ninth birthday that August. Each of the three women wanted to celebrate it with him. He was used to eluding two women in order to be with the third. It was just as easy to elude all three.

He spent the day alone, and it was like playing hooky. He drove to a lake outside the city, swam, lay in the sun, drank red wine, slept, swam another lap. That evening, at the far end of the lake, he found a restaurant with a terrace. He ate, drank red wine, and gazed out into the evening. He was satisfied with himself and his world.

Was it the red wine? The beautiful day and evening? His success at his profession and his good fortune with women? He had another year before he was fifty and would have to take stock. But the entries in the book of his life would be no different then. Thirty years before, he had set out into the world to make it better and more just. Because there is bread enough for everyone on this earth, and roses, myrtle, beauty, desire, and sugar peas, too. Back then he had been more attracted by the sugar peas in Heine's poem than by Marx's communist society, even though he had no notion of how they looked, tasted, or differed from ordinary peas. But then, he had also had no notion of how a communist society would look, taste, or differ from an ordinary society. Sugar peas? Yes,

> *sugar peas for everyone,*
> *when once the shells burst open!**

Should he take up politics again? Get involved with the Green Party, now home of his former friends? With the Social Democrats, home of his current friends? They were inviting him to become politically active. East and West Berlin, joined under a single administration, needed to grow together politically and architecturally as well. The one wouldn't work without the other, and neither without men like himself. Men—he would prefer to encounter women in politics. An emancipated, political woman with nickel-frame glasses and a bun, from which, when she undid it, red hair would fall luxuriantly down over her shoulders, and whose eyes, with the glasses removed, would look astonished and seductive.

He laughed to himself. That was the red wine now. But was that all? Was there not a deeper wisdom hidden in red wine, revealed to those who are ready? Sugar pea wisdom? You have to be happy to make others happy. You need to let life be good to you, so that you can enjoy it and be able to help it be good to others as well. And even if

---

*Heinrich Heine, *Deutschland: A Winter's Tale* (Chester Springs, Pa.: Dufour Editions, 1997).

you only make yourself happy—every speck of happiness that enters the world makes the world a happier place, whether it was your own speck or someone else's. The one thing you may not do is hurt anyone. He wasn't hurting anyone.

So Thomas sat there on the terrace. The moon was shining and the night was clear. Ah, how good it felt to be satisfied—and with good reason—with yourself and the world.

6

THAT FALL HE had to go to New York. Negotiations with the bridge consortium took several weeks, and he detested the style in which things were handled. The false intimacy of calling people by their first names, the false intimacy of conversations about wives, children, and weekend trips, the false sincerity of the greetings each morning—he'd had enough. He'd also had enough of finding only half of what was agreed to one day in the next day's written contracts and then having to renegotiate the other half. Besides, when the day's negotiations were finished in New York, the workday was just beginning in Tokyo, and everything had to be hashed over again on the phone with his Tokyo partner until the early morning hours.

Then one day he drew the line. There were political

problems with New Jersey that only the governor could solve. When it became clear that he would not solve them before the next morning, Thomas saw no reason to sit there with the others and wait. He left.

He let the city take him where it would, strolled through the park, took a peek into the Metropolitan, passed the buildings where Jutta would have loved to live, crossed through a neighborhood where he heard only Spanish, and finally found a café he liked opposite a large church. Not one of those trendy cafés where you're served promptly and then handed the bill equally promptly and expected to leave. The guests here sat, read, wrote, and talked the way people do in a Viennese café. As if there was no rush. The sidewalk tables were occupied, so he took a seat inside.

Along the way he had bought three postcards. "Dear Helga," he wrote on the first one, "the city is hot and loud, and I don't understand what people find in it. I'm sick of the negotiations. I'm sick of Americans and Japanese. I'm sick of my life here. I long to paint, and more than anything else I long to be with you. When I get back, we'll start fresh, okay?" He wrote that he loved her and signed his name. He saw Helga before him, soft and hard at the same time, both calculating and calculable, often loveless and yet often so in need of love, so ready for love. Ah, and the nights with her! "Dear Veronika," he wrote on the next postcard, and then didn't know how to go on. His last visit with her had ended in an argument. She had treated him badly, but he knew that she had done it out of desperation. Then she had stood at the door and called after him, telling him to go to hell, over and over, and waiting for him to turn back and take her in his arms and whisper in her ear that everything would be all right. "When I get back, let's start fresh, okay? I long to be with you. I long to paint again too, but above all long to be with you. I'm sick of living like this. I'm sick of work, the negotiations, of Americans and Japanese. I'm sick of the city. It's hot and loud, and I don't understand what people find in it. I love you. Thomas." He sat a long time looking at the third card. It showed the Brooklyn Bridge by sunset. "Dear Jutta, do you remember the city in spring? It's hot and loud now, and I don't understand what people find in it. I'm sick and tired of the negotiations and of the Americans and the Japanese I'm dealing with. I'm sick of my life here, too, and that there's no room in it for painting. And that you have no place in it. I love you and miss you. When I get back, we'll start fresh, okay?" He knew how she'd smile reading it— amazed, happy, a little skeptical. That was the smile he'd fallen in love with, twenty years before, and it still enchanted him. He stuck stamps on the postcards, left his jacket hanging over the back of his chair and his newspaper lying on the table, crossed the street to a mailbox, and dropped the postcards in it.

He came back to his table and through the window watched the hustle and bustle on the sidewalk. The window was open; he could have called out to passersby, engaged them in conversation. They were only a few yards away. A few steps outside and he would be one of them. A few steps and they could have entered the café and sat at a table just like him, maybe across the way or next door. At that moment a man veered from the sidewalk into the café, ordered a pastry and a coffee at the counter, gave his name, found a table, pulled out a book, paper, and pen, and waved to the waitress carrying a tray with his order and calling out "Tom." Tom. The same name as his.

He went back to looking outside. The sidewalk was full of people. What were they all doing? Of course he knew that those two were walking with their arms around each other, gazing into each other's eyes, and kissing, that that father, mother, and child there were on the way home with shopping bags stuffed full, that the shabbily dressed black man who kept ducking into view on the left was begging, that these were tourists strolling past now, that those were schoolkids, and that the man in the brown pants and shirt was delivering packages for UPS. But why were they doing what they were doing? Why was that sweet, pretty girl wrapped arm in arm with that pimple-faced bully? Why had those parents added that whining brat to the planet's population, why were they raising it and buying things for it? What were they themselves doing on the planet? You could see that he was an unsuccessful, academic blowhard and that the child was obviously too much for her. What did the beggar expect, how was it that he had come to expect anything, and why should anyone care? Who would miss those pointlessly happy tourists if they were suddenly swallowed up by the earth? Or the schoolkids, if they suddenly fell dead? Their parents? But did it even matter if their parents were to miss them or, later, their own children, or later still, their grandchildren? The tragedy of an early death? That someone would have his life curtailed by early death seemed no more tragic to Thomas than having it ended by old age, or being deprived of life before birth.

The UPS man tripped on the sidewalk and went sprawling with the package he was carrying. Why was he cursing? If death is something awful, then he should be happy he's alive, and if death is beautiful, then in light of its eternity the present or this momentary stumble shouldn't matter to him. A beautiful couple walked past, slender, energetic, happy, with clever, alert faces. Her arm wasn't around some pimple-faced bully his around some dumb blonde. But that didn't make them any better. Thomas saw futility and nothingness even where they were not obvious. He saw them everywhere.

He asked himself whether, if he had a gun, he would be able to blast these passersby to pieces the way his sons did on the computer. It would cause trouble, and he didn't want trouble. But these people framed in the window were no closer, no more real or alive than figures on a computer screen. They were like him. But that did not bring them any closer to him.

7

LOOKING BACK LATER, he saw that this day and this place marked the beginning of his fall. From then on he was a man falling—like the one in the painting by Max Beckmann that he had seen in the home of the president of the bridge consortium. He was tumbling head over heels, helpless despite the strength in his muscular body, flailing his arms and legs as if to swim. He was tumbling between burning buildings, his burning buildings, those he had built and those he lived in. He was tumbling amid birds that mocked him, angels that could have saved him, but didn't, boats floating safely in the heavens, the way he could have floated safely if he had not got involved with buildings.

He returned home and took up his life again. His Berlin life with a family, office, and friends, for whom he was Jutta's husband, the father of three children, architect and amateur painter. He had long been part of their and their families' lives, too, had spent vacations with them, survived marital crises with them, and shared their worries about their children. He moved among them like a fish in water, certain of a mutual trust, even if he preferred not to put it to the test, and certain also of their shared treasury of memories, anecdotes, and jokes. It was different in Hamburg. He had friends there, too, not as many as in Berlin, not by way of his profession, but through Veronika, most of them single, some with a child. For them he was the artist whom Veronika had under contract and who was the father of her child, who was pleasant enough to be around, but who had another life as well, from which he erupted into their world, a stranger really. A warm, trusting relationship had grown up between him and a woman who was Veronika's best friend, a pediatrician—and yet even here his other life was something apart. His second Berlin life was again very different. Like Helga, most of her friends were almost twenty years younger than he, concerned about finishing studies and starting a professional life, their world still not firmly fixed, open for many things, including this older friend of Helga's, a generous man of many talents and a friendly, wise adviser in matters of establishing a medical practice or buying a condo. They were glad when Helga brought him along or he was present when Helga invited them to her place. But his contact with them carried no commitment, just as they perhaps did not feel particularly committed to one another.

Despite the lack of commitment and despite that final distance between himself and his Hamburg friends, and, if he was honest, his Berlin friends as well, being with them all was stressful. He didn't know why. It had still been easy in the summer. Now he felt as if he had to constantly reinvent himself: Helga's, Veronika's, Jutta's Thomas, the architect and artist Thomas, the father Thomas with three growing children and the father Thomas who could almost be a grandfather Thomas of a one-year-old. At times he was afraid he wouldn't be able to reinvent himself quickly and completely enough, and might still be Berlin Thomas in Hamburg or Jutta's Thomas when he was with Helga. After one late night of exhaustion and too much alcohol, when he unfolded to one of Veronika's friends how he imagined life in New York for a German family with school-aged children, and another when he explained at length to a couple with whom he and Jutta had been friends for years just how difficult it was to be a single mother running an art galley, he became more cautious about his drinking. When changing from one life to the other, he got used to concentrating the same way he did before business negotiations, emptying his brain of everything except what he would need next. But that, too, was stressful.

His dreams became stressful, too. He actually began to dream of being a juggler, not with rings but with plates, like the ones Chinese jugglers stack on long poles, or with knives or burning torches. At first it would go well, then he would increase the number of plates, knives, or torches until he could no longer handle them all. As he lay there buried under them, he would wake up drenched in sweat. He often slept only a few hours.

One morning on the train from Hamburg back to Berlin he found himself engaged in a conversation with the man across from him. He represented a company that made blinds, talked about blinds for home and office, wooden and plastic blinds, blinds to absorb heat and noise, about the invention of the blind and its superiority to curtains, about his trips and his family. It was a nice, diverting, inconsequential conversation. For a long while Thomas merely listened. When asked about his own whence and whither, his job, family, and the circumstances of his life, he heard himself talking about his factory in Zwickau, about the drafting instruments he produced, about the problems he foresaw as people switched from drawing boards to computers, about his family's struggle to keep the company going in the fifties and after the wall came down. He told about his house on the river, his wife, who was confined to a wheelchair, and his four daughters. He was returning from Hamburg, where he had bought sandalwood and cedar he was using for a new line of high-end pencils. Sometimes he traveled as far as Brazil and Burma for wood for his pencils.

8

HE RESOLVED that he would end his relationship with Veronika. Each time he would arrive in Hamburg with the intention of telling her—after their daughter was in bed and they were sitting at the kitchen table—that he wanted to go back to Jutta, that of course he was ready to talk with her whenever she liked about child support, his contact with his daughter, and the sale of his paintings, and then calmly leave. But as they sat there at the kitchen table, with Veronika so happy that the day was over and

he was there, he couldn't get the words out of his mouth.
And if she was unhappy, then he certainly couldn't talk
about it, because he didn't want to make her unhappier.
He postponed the talk till morning. But mornings belonged to their daughter.

He told himself everything there is to be said in such
situations. That it was merely a matter of ending a state
of affairs that had become unbearable. That if he didn't
really want to remain with Veronika, then he should not
hold on to her any longer, but let her go and live her life.
That a horrible ending is better than unending horror. Or
might he stay with her after all? No, he was already so
psychologically and physically removed that he couldn't
stay with her any longer and would never find his way
back to her. No, there was nothing, nothing that he could
offer as an excuse for his inability to talk with her. He
experienced it as something physical, as if he wanted to
speak but his mouth, tongue, and throat wouldn't obey,
the way a paralyzed arm won't obey the command to lift
and move. But his mouth, tongue, and throat weren't
paralyzed. He would sit on the train to Berlin and feel
ashamed.

Then he decided to put the easier task before the
harder and end his relationship with Helga first. He managed to speak with her. He explained to her that he
wanted to go back to his wife and family. Granted, nothing would come of their ambitious plans. But he would
like to remain her friend and help her out as a friend.

Hadn't they spent lovely times together? Shouldn't their good-byes be just as lovely?

Helga listened attentively. When he was finished, she stared at him wide-eyed. Her eyes welled up and overflowed, big tears rolling down her cheeks and dropping on her skirt. Then she threw herself in his arms with a sob, and he held her, felt her soft body, tried to say something to comfort her, but she shook her head and pressed her mouth against his. At breakfast the next morning she told him about her latest idea for the dental clinic. Did he think it was feasible?

He didn't even try to talk with Jutta. As he sat across from her one evening, he pictured to himself how she would react, what she would say, and then how he would fold his tents. Yes, he would fold his tents with Jutta as well and be happy to have a reconciliation and then finally be taken in her arms. The pitifulness and pointlessness of his decisions, this ridiculous back and forth—he began to laugh, and couldn't stop, laughed hysterically, until, at her wit's end, Jutta slapped him twice, which brought him to his senses.

He was amazed how much he accomplished despite everything. He revised the plans for the bridge over the Hudson and designed a new bridge over the Drina. He painted a new series of pictures—all of women paddling canoes, some standing, some sitting, some clothed, some nude, some dark, delicate-limbed, and delicate-nerved, some blond and soft, some redheaded and energetic. Veronika exhibited the first paintings even before the series was complete, and a collector immediately expressed interest in the entire series.

The appendicitis attack came like a stroke of salvation. He was driving from Dresden to Munich when the pain started. He first thought it was a stomachache, but it was soon apparent that it had to be something different, more serious, far worse. Terrified and hunched over the steering wheel, to ease the pain, he made it to a district hospital on the far side of Hof. He was operated on at once. The next morning the doctor making rounds told him that his symptoms could have indicated pancreatic cancer and how pleased he was that it was only an inflamed appendix.

Thomas stayed in the hospital for a week. He imagined the doctor opening him up, discovering inoperable pancreatic cancer or an abdomen full of metastases, and sewing him up again. He would then have only a few weeks or a few months to live. He would be free of responsibilities, owe no one anything, be treated considerately and attentively by everyone, perhaps even admired for how he was conducting himself. He would be able to say good-bye to Helga, Veronika, and Jutta, without their being able to reproach him or any self-reproach on his part. He would paint a picture, his final and most profound work. He would spend time with his children, time so beautiful and close that it would illuminate their lives long after his death. He would write an essay on the bridge, his theoretical legacy to architecture. A few months—that was all he needed for closure, for finding peace. And happiness. He envied any man with only a few months to live as a happy man. Truly a man with his cares behind him.

Why shouldn't he be that happy man? He had called Berlin and Hamburg to report about his appendectomy. But that would also fit in with how he would conduct himself if he were going to die in a couple of months— first talk about an appendectomy so as not to frighten anyone, and then confide the truth later, softening the blow.

And so he returned to Berlin and was the same man as always, except a little quieter, a little more downcast, more dignified, distracted at times—like a man, that is, who has been singled out by death. Then he told them. He withstood their dismay, their insistence that he consult other doctors, their helpless concern. Each of the three asked him what he was going to do now, and he told each of them that he would go on living as before— what else? Doing what was essential and leaving whatever was unessential aside. Paint a picture. Write an essay on bridges. Spend time with his children. And in fact he did set a new canvas on his easel, buy a new fountain pen, and make plans with his children.

9

NOT THAT HE had actually begun to believe he had cancer. But when Veronika barked at him one weekend in Hamburg—for sitting at the table after their meal instead of helping with the dishes—he was outraged. How could she demand he help with housework knowing that he had cancer? Besides, the incision really did still hurt; if they had opened him up for an appendectomy and sewed him up with metastases still inside, it couldn't have hurt any more than it did now without them. And he still felt weak, overtaxed, exhausted.

No, the way Veronika had treated him wasn't right, and Jutta and Helga really ought to have shown him more consideration, too. Jutta, who saw him at home now more than ever in the last few years, asked him to help his sons with their homework, to pick their daughter up from her music lessons, to repair the blinds, and hang up the laundry. "That isn't too much for you, is it?" Helga, who wanted him along for meetings and inspections of possible sites for her dental clinic, was happy to play chauffeur—but he suspected that this was less to spare him and more to be able to drive his BMW. But whenever he wanted to sleep with her, she would shake her head and ask, "Can that be good for you?"

He himself noticed that he was getting whiny and grouchy. But he considered what was happening to him simply unjust. He had drudged away for three women, and now, when he was having a rough time and could have used them, they simply went on living their lives. He had made Jutta an equal partner in the firm, sharing with her the profits of his success, and had allowed Veronika to earn more from his paintings than galleries usually take, and had coddled Helga with gifts the way a petty prince coddles his mistress. True, each would have liked to have had more of his time. But on the days he spent with each, he had made her happy. Besides, all women complain that their husbands have too little time for them, even those whose husbands don't have other women. No, he had done all he could for them, and they were not repaying him as they should. They had forced him into a situation from which his only escape was cancer and death. What was he actually going to do in a few weeks or months? Healthy as he was? They had driven him into a dead end.

One day he visited his tailor. The sign over the door of the little shop, which you reached by descending a few stairs, read Alterations, but the mustachioed Greek who owned it could not only alter and repair, but made the finest shirts, suits, and coats as well. Thomas regularly had him make his ankle-length nightshirts, because they were unobtainable in regular stores. Only as he stood there in the shop, ordering a new nightshirt, did he realize for the first time what an absurd order it was. For a man who would die in a few weeks or months.

Then he saw a roll of heavy wool, a radiant dark blue.

"That's material for a coat or jacket. A customer wanted me to make a cape for him, but then changed his mind."

"Can you make something from it for me?"

"What would you like?"

"A cassock, like the ones monks wear, ankle-length like my nightshirts, with an attached hood and deep pockets."

"With buttons? A lining? With loops for a belt or a cord?"

Thomas thought it over. Did monk's cassocks have buttons? Or a lining? He decided for a lining and loops, but against buttons. He wanted to pull the hood up over his head. He also decided for a dark green cord and dark green along the seams and for the lining.

"Would you also like . . . ," the Greek signed a cross on his breast with one hand, "embroidered in the same color?"

No, Thomas didn't want a cross.

"Yes, well then I know all I need to know."

"How long will it take you?"

"A week."

A week. "I need to be alone for a while," he said over the next few days to Jutta, to Veronika, and to Helga. "I don't know where I'll go, but I know I have to get away. It's all been too much. I've got to get hold of myself." He thought they would protest, hold him back or want to go along. But they simply took note of it. Jutta's only demand was that he postpone his departure for two days to deal with the workers who would be repairing the roof. Veronika said fine—that way she would be able to put a girlfriend of hers up in his studio for the next week. Helga asked if he was taking his car or if he would leave it for her.

He bought a long, lightweight, dark raincoat. He packed the coat, a second pair of shoes, a sweater, a shirt, underwear, black socks, and a pair of jeans in a leather satchel, along with his toiletries and shaving gear. He postponed his departure two days, let Helga have his BMW, and cleared all the finished and unfinished paintings out of the way in his studio—including the easel with the empty canvas for his final, most profound chef d'oevure. Carrying his leather satchel and a large plastic bag, he entered a rest room at the Zoo train station. When he came out he was wearing the cassock, and in its place had stuffed what he had put on that morning into the plastic bag. He dropped the bag into the garbage, bought a ticket, and boarded the train.

10

He traveled for a whole year.

At first he spent money like water. He stayed a few weeks in Brenners Park Hotel in Baden-Baden and a couple more at the Baur au Lac in Zurich. The personnel and the other guests first eyed him in astonishment, but then were happy to enter into conversation and came to trust him. He listened to life stories, stories of pain and guilt, of the blisses and misfortunes of love, marriage, family, everyday life. The head of reception once called him in the night to care for a woman who had been about to hang herself, but was accidentally found in time by a chambermaid and cut down. He talked with her on into the morning hours. The next day she departed, leaving behind a check for several thousand dollars made out to his religious order.

Sometimes he sent postcards to Berlin and Hamburg, not to Jutta, Veronika, or Helga, but to his children. When he called Helga once, the first thing she asked was whether he wanted his car back. Her next topic was payments he owed as part of his silent partnership. He hung up. When his credit card was about to expire, he began to worry and withdrew all the cash he could.

But there was no need to worry. Once he had had enough of expensive hotels, he needed hardly any money. He usually spent nights free of charge in monasteries and ate meals there for free as well. At first he hesitated telling his story of the Order of Saint Thomas, which had survived both the Reformation and Communism among the Saxons of Transylvania, but which now counted only five brothers, and which he, as a descendant of Transylvanian Saxons, had joined a few years before. But he grew more assured with each telling, allowed himself embellishments, and calmly parried all questions. Often the monks did not want to know much. They showed him his cell, nodded to him in the chapel and at meals, and responded to his farewell greeting. When he had had enough of monastery life, he would spend the night in small hotels and pensions. Both there and on his train trips, people sought out conversation with him. He judged no one, commended no one, felt sorry for no one. He listened, and if he was asked something, hit the ball back.

"What should I do?"

"What do you want to do?"

"I don't know."

"Why don't you know?"

He almost made love to a woman once. Whenever he had to have his cassock cleaned, he would go to the cleaners in the afternoon, asking that his cassock be ready by evening and that he be allowed to sit in the corner and wait. Once, in a small town in the Hunsrück Mountains, it was very late before the cassock was ready. The woman closed the shop and let down the blinds. Then she came to him and hitched up her smock a bit, sat astride his knee, and clasped his head between her arms and breasts. "My little chicken," she said in sad sympathy—because in his white T-shirt and jeans, both of which had become too big for him, and with the bad cropped haircut he had given himself, he reminded her of a plucked chicken. He spent the night with her, but without having sex. The next morning, as he sat across from her in her late husband's bathrobe, she asked whether he might not like to stay on a while.

"You wouldn't have to hide. You can wear my husband's clothes, and I'll say you're my brother here visiting me. How strange—you're the same man without your cassock . . ."

He knew that. At the very start of his journey on the train he had sat across from a construction contractor from Leipzig for several hours, a man he had often done business with, who looked him over but did not recognize him.

But he didn't want to stay. He gave the woman a wry smile and a shrug of regret. "I have to move on."

He realized that if he were to stay, he would have to sleep with this woman. But he didn't want to. Years before he had given up smoking, from one day to the next, and the ease of living without the fifty or sixty cigarettes he had previously smoked each day had left him pondering the question of what was essential. To give up alcohol next, then love, then food—to him these seemed easy, natural steps, and once he took the last one his physical existence would be unessential. When he had first set out in his cassock, he had given up alcohol and found it easy to live without the bottle of red wine he used to empty every evening. In assuming the celibate life, he had made the next step as well, and food had come to mean less and less to him in any case.

He often felt as if he were floating. As if his feet weren't touching the ground. As if people didn't truly notice him or as if the faces and bodies he saw were not real, live human beings, but phantoms, structures that formed and melted only to form and melt again.

Occasionally he would touch them, by chance or intention, to be sure their bodies offered resistance. He also had no doubt that they would bleed if wounded. They would scream perhaps and, if the wound was bad enough, cease to move. But whether they moved or didn't move—what did that mean? Wasn't the world already full to overflowing with structures that moved?

His life in Berlin and Hamburg truly seemed a phantom world now. What had he been doing with those three women? Why had he painted pictures and built bridges? What sort of drive had kept him moving along with so many others? What had been all the fuss in his office or at the gallery or the plans and projects with Helga? His children didn't make any sense to him, either. What was it they wanted on this earth? Who had called them into being, who needed them?

He watched a boy fall from a pier into the water of Lake Como. The boy screamed, briefly flailed at the water around him, and went under. There was no one around to help him. Thomas at last stood up from the bench where he had been sitting, ran to the pier, jumped into the water, rescued the boy, and got him breathing again—but he had done it all because he didn't want any trouble. If anyone had seen him sitting there and not moving and then reported it to the police, his life in a cassock would have soon come to an end.

11

HIS LIFE IN A cassock came to an end. On the way from Como to Turin he changed trains in Milan. The doors of the train from Milan to Turin had snapped closed automatically just as he was about to board. He stepped back and noticed that his cassock was caught in the door. He tried vainly to get the door open again, tugged at the cassock, tugged as he ran alongside the train as it began to pull out, and as the train moved faster and faster he soon had to run so fast that he could no longer try to free his cassock from the door. He heard laughter from travelers on the platform, who did not understand his plight and found a running blue monk hilarious. No longer able to keep up with the train, he threw himself backward in desperation and in the hope that his cassock would rip. But the heavy woolen fabric held, and the train pulled away, dragging him with it the length of the platform and then over the gravel beside the rails. Someone leaning out of a carriage window became aware first of the sudden horror of the travelers on the platform and then of the emergency itself and pulled the emergency brake, but before the train finally came to a halt, Thomas was nothing but a bloody sack.

They took him to the hospital. Days later, when he returned to consciousness, the doctor told him that his spine had been injured and he would be paralyzed from the chest downward. His only reason for going to Turin had been to see if there were still horse-drawn cabs there and worn-out horses to pull them, like the one that the mad Nietzsche had hugged.

All patients are equal in intensive care. But when Thomas was transferred to a regular ward, he was placed in one of sixty beds in a large hall that had been constructed in the twenties as an emergency ward in the event of catastrophe and was now used for patients at the low end of the insurance scale. It was loud, even at night. Soldiers, who were already well but still playing sick because they would rather be in a hospital than in their barracks, drank and partied and sometimes even brought in girls for the night. By day it was hot and stank of food, cleansers, disinfectants, and excrement. Thomas's bed stank; he had no control over his excretory functions. The nuns who ran the hospital tried to look after the blue monk, but they spoke no German and he spoke no Italian. One day a nun brought him a German Bible. He was amazed at how much life there was in the book. But for that very reason, he didn't want to read it.

His injuries healed. After three weeks he knew he could endure the noise and stench no longer. Hadn't life before the accident become a phantom and an irrelevance to him, hadn't he felt removed from it and from himself? Now life was very immediate, real, palpable—but it was the life of a cripple in a sewer. Only that sense of floating that he had known before the accident held true. He had felt as if his feet weren't really touching the ground, and that was the case now—his feet would never really touch the ground again.

Four weeks later, with no announcement, he was taken away. One day men were standing beside his bed with a gurney; they put him on it and wheeled him away.

"Where are we going?"

"We're supposed to bring you to a rehab clinic near Berlin."

"Who sent you?"

"If you don't know—our boss didn't tell us either. But if you don't want to come, we'll leave you here." The attendants came to a halt. "Do you want to leave or not?"

They were standing in the door to the hall where he had lain for almost four weeks. No, he wasn't going to stay here, no matter where they were taking him.

12

HE SPENT two months at the rehab clinic. He learned to deal with the inert and unfeeling half of his body, with his excretory functions, with the sores from sitting and lying, with his training equipment, with his wheelchair. He spent a lot of time in water, at first in a swimming pool and then in the lake on whose shore the clinic was located. He made such progress with his exercises that he thought he would have will and discipline enough to reconquer everything—water with the help of water wings, land with his wheelchair—and to restore speed and mobility to his crippled body with the strength of his arms. But when, despite his learning, his will, and his discipline, he developed the third of the sores common to paraplegics, he knew that he would no longer be able to depend on his body.

He had learned that his doctor, a friend of many years, had arranged for him to be transported from Milan to the rehab clinic. His own insurance had paid for the journey and the stay. When he wanted money to buy underwear, shirts, pants, books, and a CD player, he called his bank. His account had been closed. But then several thousand marks were wired into it and made available to him. Six weeks into his time at the clinic, he had his fifty-first birthday. That morning he received a bouquet of fifty-one yellow roses. The card attached identified them as coming from TTT, a licensing and marketing agency that he had never heard of. That afternoon his doctor friend paid him a visit.

"You look good—tanned, healthier, and stronger than the last time. Was that a year and a half ago? Or was it at your vernissage in the spring? At any rate, what a fine thing that you'll soon be home again."

"I have no idea what's going to happen with my life. I didn't want to call Jutta, but I'll have to do so at some point. I'll probably get a disability pension and an apartment through the welfare office, and a conscientious objector—do you think I'll get one?"

"They're called alternative service aides, and if

you're entitled to one, then Jutta has already taken care of it. She's looking after everything."

They sat beside the lake, Thomas in his wheelchair and his friend on the bench. Thomas had a sense that he had best be careful about what he said and asked. But he was curious. He cautiously said, "There are a lot of things I'd like to know about."

"That'll take care of itself. I think it was wise of you to leave everything to Jutta and not worry about any of it yourself. The daily routine will start soon enough, and be difficult enough." His friend put an arm around Thomas. "I've also been impressed by your not wanting to meet Jutta until you've put yourself back together."

"When is that going to be?"

"Finish your two months. I've spoken with your doctors. They think you'll improve even more, and it'd be a good idea if they can keep an eye on your heart for a while yet."

The friend left him a package from Jutta. Thomas opened it and found the catalog from his show last spring. There had actually been one in Berlin, arranged by Veronika's gallery in Hamburg. His drawings—Veronika had collected his sketches, roughs, and first drafts and tagged them with audacious prices. Thomas also found a small brochure that identified him as the author of "Thoughts on Building a Fantasy Bridge over a Fantasy River." It was a lecture that Jutta had delivered for him in Hamburg the previous spring. He recognized ideas he had occasionally played with and jotted down in a notebook; Jutta must have found the notebook and assembled the ideas into a lecture. Her lead-in to the lecture had been printed as a foreword to the brochure. Jutta had known how to present him to the audience as a man who had broken out and away from a fulfilled life in order to use freedom and isolation to gain a deeper understanding of the architecture of bridges and to give shape to that vision. Which was why he was not giving the lecture himself; parting with his manuscript and entrusting it to her was already a worldly compromise. Which was also why he would not be building the bridge over the Hudson himself. He was leaving that to her, so that he could immerse himself in the idea of the project and not have to wrestle with its bureaucratic, political, and financial aspects. Thomas laughed, he had not imagined Jutta capable of licensing and marketing him so acutely, or of seizing the bridge over the Hudson for herself. And Veronika—she had also revealed a talent for licensing and marketing that he would never have expected of her. He laughed some more. The only one missing was Helga.

13

HELGA ARRIVED in a new BMW. "I traded your old one in for it."

"Why are you picking me up? Why didn't Jutta pick me up?" In the old days he was a man who packed at the last minute, arrived on the train platform or checked in at the airport at the last minute, but he had been waiting with his bag packed since early morning for Jutta to pick him up. He was excited.

"Jutta is up to her ears. Don't you want to ride with me? Should I call a taxi or order you a car and driver?"

"No, but if I . . ." He looked down at himself.

"If you have problems with your catheter? As if I've never seen your weenie!" She laughed. "Climb in and don't hold up production."

She was a fast but safe driver, and at once started in talking about her dental clinic. "We're having the roof-raising party in a few weeks, and you'll have to come and give a speech. You've also got to get to work on plans for dental clinics in Hanover and Frankfurt. Professional ethics don't permit franchising, but I've got an idea how we—"

"Helga!"

"—can achieve the same effect. All we have to do is—"

"Helga!"

"Yes?"

"Were you hurt when I just slunk away like that?"

"That's okay. You had got the dental clinic well on its way, we managed the rest of it fine without you."

"I'm not talking about the dental clinic. I'm—"

"The others can talk about the other stuff. Not that I couldn't, but it would be unfair."

They got caught in a traffic jam, and the drive took

longer than expected. He had problems with his catheter; Helga provided efficient assistance—without revulsion, without compassion, as if it was the most normal thing in the world.

"Thanks." He was ashamed. Eroticism and sexuality had not come to an end, as he had sometimes hoped and sometimes feared. He simply could not live them out any more. He was impotent; his head wanted to, but his body couldn't. It didn't help that he could no longer feel his inert penis. It didn't help either that Helga was so cool and distant.

His wheelchair just fit into the elevator. Helga took the stairs. But when he arrived at the top, Jutta and Veronika were standing at the door. "Welcome home!"

He looked uncertainly from one to the other. "Hello." Veronika wanted to push him, but he declined and rolled himself into the apartment alone, down the hall to the terrace—the familiar view across the Spree and the Tiergarten, to the Brandenburg Gate and the Reichstag. The new dome was finished.

He turned his head. Jutta was leaning in the doorway. "Where are the children?"

"Ours are on summer vacation. The boys are in England, and Regula is with my parents. Your little daughter is at child care."

"How is it that . . . how have you . . . How did you come to know one another?"

"Helga brought us together. She simply invited us over one day."

Thomas heard Helga come up the stairs, enter the apartment, and be greeted by Veronika. He turned his wheelchair around and halted in front of Jutta. "Can't we talk in private? I want to explain how it all happened. I didn't mean to hurt you, all I really wanted to—"

Jutta waved him off. "That's water under the bridge. You don't need to apologize. Come on, we have to hurry. Veronika has to leave soon." She took hold of his wheelchair, paying no attention to whether he wanted to push it himself, called out to Helga and Veronika, and rolled him into the adjoining room.

He no longer recognized it. The living room had been turned into a studio, with easels, canvas stretched on wooden frames, paints and brushes, and a sketch or two of his own on the walls. "No need to stare. They're your old things from the studio in Hamburg." Veronika pointed to a sketch. "I didn't put it in the show because I thought you could use it. The railroad motif—you can develop your next series from it. The artist struggling to grapple with the railroad that left him a cripple—the paintings should sell like crazy."

Jutta rolled him through a sliding door into what had been the dining room. His drawing table was at the window, the bookcases contained his office library, and where the dining table had been was now a conference table with six chairs. Jutta pushed him to the head of it. The women sat down.

"This will be your apartment. You've seen the two work spaces. The bedroom is the same, your nurse will sleep in the boys' room, and Regula's room is for whichever of us happens to be looking after you at the moment."

Helga interrupted Jutta. "I'm sorry to press ahead, but Veronika has to leave in a minute and so do I. He'll catch on to the apartment and the housekeeping arrangements. There's a rush on the design. We've promised it to the English by fall, and I've arranged for Heiner to come by here tomorrow to show Thomas what he's done. Heiner," she said, turning to Thomas, "has already done a little preliminary work on the design. And next Monday the journalist from *Vogue* will be here. There ought to be something on the easel by then. If we start the media campaign now, we'll have wild momentum going by the time of the show this winter." Helga paused to think. Then she looked from Jutta to Veronika. "Is there anything else?"

"A couple of words about the whole package?"

Helga nodded. "Veronika's right. You know about our licensing and marketing agency from the flowers on your birthday—TTT, the three Thomases. You transfer the rights to your work to us, and we take care of you."

"The rights to my—"

"To be more precise, you've already transferred them. When you just vanished like that, without so much as a thought about your children, us, your firm, your studio, or my clinic, life had to go on, and it wouldn't have gone on without your signature on things. Don't get upset, it's not good for you. We didn't plunder your credit cards or your bank accounts. We didn't abuse your signature, but we used it when we needed it."

"And what if I want to do my own licensing and marketing? What if I don't go along with you? After all, I'm not—"

"Oh, yes you are. You're a cripple in a wheelchair and you need help. You're going to have to have around-the-clock help. And we'll take you on vacations and for rides, and if you want a particular video or want to eat spaghetti alla puttanesca, you'll get whatever you want. Don't be silly and force us to turn off the elevator and cut telephone service or let you develop a bed sore or two or a urinary tract infection. Besides, you'll have your reputation as an architect, an artist, and the founder of a dental clinic empire. If you won't play along, then we'll find a young artist who can paint in your place, and Jutta will design the bridges, and I'll take care of myself and my dental clinics. Meanwhile you'll be stuck up here, without an elevator or telephone, and we'll have shutters put on the windows. If you want to be that stupid, then be that stupid. I for one am fed up with your stunts. We're all fed up with your stunts. We've played your game long enough, we've tolerated your escapades, put up with your moods, listened to your bullshit and your—"

"Hey, Helga," Veronika laughed, "slow down. He'll play along. He's just acting coy."

"I'm leaving." Helga stood up. "Are you two coming?" She turned to Thomas. "Someone will be here at six, who'll stay till morning. For the next few days, too.

It'll be better that way at the start." Helga and Veronika left without saying good-bye. Jutta stroked his head. "Don't do anything foolish, Thomas." Then she was gone, too.

He rolled himself through the apartment. Everything he needed was there. He rolled out of the apartment to the stairwell and pushed the elevator button. The elevator didn't come. He rolled onto the terrace, stuck his head over the railing, and called down, "Hello, hello!" No one heard him. He could slide down the stairs without his wheelchair. He could throw things down onto the street until some pedestrians noticed. He could use large drawing paper to make a Help! sign and hang it from the terrace railing.

He sat there on the terrace and thought of the speech he was supposed to give for the clinic roof-raising. He thought of paintings he could paint and of what sort of bridge the English clients might want. Over the Thames? Over the Tay? He thought of sugar peas. He had time for politics now. First he would campaign for a seat on the district board, and then for the Berlin parliament. And why not for the Bundestag? If things were working okay, the quota for the handicapped should take precedence over any quota for women. And if there was still no quota for the handicapped, he would demand it. Sugar peas for everyone!

Then his thoughts ran out. He looked over to the Reichstag. Tiny people were moving up and down the spiral staircase inside the glass dome. They had healthy legs for walking. But he didn't envy them. He didn't envy the pedestrians on their healthy legs walking along the street and along the riverbanks below, either. The women would have to get him a cat or two. A couple of kittens. If they didn't, he would go on strike.

THE CIRCUMCISION

1

THE PARTY was over. Most of the guests had left, most of the tables had been cleared. The young woman in the black dress and white apron who had been serving them opened the curtains and windows to let in sunlight, air, and noise. The raucous traffic on Park Avenue lurched to a halt at stoplights, let the impatient, honking press of traffic from the side streets pass for a moment, and surged ahead again. The breeze entering the room stirred up the cigar smoke before wafting out the smell.

Andi wished that Sarah would come back so they could leave. She had vanished with her little brother, whose bar mitzvah the family was celebrating, leaving him alone with Uncle Aaron. Uncle Aaron was friendly, the whole family was friendly, including Uncle Josef and Aunt Leah, who, as Andi knew from Sarah, had been in Auschwitz and lost their parents, brothers, and sisters there. People had asked what he did, how he lived, where he came from and where he was headed in life—the things you ask a young man that your daughter or niece or young cousin has brought to a family gathering for the first time. No difficult questions, no provocative remarks, no embarrassing allusions. Andi had not sensed that anyone expected him to feel any different than if he were Dutch or French or American: welcome, viewed with generous curiosity, and invited to take a curious look of his own at their family.

But it wasn't easy. A wrong word, a false gesture—they might ruin everything. Was their generosity credible? Could he count on it? Might it not be recanted and withdrawn at any time? Didn't Uncle Joseph and Aunt Leah have every reason to say their good-byes in a way that would make it clear they didn't want to see him again? Avoiding the wrong words and wrong gestures was stressful. Andi didn't know what might be taken amiss. That he had served in the army rather than having been a conscientious objector? That he had no Jewish friends or acquaintances in Germany? That everything at the synagogue had been new and strange to him? That he had never been to Israel? That he could not remember the names of everyone here?

Uncle Aaron and Andi sat across from one another at one corner of a long table—between them were the white tablecloth with its spots and crumbs, the crumpled napkins, and empty wine glasses. Andi twirled the stem of his glass between his thumb and forefinger, while Uncle

Aaron talked about his trip around the Mediterranean. He had allotted himself eighty days, like Phileas Fogg for his trip around the world. And like Phileas Fogg he had found his wife on his trip, the daughter of a Jewish family that had emigrated from Spain to Morocco around 1700. Uncle Aaron was a spirited, witty storyteller.

Then he turned serious. "Do you know where your ancestors were from and what they did?"

"We—" But Andi never got to answer the question.

"Ours were the only two people in the shtetl to survive the great plague of 1710, and they married—he was from a simple family and she was the rabbi's daughter. She taught him to read and write, and he started a lumber business. The business grew under their son, and their grandson owned the largest lumberyard in the district, maybe even in the whole provinces of Poland and Lithuania. Do you know what that means?"

"No."

"It means that after the fire of 1812, he rebuilt the synagogue with his own lumber, larger and more beautiful than before. His son expanded the lumber business even more. Until in 1881, his lumberyards in the south burned, and he never recovered from it, neither commercially or personally. You know what happened in 1881?"

"A pogrom?"

"A pogrom, a pogrom. The worst pogrom of the century. After that, they emigrated; his two sons took him and his wife with them, even though they didn't want to come. On July 23, 1883, they arrived in New York." He paused.

"And then?"

"And then? That's what the children always asked. What it was like in the district and what caused the great fire to break out and what the rabbi who died of the plague wrote, for he was a writer—all this they didn't want to know. But then the family arrives in New York, and they prod you with their questions. And then? And then?" He paused again and shook his head. "They lived on the Lower East Side and worked as tailors. Eighteen hours or fifty cents a day, six days or three dollars a week. They saved enough that after 1889 Benjamin could study with the Educational Alliance. Samuel first threw himself into politics and wrote for the *Naijen Tsaijt*. But when Benjamin, after some bad luck in both the lumber and old clothes businesses, had success in scrap iron, Samuel joined him. In 1917 they sold their scrap iron business and used the profits to make a fortune in the crazy stock market of one single war year. Can you imagine that? Making a fortune in just one year?"

He didn't wait for an answer. "In September 1929, two months before the crash, they sold all their stocks. They had fallen in love, both of them, with two young sisters who had arrived from Poland in 1924. They had fallen in love and all they cared about was the two sisters, not about stocks."

"Aha, love conquers the market." For a moment Andi feared his remark was too flip.

But Uncle Aaron laughed. "Yes, and with the cash, which was scarce at the height of the Depression, they bought the same scrap iron business in Pittsburgh that had bought them out in 1917, and one in Dallas, and were very happy husbands and very successful businessmen at the same time."

"Do the two always go together?"

"No, but wouldn't it be nice. And there's hardly a happiness without a drop of bitterness. Samuel and Hannah had no children. But Benjamin and Thirza had three. You've met my brother, the doctor." He pointed to Sarah's father, who sat dozing in an armchair by the window. "You know me now, too, except you don't know that I'm the schlemiel of the family and have contributed nothing to its fame. You've yet to meet my sister Hannah. Believe it or not, she runs the business, has expanded it, though how she does it is a mystery to me, but a beneficial mystery that we all live from, including cousin Joseph and Leah, who survived and came here. What did your father do during the war?"

"He was a soldier."

"Where?"

"First in France, then in Russia, and finally in Italy, where he was taken prisoner by the Americans."

"If Joseph hears that he's sure to ask you if your father came through Kosarovska, but you can't know that."

"I haven't any idea. My father told me hardly anything more about the war than what I've already told you."

Uncle Aaron stood up. "We're all about to leave. Josef and Leah want to go to synagogue."

Andi looked astonished.

"You mean, four hours this morning were enough? They are for me and for most of us. But Josef and Leah like to go more often, and today is David's bar mitzvah."

"I really liked the . . ." but Andi couldn't come up with the word and blushed, "the little speech that David gave at dinner."

"Yes, David's *derasha* was good, both the exposition of the Torah and what he said about the love of music. He read well in this morning's service, too." Uncle Aaron gazed into space. "He must not be lost. Not one more must be allowed to be lost."

2

ANDI AND SARAH walked across Central Park. Sarah's parents lived on the East Side, their apartments were on the West Side. The late, low sun cast long shadows. It was cool, the benches were empty, with only a few joggers, skaters, and bikers around. He had put his arm around her.

"Why did Uncle Aaron tell me your family history? It was interesting, but I had the feeling that wasn't why he did it."

"Then why did he tell it to you?"

"You shouldn't answer my questions with questions of your own."

"And you shouldn't play schoolmaster with me."

They walked on without talking, each with a little grudge against the other in his or her heart and each unhappy to find a grudge in both their hearts. They had known one another for two months. They had met in the park, the dogs that both of them were walking for out-of-town friends knew each other. The date they made for afternoon coffee a few days later didn't end until after midnight. He knew that same evening that he had fallen in love, she knew it the next morning when she woke up. Since then they had spent their weekends together, plus one or two evenings that stretched into nights. They both had a lot to do; he had received a fellowship from the University of Heidelberg to spend a year in New York writing his thesis for his law degree, and she was working on a program for a computer game that had to be finished in a few months. Time was slipping away, time they needed for their work and for each other.

"It was a lovely party, and I want to thank you for taking me along. The synagogue was lovely, and the food and the conversation. I appreciate the cordial way they all received me. Even Uncle Joseph and Aunt Leah were friendly, although it surely wasn't easy for them." He remembered how on their first evening together Sarah had told him about Uncle Josef and Aunt Leah and their family, who had been murdered in Auschwitz. He hadn't known what to say. "How awful" had seemed too feeble, but to ask "How big was the family?" would have seemed improper, as if he were implying that the murder of a small family wasn't as bad as the murder of a large one.

"He told you our family history so that you'd know who you're dealing with."

After a while he asked, "Why didn't he want to know who you're dealing with?"

She pulled up short and gave him a worried look. "What's wrong? Why are you so touchy? What's upset you?" She threw her arms around his neck and kissed him on the lips. "Everybody liked you. I got so many compliments about you, how good-looking you are and how clever, and what a charming and modest and polite way you have about you. Why should they pester you to tell your story? They know you're German."

In view of which all else is irrelevant, is that it? It was only a thought, he didn't ask it.

They went to her place and made love as dusk fell. Before it grew dark in the room, the streetlight outside the window went on, bathing everything—walls, wardrobe, bed, and her body—in a hard, white light. They lit candles, and the room turned warm and soft.

Andi woke up in the night. The light from the streetlight filled the room, reflecting off the white walls, illuminating every corner, swallowing every shadow, making everything look flat and weightless. It took the wrinkles from Sarah's face and made her look very young. Andi gazed happily at her, until suddenly a wave of jealousy came over him. He would never experience Sarah the

first time she danced or rode a bike or saw the sea. Other
men had received her first kiss, her first embrace, and in
the rituals of her family and faith she had a world, a treasure, that would always remain closed to him.

He thought about their argument. It had been the first
time they had ever argued. Later it seemed to him the precursor of all the arguments to come. But it's always easy
to see precursors when you look back. In the fullness of
the things you do together there's always a precursor for
everything that happens—or doesn't happen—later.

3

HE HAD MET Sarah's sister, Rachel, at the bar mitzvah.
She was married, had two sons, three and two years old,
and didn't work. Would he like to rent a car and go for a
drive with her? Would he like her to show him some
things he hadn't seen? One of the splendid mansions up
along the Hudson? Sarah encouraged him. "She'll tell
you she's doing it for you, but she never gets out of the
house, and would love to. Do it for her sake, and mine too.
I'd love for you two to get acquainted."

He picked her up. The morning was clear and fresh,
and since he had had to park a good distance from her
house they were both glad of the warmth in the car. She
had brought along coffee and chocolate cookies and while
he concentrated on city traffic, taking a sip or a bite only

now and then, she didn't say much, but ate the cookies and drank the coffee, warming her hands on the cup and gazing out the window. Then they were driving north along the Hudson.

"That did me good." She put the cup away, stretched, and turned to him. "You're in love, you and Sarah, aren't you?"

"We've never said as much, to each other. She's a little anxious, and I am too." He smiled. "It's strange to tell you that I love her before I've told her myself."

She waited to see if he would say anything more. Then she started talking herself, told how she and her husband had fallen in love, talked about her father-in-law, a rabbi, and what a fine cook and baker her mother-in-law was, about her husband's job in research and development at an electronics firm, and about how she had previously worked at a library for a foundation and how she longed to work again. "There are too many people who love books and know something about them, they're like pebbles on the shore. But often they aren't even hired where they're needed, and instead the jobs are taken by rich women who don't know anything and don't cost anything, but have an outlet for their boredom because their men are on the board or among the sponsors. I like taking care of the boys, you know, and every day during those first years is full of wonders. But for a job two days a week, or even one day a week, I'd give my—no, not my left arm, but the little toe on my left foot or even on the right. It would be better for the boys, too. I think about them too much, worry so much that they sense it and it's not good for them."

Andi talked about his childhood in Heidelberg. "Our mother never worked. I know that mothers have every right to work, but my sister and I loved the time our mother had for us. And then we could play outside—the woods began just behind our house—and we didn't have to be carted around to athletics, to music lessons, to friends, and even to school like kids in New York."

They talked about growing up in big cities and smaller towns, and the problems of growing up in both. They agreed that they wouldn't want to be young again, in New York or Heidelberg or anywhere else.

"When do the kids go off to college? Isn't the worst over by then? Isn't the kid who doesn't end up taking drugs in high school protected against it later, and don't most kids who make it into college graduate?"

"Are those the worst things possible? Drugs or failing at college?"

Andi shook his head. "It's what parents try to protect their kids from, isn't it? That and a few other things. Sure, there are worse things, but they're not in the parents' control." He wondered if what he had said was true, and wasn't sure. "What would be the worst thing for you?"

"That could happen to my children?" She looked at him. Later he regretted not being able to recall her face better. Was it a questioning look, because she was asking herself what precisely he wanted to know. Was it a hesitant look, because she was unsure if she should answer his question honestly? Or was it hesitant because she was uncertain what the worst thing was? But he could recall precisely the spot they were passing when her answer came. From the road that followed the curves in the shore, another road branched off to the left, leading to a long bridge over the river. The bridge, its arches and struts constructed of iron or steel, was coming directly into view as Rachel said, "The worst thing would be if my boys were ever to marry a woman who wasn't Jewish."

He didn't know what to say or think. Was what Rachel had said the same as if he'd said the worst thing for him would be for his son to marry a non-German, a non-Aryan, a Jew, or a black? Or was it purely about religion? And how bad would it be for Rachel, if he and Sarah were to marry? He assumed that something would follow now, some explanation, a request that he not misunderstand her or think her answer was directed at him. But nothing followed. After a while he asked, "Why would that be so bad?"

"They would lose everything. Lighting candles on Friday evening, saying the Kiddush over the wine and the blessing of the bread, eating kosher, hearing the shofar on Rosh Hashannah, making amends at Yom Kippur, building a hut at Succoth to decorate and live in—how could my sons do that with anyone except a Jewish girl?"

"Maybe your sons, or one of them, won't want to do

any of it. Maybe he'd enjoy deciding with his Catholic wife how to celebrate which holidays, Jewish or Catholic or something else, or deciding which child to raise what way. Why shouldn't he take his son to the synagogue on Sabbath and she take her daughter to church on Sunday? What's so bad about that?"

She shook her head. "It doesn't work that way. Mixed marriages don't produce a particularly rich spiritual life, they produce none at all."

"Maybe they'd both be happy not to be either Jewish or Catholic. But that doesn't make them bad people; surely you admire and like people who are neither Jewish or Catholic. And their children might discover a rich spiritual life as Buddhists or Muslims or Catholics or Jews."

"How can my son be happy if he's no longer Jewish? Besides, what you're saying simply isn't true. The second generation doesn't return to Judaism. Sure, there are individual cases. But statistically the person who enters into a mixed marriage is lost to Judaism forever."

"But maybe he or his children would be won over to something else."

"What are you? Catholic, Protestant, agnostic? In any case, there are already so many of you that you can manage without those of you who make mixed marriages. We can't afford to lose anyone."

"Is the number of Jews in the world decreasing? I don't have the statistics in my head, but I can't imagine that's the case. Besides—if someday nobody wants to be Catholic, Protestant, agnostic, or Jewish anymore, what's there to say against that?"

"What's there to say against there being no more Jews?" She gazed at him incredulously. "You can ask that?"

He was growing annoyed. What was her question supposed to mean? As a German, wasn't he allowed to think that like every other religion Judaism lives from being voluntarily chosen and dies when that is no longer the case? Did Rachel believe the Jewish religion was something special? That the Jews were in fact a chosen people?

As if she had heard his question, she said, "If you have no more faith in your religion and you can let it die out, that's your business. I want mine to live and my family to live with it and in it. Yes, I consider my religion unique, and I don't understand why you're annoyed—I don't deny anyone else the right to consider his religion unique. And it's the same with my family. But look," she laid her left hand on his arm and pointed ahead with her right, "there's the entrance to Lyndhurst. We're here."

They toured the neo-Gothic splendor of the mansion, inside and out, strolled through the garden with its profusion of blooming roses, had lunch, sat beside the Hudson, and talked about all sorts of things—books and paintings, baseball and soccer, school uniforms and country mansions. It turned into an easy, intimate, and happy day. But on the drive home, when he thought of asking her whether she thought it was a bad thing that he and Sarah loved each other, he decided to keep quiet.

4

HE HAD NO friends in New York that he could introduce to Sarah, and it took a while before she began to introduce him to hers. During their first months together they were happy being just the two of them. There was too much to discover together and about each other for them to need any company. They walked together in the parks, Central Park and Riverside, went to movies, the theater, and concerts, rented and watched their favorite films on video, cooked together, talked together—they had so little time for themselves, how could they have time for others?

During their first night together, Sarah had gazed at him until he had finally asked what she was thinking, and she said, "I was just hoping you'll never stop talking with me."

"Why should I?"

"Because you might think you already know what's going on in my head and don't want to hear it from me anymore. We come from two different cultures, we speak two different languages, even when you're good at translating from yours into mine, we live in two different worlds—if we ever stop talking to each other, we'll drift apart."

They had different ways of talking with each other. One was light and fast and, being impulsive, could sometimes involve corrections, offenses, and apologies. But it left no traces behind. The other was slow and cautious. When the conversation turned to different religions or to what was German in his world or Jewish in hers, they were careful not to challenge one another. When he went with her to synagogue, he found it impressive; when he joined her for a lecture on Hassidism, he found it interesting; he found the Friday evenings they spent with her parents lovely. He really liked going along; he wanted to get to know her world. Whatever he found strange he kept not only from her, but from himself as well; he simply did not acknowledge it to himself. He likewise repressed his conversation with Rachel. "It was lovely," he said when Sarah asked him about the trip to Lyndhurst, and since he and Rachel were even more cordial to one another afterward, she was satisfied. On the other hand, she enjoyed the German literature he found for her in translation, the programs at the Goethe Institute to which he took her, and the services at Riverside Church.

His birthday was in April, and she surprised him with a little party. She invited the two American colleagues with whom he shared an office at the university, and her own friends: two programmers, an editor and her husband, an artist who made his living restoring paintings,

Rachel and her husband, Jonathan, and a couple of former students from the days when she had taught computer science. She had made salads and some cheese pastries, and the guests stood around in the living room with their plates and glasses and sang "Happy Birthday, dear Andi" when he arrived. Sarah proudly introduced him, and he smiled at everyone.

The conversation turned to Germany. One of Sarah's ex-students had spent a year in Frankfurt as an exchange student. He was enthusiastic about German trains, how punctual, comfortable, and clean they were, about German bread and rolls, about the local cider, onion tarts, and sauerbraten. But certain turns of phrase had often bothered him. Germans talked about "Polish sloppiness" or said "Jewish haste." And when they did something to excess, they did it till they were "gassed."

"They were 'gassed'?" The painter interrupted and looked at Andi.

Andi shrugged. "I have no idea where the expression comes from. I would guess it's older than the Holocaust and either comes from the First World War or from suicide by gas. I haven't heard that in a long time. Nowadays you're more likely to do things 'till you drop,' or 'till you puke,' or 'till you're blue in the face.' "

But the painter was flabbergasted. "When they've had enough of something, the Germans say they'll gas it? And what if they've had enough of other people?"

Andi interrupted. "Till you can't do it anymore—the phrase is about what you do when you can't go on. Till you vomit, because you can't eat anymore. Till you die, gas yourself, because you can't deal with life anymore. It's about yourself, not about what you do to other people."

"I don't know. It sounds to me like . . ." The painter shook his head. "And what about 'Polish sloppiness'? And 'Jewish haste'?"

"Those are harmless ethnic jokes, the same kind the Germans apply to themselves when they say 'stubborn as a Westphalian' or 'merry as a Rhinelander' or talk about 'Prussian discipline' or 'Saxon sloppiness.' All over Europe people tell jokes nowadays about cars stolen by Poles and smuggled back into Poland." He had no idea if Germans actually talked about "Saxon sloppiness" or if other Europeans told jokes about Polish car thieves. But he could imagine it was the case. "We're crowded together in Europe, a lot tighter than you here in America. So we poke fun at each other more, too."

The editor challenged this. "I think it's just the opposite. Precisely because so many different ethnic groups live so close together in America, ethnic references are taboo here. Otherwise we'd be constantly at odds."

"Why at odds? Ethnic references don't have to be rude, they can be witty, too."

One of Andi's colleagues chimed in. "But whether they're witty and welcome or rude and hurtful can only be decided by the person who is the object of them, right?"

"It depends both on who makes the comment and on who it's intended for," his other colleague corrected.

"Contracts, bids, resignations—take whatever example you like, it depends on both sides." His colleagues began to shop-talk.

Andi breathed a sigh of relief. When he told Sarah about the letter he had received that same day extending his fellowship and his study in New York for another year, she hugged him with tears of happiness in her eyes and called them all together. There were cheers and toasts, and the artist's toast to Andi was especially cordial.

That evening, as Sarah and Andi talked about the party and the guests, Sarah couldn't help remarking, "You're such a trouper, why do you do battle for something that you don't even approve of yourself? You don't owe a thing to someone who tells rude ethnic jokes. About gassing or Jewish haste—they're simply offensive."

Andi didn't know what to think. He remembered the American and English war films he'd seen as a boy. He had known that the Germans were justifiably presented as the villains, but had felt torn all the same. When it came to "Jewish haste" he didn't even know if it was intended as a slur or was perhaps truly harmless.

In bed he asked her, "Do you love me?"

She sat up and laid a hand on his chest. "Yes."

"Why?"

"Because you're sweet and clever, honest, generous. Because you're such a trouper and make life so difficult for yourself. You want to make everything right for everybody, and although you manage a lot of things, you can't do it all, how could you, but you try all the same, and that touches my heart. Because you're good with children and dogs. Because I like your green eyes and your curly brown hair, and because my body likes yours." She stopped and kissed him. She whispered, "No, it doesn't just like yours. It needs yours."

Later she said, "And you? Do you know why you love me?"

"Yes."

"Are you going to tell me?"

"Yes." He waited a long time before going on. Sarah thought he had fallen asleep. "I've never met a woman who sees so much, who looks at things with so much care and sympathy. I love you for that. I feel safe within your gaze. And I love you for the computer games you invent. You use your brain to make other people happy. You'll be a wonderful mother. And you have . . . you know who you are, where you come from, where you're going and what you need to make life work. I love you for the firm footing you have in the world. And you're beautiful." His hand traced the contours of her face, as if the room weren't bright but dark and he could see nothing. "You have the blackest hair I've ever seen, and the cutest nose and the most exciting lips, you're so sensual and so wise at the same time that I still can't grasp it all." He cuddled up against her. "Will that do?"

5

IN MAY, with the semester over, Sarah and Andi took a trip to Germany. They arrived in Düsseldorf before daybreak and took the train to Heidelberg. As they were crossing the Rhine at Cologne, the cathedral and the museum sparkled in the light of the rising sun.

"Hey," Sarah said, "that's beautiful."

"Yes, and it will get even more beautiful." He loved the train trip along the Rhine, the winding river and the way the land sometimes curved down to the water and sometimes made a sheer drop, the vineyards and wooded slopes, the castles and small towns, the freighters moving fast downstream and working their way slowly in the opposite direction. He loved this stretch in the winter when steam rose from the river into the cold morning air and the sun fought its way through the fog, and in summer when the dollhouse world of castles, towns, trains, and cars on the far side of the river lay dependable in the bright light. He enjoyed the blossoms in spring, and the yellow and red foliage of fall.

The day was cloudless, and in the clear air under a blue sky what they saw was dollhouse Germany. With a child's eagerness Andi showed it all to her: the tree-lined avenue of the castle at Brühl, Nonnenwerth Island, the Lorelei, and Castle Pfalz near Kaub. As the train wound its way down to the Rhine plain his heart was gripped with a melancholy homesickness. The wide plain, the mountains to the east and west, the red sandstone quarries as the train moved on from Mannheim toward Heidelberg—this was where he came from, where he belonged. He was taking Sarah there now. In Heidelberg he kept her distracted as the taxi drove through town and up to the hill on the far side of the river. They got out, walked to Philosophen Weg, and then he proudly laid his hometown at her feet: the castle and old city, the Old Bridge and the Neckar River, the high school where he had been a student, the Municipal Auditorium where he and another classmate had played a concerto for two flutes at their graduation ceremony, and the cafeteria where he had eaten as a college student. He talked and talked, trying to make it all interesting and familiar to her.

"Sweetheart," she said, laying a finger to his lips, "sweetheart, you needn't be afraid I won't like your town. I see it and I can see little Andi going to school here and eating at the cafeteria, and I like it, and I love you."

They arrived at his parents' house just as his sister, her husband, and their two children drove up. A little later his uncles and aunts, his cousins, and a few family friends arrived. His parents had invited twenty guests for their "marble" wedding anniversary, as they called their fortieth. How easily Sarah moves in my family, he thought, how wonderfully she speaks with everyone in her mix of German and English, how fresh she looks, though she's hardly slept. What a marvelous woman I've found!

Before lunch they were sitting with his father and brother-in-law.

"Where does your family come from?" Sarah asked his father.

"From Forst, on the other side of the Rhine plain. As far back as we can remember, we were vintners and innkeepers. I'm the first to break the chain. But to make up for it, my daughter has returned to making wine."

"Didn't you like the taste of the wine?"

His father laughed. "Oh yes. The wine tasted fine, and I was tempted to be a vintner. But before I could decide, I had to go off to war as a solider, and there I realized what fun it was to organize things, and so after being held prisoner of war I went into business. Besides, my cousin who had a bad leg and couldn't go to war, had been running the vineyards for seven years, and I didn't want to take that away from him. But I missed it. That's also why I married so late. Getting married, but then not taking my wife to live in our vineyards—for a long time I couldn't imagine it."

"What did you organize in the war?"

"All sorts of things. In Russia, it was art. The Communists had turned the churches into warehouses, workshops, barns, and stalls, and we dug out the most wonderful icons, candelabra, and vestments from under the rubble and trash."

"What happened to it all?"

"We inventoried them, packed them up, and sent them to Berlin. What happened to them in Berlin I don't know. In terms of organization, France was more interesting, which was where I dealt with deliveries of grain and wine."

"And Italy?"

"Italy?"

"Andi mentioned that you were a soldier in France, Russia, and Italy."

"In Italy I was a kind of trade attaché to Mussolini's last government."

Andi listened in amazement. "You've never told me this much about the war."

"I had to or she'd be mistrustful forever." His father gave them a knowing, friendly look.

As Sarah and Andi lay in bed that evening, she got around to mentioning his father's knowing, friendly look. He was a good-looking man, she said, with that striking head and close-cropped white hair, and in his face you could see his farming background so nicely joined with a sharp mind. But something about that look had unsettled her. "How does he know that I'm Jewish? Did you tell him?"

"No, but I also don't know if that's what he meant when he talked about mistrusting him forever. The way you asked things left no doubt you expected answers."

"But what sort of answers did I get? What's a German trade attaché doing with a Mussolini who exists only at the whim of the Germans? What does that mean, dealing with deliveries of grain and wine from France? It was all about war booty in France and in Russia, about pillaging and plundering."

"Why didn't you ask him?" But Andi was glad she hadn't asked his father, that he hadn't answered her or shown her the icon in his study.

"That's why I'm talking about the look he gave me. It told me that he would have an answer for everything that would put me and my mistrust in the wrong, but would never tell me anything."

Andi remembered arguments with his father that had left him feeling like that, too. At the same time he didn't want to let his father be implicated in the charge of pillaging and plundering. "I believe him when he says those treasures from Russian churches would have been destroyed if he and his men hadn't saved them."

Sarah, who was lying on her back, raised her hands as if preparing for some fundamental statement. But she dropped them again. "Maybe. I don't care about all that—the Russian icons, the French wine and grain, or trade with Mussolini. And as long as you don't give me looks like your father's, let him look any way he wants. Your mother is sweet, and I like your sister and her kids." She gave it some thought. "And your father is a character, God knows." She rolled over on her side and looked at Andi. "And that train trip was beautiful! And the view from the hill. Shall we walk down into town tomorrow? And make love now?"

6

THE FIRST time he felt afraid that the difference between the worlds they came from could threaten their love was in Berlin. They had been in Munich and Ulm, on Lake Constance, in the Black Forest, and in Freiburg, and Sarah had taken it all in with attentive, friendly eyes. She liked the landscape more than the cities, and made a place in her heart for the country on the edge of the Rhine plain that Andi loved—the Berg Strasse, the Ortenau region, the Markgräfler Land. They spent one entire day at the thermal baths in Baden-Baden. They entered through the separate doors for men and women, were rubbed down separately, sweated separately in dry Finnish and damp Roman heat, and then met again in the middle of the old building, in the bathing pool surrounded by columns beneath its high dome. Andi arrived before she did and was watching for her. He had never before seen her walking naked toward him for any distance. How beautiful she was—her shoulder-length black hair, her open face, the curve of her shoulders, her full breasts, soft hips, and beautifully shaped, if somewhat short, legs. How gracefully she moved—proud of her beauty and at the same time embarrassed by his candid inspection of her. How enchantingly she laughed, a teasing laugh—because she always knew to tease—that also delighted in his admiration and was full of love.

In the cities they visited she made fun of how you could depend on the Germans to remark on the destruction of the Second World War. "The war was fifty years ago. Are you so proud that in the end you've become the greatest nation in Europe after all?" When they drove through suburbs she made fun of the little white houses with their tidy yards and proper fences, and when they drove through the countryside, she made fun of how there was no trace of the rubbish, rusting cars, and moldy sofas you see scattered around little farms in America. "Everything here looks as if you'd just finished the job." She made fun of the traffic markings, and kept calling Andi's attention to how carefully a parking zone ended in a diagonally striped triangle and how an intersection was marked with stripes for turning traffic that crossed the stripes of cars moving in the other direction. "You should keep traffic off the streets and take aerial photographs—they'd be works of art, true works of art."

Sarah laughed when she made fun of things, and her laugh invited him to make fun and laugh along with her. Andi noticed that. He also knew that for Sarah making fun of things was a way of making the world her own, and that she liked to make fun of things in New York as well—of the conductor, although she would rave about the concert afterward, of a kitschy movie, although she cried at the end and could turn misty-eyed the next day recalling it. She had even made fun of her brother's bar mitzvah, but at the same time had shared his fears when he had to read aloud in the synagogue or make his speech at dinner about the Torah and his love of music. He knew all that, and yet he was having trouble with the way her mockery spared nothing. He laughed along with her, but his lips were tight and his cheek muscles clenched.

In Berlin they stayed in Grunewald with an uncle who had inherited a villa that contained a small apartment—with living room, bedroom, kitchen, and bath—that he let them use. He invited them one evening to a dinner he cooked himself, but otherwise let them go their own way. On the evening before they were to go to Oranienburg, they ran into him at the front door.

"Oranienburg? What are you going to Oranienburg for?"

"To see what it was like."

"What do you suppose it's like? It's the way you imagine it, but only because you imagine it that way. I was in Auschwitz a few years ago, and there's nothing to see, I mean nothing at all. A couple of brick barracks, grass, and trees here and there—and that's it. The rest is all in your head." The uncle, a retired teacher, gave them a look of sympathetic dismay.

"Then we'll see what we see in our heads," Andi said with a laugh. "Shall we turn it into a problem of epistomology?"

The uncle shook his head. "What's the point? That was fifty years ago. I don't understand why we can't let the past be. Why we can't let it be the same way we let the rest of the past be?"

"Maybe because it's a special past?" Sarah asked in

English. To Andi's surprise she had been following their conversation in German.

"A special past? Everyone has a past that's special to him. But aside from that, it is we who make the past, in general and in particular."

"Yes, the Germans made a particular past for my relatives." Sarah gave Andi's uncle a cold stare.

"Of course that was dreadful. But is that any reason why the people in Oranienburg or Dachau or Buchenwald have to have a dreadful present? People born long after the war and who've never done anybody any harm? Because the special past of their towns is remembered and forced upon them?" The uncle pulled his key from his coat pocket. "But what's the point? Your friend is an American, and American tourists see Europe differently from the way we do. Are you going to the Italian restaurant on the corner? Enjoy your meal."

Sarah said nothing until they had found a table and were seated. "You surely don't agree with your uncle, do you?"

"In what way?"

"That we should let the past be, and that it would be left alone if the Jews didn't stir things up."

"Haven't you been saying that the war was fifty years ago?"

"So you do agree."

"No, I don't agree with my uncle. Nor is it as simple as you make out."

"How complicated is it?"

Andi was not in the mood to argue with Sarah. "Do we have to talk about this?"

"Just answer that one question."

"How complicated is it? The past has to be remembered, so that it's never repeated; it has to be remembered because the respect we owe the victims and their children demands it; both the Holocaust and the war were fifty years ago; whatever guilt fathers and sons of those generations brought upon themselves, the generation of their grandchildren has nothing to feel guilty about; anyone who has to admit outside of Germany that he's from Oranienburg has it rough; teenagers become neo-Nazis because they've had enough of hearing about coming to terms with the past. And trying to deal with all of that doesn't seem simple to me."

Sarah was silent. The waiter came and they ordered. Sarah continued to be silent, and Andi saw that she was crying softly. "Hey," he said, bending across the table to her and laying his arm around her neck, "you're not crying because of us, are you?"

She shook her head. "I know you mean well. But it's not complicated. What's right is simple."

7

ANDI DIDN'T dare tell her that he was experiencing Oranienburg just as his uncle had predicted. What he saw wasn't shocking. What was shocking was what went on in his head. That was dreadful enough. Sarah and Andi walked mutely through the camp. After a while they were holding hands.

Also visiting the camp that day was a school class of about thirty twelve-year-old boys and girls. They behaved the way twelve-year-olds behave—they were loud, they giggled and sniggered. They were more interested in each other than in what the teacher was showing and explaining to them. What they saw was an opportunity to impress and embarrass one another, to get laughs. They played guards or prisoners and moaned in the cells as if they were being tortured or dying of thirst. The teacher did all he could, and it was apparent from what he said that he had amply prepared his students for the visit. But all his efforts got him nowhere.

Does Sarah see us the way we see these kids? There's nothing wrong with kids behaving like kids, and yet I can't tolerate them. There's nothing wrong with the fact that Father discovered he liked organizing things during the war or that my uncle wants to be left in peace and that I differentiate complicated things into an "on the one hand" and "on the other." And yet it drives her to despair. How would I feel if one of these kids were my own?

Andi was glad they didn't encounter his uncle that evening. He was glad they would be touring the new eastern part of the city the next day, gathering new impressions. He had been working in Berlin when the wall came down and wanted to move back to Berlin and to awaken in Sarah his enthusiasm for the city. He was glad that he could show her all its many different facets—you'll see, he had often told her, Berlin is almost like New York. But when he pictured to himself touring with her all the construction sites at Potsdamer Platz, on Friedrich Strasse, around the Reichstag, and just about everywhere, he knew what Sarah would say, or if not say, then think. Why must it all be finished by tomorrow and look as if the city has no history? As if it has no wounds and scars? And why does the Holocaust need to be encased and stored under a monument? He would try to explain, and what he would say wouldn't be stupid or false, but to Sarah it would still sound strange.

Is there only an either-or? Are you either a man or a woman, a child or an adult? Either German or American, Christian or Jew? Are words pointless because they help you to understand another person, but not to tolerate him, and because what really counts isn't understanding but tolerance? But as for tolerance—do we ultimately tolerate only those who are like us? Of course we can deal with differences, presumably we couldn't get along without them. But doesn't that have to be kept within certain bounds? Can any good come of it if our differences call fundamentals into question?

No sooner had he put the question to himself than he was afraid. We tolerate only those who are like us—isn't that racism or chauvinism or religious fanaticism? Children and adults, Germans and Americans, Christians and Jews—why shouldn't they tolerate each other? They tolerate each other all around the world, at least wherever the world is the way it's supposed to be. But then he asked himself if they tolerate each other only because one side or the other abandons what they are. Because children become adults or Germans become like Americans or Jews like Christians. Doesn't racism or religious fanaticism begin wherever someone is unwilling to do just that? Like my own unwillingness to become an American and a Jew for Sarah?

The next day turned out just as he had imagined it would. Sarah was interested in everything that he showed her, expressed her amazement and admiration of the construction on Potsdamer Platz, of the determination with which Friedrich Strasse and the Reichstag area were being rebuilt. But she also asked him about the wounds and scars and why the city couldn't put up with them and if the planned monument to the Holocaust wasn't a way of repressing it. She asked him why Germans can't tolerate chaos and if something essentially German had not found characteristic expression, though admittedly in an abnormal way, in the Nazis' fanatic passion for tidiness and order. Andi didn't like Sarah's questions. But after a while he liked his answers even less. He was tired of his efforts to weigh his words and provide differentiated responses. In fact, he himself didn't like what he was showing Sarah, didn't like the pomposity and haste with which every hole was being crammed full with buildings. Sarah was right—why did he go to battle for things he didn't believe himself? Why had his uncle's words resulted in complicated explanations, instead of his simply saying that he found them outrageous and offensive?

That evening they went to the Schauspielhaus to hear Bach's Mass in B Minor. She didn't know it and he was afraid—the way you always are when you first share your favorite books and music with someone you have fallen in love with. He was afraid that she would find the music too Christian and too German. That she would sense that this music didn't belong in a concert hall but in a church, and that she would feel he was trying to deceive her, trying to play down his churchly, Christian, German world. He would have liked to talk with her about all this. But he was afraid of doing that as well. He ought to have explained why he liked this music so much, and yet he could not have done so. *Incarnatus est, crucifixus, passus et sepultus est et resurrexit*—the text carried no significance for him, and yet the music composed for it touched him, filled him with happiness as no other music did. If he were to describe these feelings, wouldn't Sarah have to think their strangeness to one another was even greater than she had ever realized, since with him it had its roots in depths that he could not understand or put into words?

But as they emerged from the subway, the Gendarmen Markt lay bathed in the soft light of the sun low on the horizon. The two churches and the Schauspielhaus, a trinity of elegance and modesty, spoke of another, better Berlin, and since the shops were already closed and the evening's revelers were not yet under way, everything was deserted and quiet, as if the city were holding its breath. "Oh," Sarah said, and stopped in her tracks.

During the *Kyrie* she looked around. Then she closed her eyes, and after a while she took his hand. Toward the end she laid her head on his shoulder. *Et expecto resurrectionem mortuorum*—"Yes," she whispered to him, as if to join him in the expectation of the resurrection of the dead or their own resurrection out of all the difficulties in which they kept getting themselves entangled.

8

THE NEXT DAY they flew back to New York. They had spent every day together for three weeks, often with a sense of perfectly normal, natural intimacy, as if it always had been, always would be that way, would always have to stay that way. The feeling was never stronger than on the flight back. Each knew how much rest the other needed, just how close each wanted to be to the other, what little gestures of affection would delight the other. They argued over the in-flight movie—because it was such fun to celebrate the ritual of arguing over a topic with no explosive force. He spent the night they arrived in New York at her place. Both were too tired to make love, but as they fell asleep she took his penis in her hand—it went hard and then soft again, and he felt as if he were at home.

It was summer. In Chinatown and Little Italy, in the Village and in Times Square and Lincoln Square, Manhattan was filled with even more people than usual. It wasn't as crowded in the area around Columbia University where Sarah and Andi lived. Tourists seldom made their way there, and the students and faculty had left town. The days were sultry; a few steps out on the street and your clothes clung to your body. It was a little cooler in the evening and at night. But the air was warm and humid, no longer that light element you take for granted, but thick and heavy, offering your body gentle, sensual resistance. Andi couldn't understand why New Yorkers left town, why they would choose to do without these evenings and nights. Since he couldn't stand the hum and hiss of the air conditioning in his office, he worked on a park bench. He would work until late in the evening, a little battery-powered lamp clipped to his book or notepad. Then he would go to Sarah's, exhilarated by his love for her, by his work, by the sultry air, by the shimmer of lights on the asphalt. The air resisting his body made him feel light. He felt as if he were floating effortlessly, moving in great long strides across the Milky Way.

He would have been content to take a walk with Sarah without saying much, or to sit at one of the tables outside the restaurants along Broadway, or to see a movie, in a theater or on video. But Sarah, always more of a talker than he, needed conversation after a lonely day at the computer. She wanted to hear what he had read and written and to report about the progress she was making on her computer game. While she programmed, a thousand things would come to her that she wanted to talk with him about. When he concentrated on his work, he was incapable of thinking about other things at the same time or in between, and so had nothing but his own work to talk about come evening. But he didn't want to talk about it. He didn't want to risk the argument it had led to once already.

His thesis dealt with how the concept of law and order had been developed in utopian communities in America—from the Shakers, Rappites, Mormons, and Hutterites, on down to Socialists, Vegetarians, and advocates of free love. Andi found the topic fascinating. He found it fascinating to learn about these utopian plans, to track down the letters, diaries, and memories of the utopians and to learn from yellowed newspapers how they were viewed by the world around them. Sometimes he was touched by utopian projects, saw them as a collective form of quixotism. Sometimes it seemed to him as if the utopians had known how futile their enterprise was and merely wanted to give a collective, creative form to a heroic nihilism. Sometimes they seemed like precocious children, living out a satire on society. When he told Sarah about his thesis and his fascination with it, she thought a while and then said, "That's very German, isn't it?"

"The topic of American utopian projects?"

"The fascination with utopia. The fascination with

transforming chaos into cosmos, with perfect order, with the pure society. And maybe also a fascination with futility—what was that saga you told me about, where in the end everyone commits heroic and nihilistic suicide together? The Nibelung?"

Andi didn't hear the argument, he heard an attack and fought back. "But there are a thousand times more American articles on the topic than German, and as for collective suicide, the Germans have nothing on the Americans at Little Big Horn or the Jews at Masada."

"Oh yes they do. That saga is your most important one, you said. Little Big Horn and Masada were just episodes. And it's not a matter of the number of published articles. I know the American literature on the topic without ever having read it—histories of this or that utopian society, about the people, their families, their work, their joys and sufferings, stories written with enthusiasm and sympathy. The German literature is thorough and factual, builds categories and systems, and any passion you find in it is the passion of scientific dissection."

Andi shook his head. "It's just a different scientific style. Do you know the joke about the scientific study of the elephant done by a Frenchman, an Englishman, a Russian, and a German? The Frenchman writes about, 'L'éléphant et ses amours,' the Englishman about 'How to Shoot an Elephant,' the Russian about—"

"I don't want to hear your stupid joke." Sarah stood up and went to the kitchen. He heard her furiously tug open the dishwasher and the clatter of plates and glasses being put away and silverware banging on the counter. She came back and stood at the door. "I don't like it when you make fun of me when I'm talking seriously with you. It's not about scientific styles. Even when you're not being scholarly, but just talking with my friends and family, you don't empathize, or at least not what we understand by that; all you do is analyze, use your curiosity to dissect things. That isn't bad, and it's the way you are, and the way we like you. In other situations and in other ways you're full of empathy. But when it comes to conversation . . ."

"You're not trying to say, are you, that what I get from your friends and family is empathy? At best it's curiosity, and very superficial at that. I—"

"Don't nitpick, Andi. My family tries to meet you with curiosity and empathy, just as you do them, and all I said was—"

"Above all they meet me with prejudices. You already know everything about the Germans. And so you already know everything about me. And so you don't have to be interested in me beyond that."

"We're not interested enough in you? Not the way you're interested in us? Why do we so often have the feeling you're examining us at arm's length? And why do we recognize this kind of cold reception only from Germans?" She was talking loud now.

"So how many Germans do you know?" He knew

that the calm tone he was taking would upset her, but he couldn't help it.

"Enough, and along with those that we've been happy to get to know, there are the ones we'd have rather not got to know, but got to know anyway." She was still standing at the door, arms akimbo, gazing defiantly at him.

What was she talking about? With whom was she comparing him? With Mengele and his cold, inhuman, dissecting, analytic curiosity? He shook his head. He didn't want to ask what she meant. He didn't want to know what she meant. He didn't want to say or hear anything, he just wanted peace and quiet, with her if at all possible—but without her if that was the only way to have peace at all. "I'm sorry." He put on his shoes. "Let's talk on the phone tomorrow. I'm going to my place."

He stayed. Sarah begged so hard he really couldn't leave. But he decided not to talk with her about his work ever again.

9

AND SO HE trimmed his love smaller and smaller. Ticklish subjects not to be talked about were: their families, Germany, Israel, Germans and Jews, his work, and hers, which easily led the conversation back to his. He got used to censoring what he wanted to say, to keeping

silent, restraining himself from this or that critical observation on life in New York and from comments on her
friends' remarks about Germany or Europe that he found
inaccurate or presumptuous. There were enough other
things to talk about, and there was the intimacy of weekends and the passion of nights together.

He got so used to censoring himself that he no longer
noticed it. He enjoyed the way being together was becoming easier. He was looking forward to the extension of
his fellowship and his stay. As a newcomer, he had often
been lonely the previous fall and winter. The coming fall
and winter would be happy times.

Until for no real reason at all, everything fell apart
again. Sarah had holes in all her sweaters and pantyhose.
It didn't matter to her, and ever since Andi had called her
attention to a hole one time, he knew that she didn't want
it to matter to him, either. But one evening when she had
changed clothes before they headed out to see a movie,
she appeared wearing a sweater with holes under both
arms and pantyhose with holes in both heels, and Andi
laughed and showed Sarah the holes.

"What's so funny about my holes?"

"Forget it."

"Just tell me why my holes are so interesting and
amusing that you have to show them to me and laugh at
them."

"I . . . Do I have to . . ." Andi made several starts at
it. "It's what we do at home. If someone's clothes have a

hole or spot, you tell him. You assume he wouldn't have put it on if he'd seen the hole or the spot, and is glad to know. So he doesn't put it on again."

"Aha, that's the interesting aspect. And what about the amusing part?"

"Good lord, Sarah. Four holes at once—it seemed funny to me."

"Are holes also funny when someone earns so little that he can't choose to be so picky about his clothes?"

"Darning holes doesn't cost a fortune. It's not a matter of witchcraft. I even darn my own holes."

"You like everything in good order."

He shrugged.

"Oh, but you do. Tina would say it's the Nazi in you."

He said nothing for a moment. "I'm sorry, but I've had enough of all that. The Nazi in me, the German in me—I've had enough of it."

She looked at him in surprise. "What's wrong? Why the violent reaction? I know that you're no Nazi, and I don't hold it against you that you're German. Tina can say—"

"It's not just Tina who keeps looking for the Nazi in me and finds it, it's your other friends, too. And what's that supposed to mean, that you don't hold it against me that I'm German? What's there to hold against me that you so generously don't hold against me?"

She shook her head. "There's nothing to hold against you. I don't, and my friends don't either. You know they like you, and Tina wants to bring Ethan to the shore with us next summer—you don't think she'd do that if she thought you were a Nazi. That people we meet wonder about you being German, that they ask themselves how German you are, what's German about you and if that's something bad—that's nothing new to you."

"Do you wonder about it?"

The look she gave him was full of surprise and love. "Hey, sweetheart! You know how much I enjoy the music and books that you like, and how happy I was with you on our trip to Germany. I love you and all the beautiful things you've brought into my life, including whatever is German about them. Don't you remember? I was head over heels in love with you after three days, even though you're German."

"Don't you understand what upsets me?"

Now her look was full of love and worry. She shook her head slowly.

"How would you feel if I were to say to you that I love you even though you're Jewish? That my friends look for what is Jewish about you? That they actually think it's a bad thing that I'm going with a Jewish girl, but still like you anyway? Wouldn't you think that's anti-Semitic idiocy? So why is it so hard to understand that I find anti-German prejudice equally idiotic, and when I hear it from the woman I love, and her friends—"

"How dare you compare the two." She was trembling with outrage. "Anti-Semitism . . . the Jews never hurt anybody. The Germans killed six million Jews. That somebody might start to wonder about things when he has to deal with one of you—are you really that naive? Or insensitive or in love with yourself? You've been living in New York for almost a year now and you're trying to tell me you don't know that the Holocaust still has hold of people?"

"What have I got to do with . . ."

"What do you have to do with the Holocaust? You're German, that's what you have to do with the Holocaust. And that sets people wondering, even if they're too polite to show it. They are too polite, and besides, they don't think they have to show it because you know it yourself. Which doesn't mean that they don't give you a chance."

He passed his hand over the slipcover of the sofa, where they were now sitting at opposite ends—she with her legs crossed under her and her whole body turned toward him, he with his feet on the floor and only head and shoulders turned toward her. He smoothed out the creases, made new creases, little waves and stars, and smoothed those out as well. When he looked up from the sofa he gazed briefly into her eyes and then at her hands, lying folded in her lap. "I don't know whether I can handle being liked or loved even though I'm German. My comparison with anti-Semitism appalled you. I'm too tired to come up with another one right now, too confused—you may not understand that, but I don't understand not being taken for the person I am, but some abstract idea, some construct, some creature of prejudice. With the chance, but also the burden of exonerating myself." He paused. "No, I can't handle it."

Her look was sad now. "If we meet someone—how can we forget what we know about his world and the people he's descended from and with whom he lives? I used to think that talk about a typical American or Italian or Irishman was chauvinistic. But there really is such a thing as typical, and it's part of most of us." She laid her hand on his, which continued to make and smooth creases in the sofa slipcover. "You're confused? You have to understand that my friends and family are also confused by what the Germans did, and ask themselves what is typically German about it and if this or that part of it is in every German, including you. But they're not nailing you to the wall with it."

"Yes they are, Tina is, and others too. Your prejudice is like every prejudice; it has something to do with reality and something to do with fear, and it makes life somewhat easier, like all the boxes and drawers you put people into. You'll constantly find something about me that confirms your prejudice, how I think maybe, or how I dress, or like just now, that I laughed at the holes in your clothes."

She stood up, came to him, knelt down before him, and laid her head in his lap. "I will try to see you less against the background of my own culture, against which things you say sometimes . . . ," she looked for a word that would not ignite the argument again, "bother me, and to see things more against yours. And I want to learn yours better."

"You're my sweetheart." He bent down to her, laid his head on hers and his arms on her shoulders. "I'm sorry I got so furious." She smelled good and felt good. They would make love. It would all be lovely again. He looked forward to it. He looked in the lighted windows of the building across the street, saw people moving back and forth, talking, drinking, watching TV. He imagined their view of Sarah's building. A couple who have argued and made up. A couple in love.

10

WHEN DO YOU have to admit to yourself that an argument is not just an argument? That it's not a thunderstorm to be followed by sunshine, and not a rainy season, followed by a barometric high, but just normal lousy weather? That making up solves nothing, takes care of nothing, but only signals exhaustion and makes room for a shorter or longer pause to be followed by more argument.

No, Andi told himself, I'm exaggerating. Sometimes we don't get along and we argue, but then we make up and get along again. Two people who love each other sometimes get along better, sometimes worse, and sometimes not at all. That's how it is. How often you're allowed to argue—there's no rule about that. Anyway, it's not a matter of whether you get along, but whether you tolerate each other. Whether you tolerate each other because you're two of a kind, or don't tolerate each other because you're not. Whether one person gives up whatever separates him from the other, or holds on to it.

All utopias begin with conversion. People say good-bye to old religions, convictions, and ways of life and consent to the new ones of the utopian project—that's conversion, not a lightning bolt from heaven, an awakening, ecstasy, or some other silliness. Those things happened too. But Andi was amazed that conversion to a utopian project was usually a sober personal decision. It was true especially for the wives and husbands of those who signed up for a utopian project. Love, the desire to live together, the impossibility of living in the normal world and in utopia at the same time, the chance of a better life for your children, the chance of professional and economic success for yourself—that was it. It wasn't enough to understand someone else's utopian enthusiasm, and it wasn't necessary to share it. What was necessary was to give up the normal world that separated you from the other person.

One day in the office Andi asked his two colleagues, "If an adult male converts to Judaism and isn't circumcised, does he have to be circumcised?"

One of them sat up straight and leaned back in his chair. "Is it true that Europeans aren't circumcised?"

The other one remained bent over his books. "Yes, he

must. And why not? Abraham circumcised himself when he was ninety-nine years old. But the convert doesn't have to circumcise himself; the mohel does it."

"Is he a doctor?"

"Not a doctor, but an expert. Cut around the upper foreskin and clip off the lower foreskin, push the skin back down below the glans, and drain the wound—you don't need a doctor for that."

Andi grabbed between his legs, his hand protecting his penis. "Without an anesthetic?"

"Without an anesthetic?" His colleague turned to him. "What sort of horrors do you suspect us of? No, adult circumcision is done with a local. Have you found a group of Jews that dispensed with circumcision? Some Jews in the nineteenth century wanted to modify or do away with it."

Andi asked his colleague about the source of his knowledge and learned that the man's father was a rabbi. He also learned that the convert who is already circumcised has to undergo a kind of symbolic circumcision. "You can't cut off what's already been cut off. But you can't do entirely without ritual, either."

Andi saw the point. You couldn't do without ritual. But to undergo the ritual of having his upper foreskin sliced and his lower clipped by a mohel using a local anesthetic, to let him push the skin back below the glans and drain the wound, to hand his body over to religious injunctions, to bare his penis to someone with whom he

had no connection—be it love or a doctor-patient relationship or the trust between friends—to let it be man-
handled and maimed, to show it not just to the mohel but
quite possibly to a rabbi and various elders, witnesses,
and godparents, to stand there the whole time with his
pants down or just in his stocking feet with no pants,
waiting for the ritual to end, while the shot wears off and
his heavily bandaged penis is crammed back into his
pants and his bloody foreskin is lying there in a ritual
bowl—no, he was not prepared to do that. If there was to
be a circumcision, it would be on his terms. He would
arrange it so that it was not so personally embarrassing
or painful. If he was to become a Jew, then a circumcised one.

Andi thought of baptism, of nuns and recruits shorn
of their hair, of SS men and concentration camp prisoners with their tattoos, of cattle being branded. Hair grows
back, tattoos can be removed, and you reemerge from the
baptismal water no different, at least externally, from
before. What sort of religion is it that isn't content with
the symbol of surrender, but instead demands that the
surrender leave an irreversible physical mark? A surrender that the mind may betray, but to which the body must
forever be faithful?

11

THAT WAS the same question that his friend, who had become a surgeon, asked when he visited him his first day back in Heidelberg. "Why do you want to get involved with a religion that starts by cutting off your weenie?"

"It's just the foreskin."

"I know. But what if the knife slips . . ." He grinned.

"Cut the jokes. I love this woman, and she loves me, and we can't handle the fact that we come from two different worlds. So I'm simply changing over to hers . . ."

"Just like that."

"Germans become Americans, Protestants become Catholics, and I've met a black man in the synagogue who's a Jew now, but was an Adventist before that. Just like I became a Christian, without believing or praying, I can become a Jew, too. I meditate in church, but why shouldn't I meditate just as well in a synagogue as in a church? The liturgy in a synagogue is no less beautiful than in a church. And the rituals at home—well, there wasn't much of that in my home, and I'd like more."

His friend shook his head.

"I mean it. Either she has to become like me, or I become like her. You really tolerate only your own kind."

They were sitting in the same Italian restaurant where they used to meet as students. There were one or two new faces among the waiters, one or two new pictures on the walls, but otherwise the place hadn't changed. Just as in the old days, Andi had ordered salad, spaghetti bolognese, and red wine, and his friend had ordered a bowl of soup, pizza, and beer. Just as in the old days, his friend had the feeling *he* was the sober and practical one, who also bore the responsibility imposed on a sober and practical mind when dealing with romantics and utopians. The ideas that Andi had got in his head over the years!

"A woman who would demand—"

"Sarah isn't demanding anything of me. She doesn't even know I want to be circumcised, and that's why I'm here. I told her that I was going to give a lecture at a conference."

"Well, okay. But what are you doing with a woman you can't speak openly with?"

"Openness presumes you're standing on common ground. Whether or not you're standing on common ground—that's not something you talk about, it's something you decide."

His friend shook his head. "Just picture it. Your girlfriend doesn't want the baby she's carrying and gets an abortion without saying a word to you. You'd be mad as hell."

"Yes, because she'd be taking something from me. I'm not taking anything from Sarah, I'm giving her something."

"You don't know that. Maybe she loves your foreskin. Maybe she doesn't share your weird theory and wants to live with you not because you're the same, but because you're different. Maybe she doesn't take things as seriously as you do when you argue. Maybe she likes to argue."

Andi gazed at him sadly. "I can only do what I think is right. You think my theory is weird—wherever I look, back in history or in the present, in the grand scheme of things and in the details, I find it's confirmed."

"Doesn't it bother you that the decisive step for applying your theory would be a lie?"

"How do you mean?"

"You want to become a Jew for Sarah, but you want to wriggle your way out of what it actually takes to become a Jew. You find it embarrassing, it might hurt more than necessary—and you don't want that." His friend teased him. "I'm beginning to understand why the Jews came up with circumcision. They don't want any limp dicks who . . ."

Andi laughed. "They don't want any uncircumcised limp dicks, that's all. That's why I want you to circumcise mine. Will you do it?"

His friend laughed, too. "Just picture it . . ."

It was like one of those discussions they had had as students. Just picture it, your friend is a terrorist, the police are looking for him, and he asks you to hide him. Just picture it, your friend wants to commit suicide, is paralyzed, and needs your help. Just picture it, your friend confesses that he has slept with your girlfriend. Just picture it, your friend becomes a successful artist—

will you tell him that his paintings are bad? That his wife is cheating on him? That some good deed he's done will ruin his life?

"You'd like to get it over with as soon as possible."

"I want to get back to New York and Sarah as soon as possible."

"Then come by tomorrow at noon. I'll give you a light general anesthetic, and when you wake up the wound will have stitches that won't need to be removed, because the part inside dissolves and the rest falls off. You'll have to change the bandage now and then, just gauze and panthenol. In three weeks you'll be good as new."

"What's that supposed to mean."

"What does it mean that your weenie will be good as new? What do you suppose?"

12

THE OPERATION wasn't bad. The pain afterward was bearable and completely gone after a few days. But Andi was constantly aware that his penis was part of him, a wounded and threatened part. When he bandaged it, when he carefully tucked it away as he put on his pants or felt the pain of it if he made a wrong move or touched it wrong—he kept trying to protect it when he moved or touched it—it commanded his attention.

He was in his hometown, where he had grown up and

worked before leaving for New York and where he would work when he returned. He stayed with his parents, who were glad to have him home, but left him in peace, and when he met with colleagues and friends, they picked up the conversation right where they had left off. Sometimes he would run into a friend from high school, a former teacher or girlfriend, who didn't know he had been gone for almost a year and would soon be leaving again, and they greeted him as if he still lived here. He could have moved through his hometown like a fish through water.

But he felt stranded, as if he had arrived where he didn't belong, as if the town and its landscape of mountains, rivers, and plain were no longer his home. The streets where he walked were full of memories—here was a cellar window beside which he and a friend had played marbles on the sidewalk, there a bike shed in a driveway where he and his first girlfriend had stood to get out of the rain and had kissed. At one intersection on the way to school he had got his bicycle wheel caught in the trolley tracks and fallen, and in the park, beyond that wall there, his mother had practiced painting watercolors with him one Sunday morning. He could paint the town with the brush of his memory and in the colors of his past happiness, of past hopes and past sadness. But it was different now, he couldn't enter into the picture. When his memories invited him in, when he tried to live in the unity of past and present that mean home, a little movement, some accidental touch of the change purse or key ring in his pants pocket would call up a very different memory—

his circumcision and, as part of his circumcision, the question of where he belonged.

In New York? In the Kehilath-Yeshurun synagogue? With Sarah? He called her every day, in the early afternoon when it was early morning there and she was still lying in bed or having breakfast. He invented a couple of conference events and told her about walks he'd taken, about meetings with friends and colleagues, and about relatives she'd met at the marble anniversary party. "I miss you," she said, and "I love you." And he said, "I miss you, too," and "I love you, too." He asked her what and how she was doing, and she told him about both their neighbors' dogs, about a tennis match with a former professor, and about the plots and intrigues that a woman working on another computer game had tried to involve their publisher in. He understood every word and yet didn't understand a thing. He had left his feeling for certain allusions, for New York irony, sarcasm, and seriousness, in New York. Or had it been cut off along with his foreskin? He assumed that Sarah meant what she said a little ironically. She usually meant what she said a little ironically. But what in fact was the point of her irony?

Sitting at work in New York, he would constantly fantasize about making love with Sarah. The fantasy didn't interrupt him in the middle of a thought or a sentence. But once the thought was completed or the sentence written down, he would look up and see the rain outside and picture himself making love with Sarah listening to the rain. Or he would be sitting on a park bench watching children and picture himself making love with Sarah, making a child with her. Or he would see a woman with her back to him, leaning against a wall and gazing out at the Hudson, and he would imagine that she was Sarah and picture himself stepping up behind her, lifting her skirt, and entering her. When he was tired he would picture her falling asleep after they had made love, his stomach against her butt and his hand between her breasts, wrapped in the scent of love. But he had left these fantasies and longings in New York, if only because of the painful erections they might cause.

Or maybe it had to be that way? Wasn't it natural for him not to belong to his old home and still not belong to his new one either? Don't you have to go through no-man's-land when you're changing sides?

13

THE PLANE above the Atlantic is a no-man's-land, too. You eat, drink, sleep, wake up, do nothing or work, but whatever you do it's all just airy potentiality, until the plane lands and you've arrived. Only after you've brought your full stomach, that feeling of relaxation, or the work you've done back to earth is any of it real. Andi would not have been surprised if the plane had crashed.

He stepped out of the cool airport terminal and into

the heavy hot air of New York. It was loud, there was a press and tangle of cars, with honking taxis and a dispatcher who kept order among taxis and waiting passengers by blowing on his whistle. Andi looked for Sarah, although she had told him that she wouldn't be picking him up, that nobody in New York picks anyone up at the airport. It was too hot in the taxi if he closed the window, and there was a draft if he opened it. "Grab a cab, and come to me as fast as you can," Sarah had said. Actually he couldn't afford a taxi. He didn't understand why he should come as fast as he could. What difference would it make if he arrived an hour later? Or three or seven? Or a day? Or a week?

Sarah had bought flowers, a large bouquet of red and yellow roses. She had put the champagne on ice and clean sheets on the bed. She was waiting for him in a short-sleeved man's shirt that barely covered her butt. She looked seductive and she seduced him before he could even feel the fear he had assumed would be part of the first time since his circumcision—fear that it would hurt or feel wrong and unpleasant or that he would be impotent. "I missed you," she said, "I missed you so much."

She didn't notice that he was circumcised. Not as they made love, not when he got up naked to open the champagne and bring the filled glasses back to the bed, not when they showered together. They went out to eat and to the movies and returned home across the shimmering asphalt. Andi knew Sarah so well, her voice, her smell, her hips when he put his arm around her. Were they closer now? Did he belong more to her, to her world, to this city and this country?

As they ate she told him about a trip to South Africa that she was supposed to take with her employer and asked if he wanted to come along. He said he regretted not having visited South Africa during apartheid, a world that he could have seen and now was gone forever. She looked at him, and he knew what she was thinking. But he realized that it didn't matter. He searched for his old sense of outrage, his old need to contradict and set things right, but found nothing. She said nothing.

Before they fell asleep they lay there facing each other. He gazed at her face in the white light of the streetlight. "I'm circumcised."

She reached for his penis. "Were you . . . no, you weren't . . . or were . . . hey, you've got me really confused now. Why are you saying that you're circumcised?"

"Oh, no reason."

"I thought you weren't. But if you are, then . . ." She shook her head. "It's not so common in Europe as it is here, is it?"

He nodded.

"I used to want to know how a man who's uncircumcised would feel inside me—if it would be any different, better or worse. My girlfriend said it made no difference, but I didn't know if I should believe her. Then I told myself that I wouldn't gain all that much with an uncircumcised man, because if it does feel some other way, that could be for any number of reasons. You can't imagine how different particular circumcised men can feel." She cuddled up against him. "And how good you feel!"

He nodded.

He woke up the next morning at four. He wanted to go back to sleep. But he couldn't. Over there, at home, it was ten o'clock and broad daylight. He got up and dressed. He opened the apartment door, set his shoes and suitcase out in the hallway, and pulled the door to so gently that it barely clicked. He put on his shoes and left.

THE SON

1

THERE HAD been no civilian air service since the rebels had shelled the airport and hit an airliner. The observers arrived on an American military plane painted white with blue markings. They were received by officers and soldiers, who escorted them across the runway, down long corridors, into a large hall, and on past out-of-service moving sidewalks, closed ticket counters, and deserted shops. Advertising signs were dark, flight information boards blank. The large windows had been sandbagged to chest level, many had no glass. Slivers and sand crunched beneath the feet of the observers and their escorts.

A small bus was waiting outside the terminal. Its door was open and the observers were politely requested to board. No sooner had the last man stepped onto the bus than two jeeps pulled up in front and two trucks with soldiers moved in behind. Then the motorcade set off at high speed.

"Welcome, gentlemen." The observers recognized the old man with white hair and a white mustache who was standing between the two front seats, clutching their backs—the president. He was legendary. He had been elected in 1969 and toppled by the military two years later. He hadn't fled the country, but instead had stayed and been put in prison. At the end of the seventies, as a result of pressure from the Americans, he was released to house arrest; in the eighties he was permitted to work as a lawyer and by the nineties had organized the opposition. When the rebels and the military were forced into peace negotiations, they agreed to install him as president. No one doubted that the planned election would confirm him in office.

The motorcade had reached the outskirts of the capital—huts constructed of planks, sheets of plastic, and cardboard; a cemetery, its mausoleums inhabited, its gravestones providing foundations for shacks; little mud-brick houses with corrugated tin roofs. Women, men, and children walked along the roads carrying containers with water. It was obviously hot and dry. Over everything, even the asphalt road, lay a coat of sandy dust that was kicked up by the passing motorcade. After a short while dust clouded the bus's windows. The president talked about the civil war, about terrorism and peace. "The secret of peace is exhaustion. But when is everyone finally exhausted? We'll be happy if the majority is exhausted. But not too exhausted—they have to prevent the fighting initiated by those who want to go on fighting." The president offered a weary smile. "Peace is an improbable state of affairs. That is why I asked for a peacekeeping force of twenty thousand men. Instead, the twelve of you have come to observe whether the agreed-upon establishment of mixed units, the election of governors, and the reinstatement of civilian administration are properly carried out." The president looked into the face of each of them in succession. "You have shown courage in coming here. I thank you." He smiled again. "Do you know what our press is calling you? The twelve apostles of peace. God bless you."

They were now in the heart of the city. It lay at the end of a valley, a couple of streets with an old cathedral, government buildings, the parliament, and courts from the nineteenth century, plus modern office and retail buildings, and apartment houses. The president took his leave. The bus drove on. Halfway up the mountain it halted at the entrance to the Hilton. The side of the hotel facing the mountain revealed bullet holes and boarded-up windows. Sandbags had been used to reinforce positions in the park.

The manager greeted them in person. He apologized for the less than perfect arrangements and service. The military had given the hotel back only a few days before. In any case the rooms were in perfect condition again. "And throw open your balcony doors. The nights are cool and heavy with the scent of flowers in our garden, and the mosquitoes stay down by the coast. You won't miss the air-conditioning, which still isn't running."

2

DINNER WAS served on the terrace. The observers sat at six tables, corresponding to the country's six provinces. Each of the two observers assigned to a province was joined by an officer of that province's military and a *comandante* of its rebels. Just as the hotel manager had promised, the temperature was pleasant, the garden fragrant. Now and then a moth burned up in a candle flame.

The German observer, a professor of international law, had stepped in for someone else at the last minute. He had already worked for various international organizations, had sat on committees, written reports, and drafted treaties. But he had never agreed to be placed in a trouble spot. Why had he always dodged such assignments? Because as an observer one enjoys neither influence nor prestige? Then why had he insisted on it this time? Because he had felt like a charlatan who had never faced the realities he managed from a desk? Maybe, he thought, maybe that was it. He was the oldest of the observers and weary from flights over the Atlantic and the Gulf of Mexico, and from an argument with his girlfriend in New York that had lasted all night between flights.

His partner was a Canadian, an engineer and businessman who had become involved in a human rights organization once his business was able to run without him. When the officer and the *comandante*, with whom they would set out for the more northern of the two coastal provinces the next day, proved uninterested in stories about his previous assignments as an observer, the Canadian pulled out his wallet and spread photographs of his wife and four children on the table. "Do you have a family?"

The officer and the *comandante* looked at each other in embarrassed surprise and hesitated. But then each reached into his jacket for his wallet. The officer carried his wedding picture with him—he in black dress uniform with white gloves and his wife in a white dress with a veil and train, both looking very serious and sad. He also had a picture of his children; they were sitting side by side on two chairs, his daughter in tulle and lace, his son in a camouflage uniform, both too small yet for their feet to reach the floor and both with that same, serious, sad look in their eyes. "What a beautiful woman!" Clicking his tongue, the Canadian expressed his admiration for the bride, a girl with black eyes, red lips, and full cheeks. The officer quickly put the picture away, as if he wanted to protect his family from such admiration. The Canadian examined the portrait of the *comandante*'s wife, a smiling student in her graduation robe and cap, and said, "Oh, what a beauty your wife is too!" The *comandante* laid a second photograph on the table, of himself and two little boys, one on each hand, beside a grave. The German saw the officer's eyes narrow and his cheeks grow taut. But the *comandante*'s wife had not been killed by soldiers, she had died giving birth to her third child.

Then everyone's eyes were directed at the German. He shrugged. "I'm divorced, and my son is grown." But he knew he could have had a photograph with him all the same. Even earlier, when his son was still small, he hadn't carried one. Why? Would it have reminded him, perhaps, that he was not much of a father to his son, who had been five at the time of the divorce and been raised by his mother, so that he saw him only seldom?

Their meal arrived. The first course was quickly followed by a second, third, and fourth, and there was red wine from the coast. The *comandante* ate and drank with concentration, head and chest bent over his plate. After each course he took a piece of bread, wiped his plate clean with it, popped it in his mouth, and sat up straight, as if about to say something, but then said not a word. Although he was scarcely any older than the officer, he seemed to come from a different generation, a generation of slow, ponderous, taciturn men who have seen everything. Sometimes his eyes would measure the others— the Canadian, who talked about his wife and children; the officer, who stuck out both pinkies when using his knife and fork and asked polite questions; and the German, who was too tired to eat and leaned back, his eyes meeting the *comandante*'s.

I should talk, the German thought, and polish up my rusty Spanish. But nothing occurred to him. True, pulling out photographs to show had not made buddies of these husbands and fathers, but he felt as if they belonged together and shared in a right to this world that he did not have.

While they were eating dessert, they heard shots, the rattle of submachine-gun fire. Conversations broke off, everyone listened into the night. The German thought he saw the officer and the *comandante* exchange glances and shake their heads.

"That was one of yours," the Canadian said, looking at the *comandante*. "That was a Kalashnikov."

"You have good ears."

"It would be good if all the Kalashnikovs were in their hands," the officer said, nodding his head in the *comandante*'s direction.

They could hear the same hum that had risen from the valley all evening—the soft hum of power stations, of air conditioners in the office, retail, and apartment high-rises, of traffic, of workshops and restaurants. And of breathing. The German thought of people in their sleep, of lovers and of the dying—it was a pleasant thought.

3

As ALWAYS after a transatlantic flight, he woke up at four. He stepped out on the balcony. The city lay dark in the valley. The fragrance of flowers wafted from the garden. The air was mild. He opened up his chaise longue and stretched out. He couldn't recall ever having seen so many stars. A light was moving; he followed it with his eyes, lost it, found it again, lost and found it once more, and stayed with it to the horizon.

It grew light around five. All at once the sky was gray instead of black, the stars vanished, and the few lights left in the city and on the hills went out. In the same moment birds began singing, all together, a loud dissonant concert, interrupted sometimes by the fragment of a melody like some secret greeting. Was that why the music of different cultures sounded different? Because the birds had different songs?

He went back into the room. Breakfast was to be at six, and they were scheduled to leave at seven. He showered and dressed. In his carry-on he found a tie he didn't recognize. His girlfriend must have slipped it in between his suits after they had argued. Should she join him in Germany or should he join her in New York, should they try to have children, shouldn't he try not to work so hard—it was a riddle to him how they could have spent the whole night talking about such things. An even greater riddle was how after the argument, which had ended in bitterness and near exhaustion, his girlfriend could have packed a tie for him as if nothing had happened.

He picked up the phone without any hope that it would be functioning. But it was, and he called the hospital where his son had begun working as a doctor only a few weeks earlier. As he waited for his son to come to the telephone, the hum on the line reminded him of the hum from the city.

"What's wrong?" His son was out of breath.

"Nothing. I just wanted to ask . . ." He wanted to ask him if he could fax him a photograph of himself, since if the phone was working the fax would be too. But he didn't dare.

"What is it, Papa? I'm on duty and need to get back to my station. Where are you calling from?"

"From America." He hadn't spoken with his son for weeks. There was a time when he had called his son every Sunday. But their conversations had been labored, and so one day he let it slide.

"Let me know when you get back."

"I love you, my boy." He had never said that before. Whenever he heard how easy it was for fathers or mothers to say it to their sons and daughters in American films, he would resolve to say it to his son. But he had always felt too embarrassed.

His son was embarrassed now too. "I—I—I also wish you all the best, Papa. See you soon."

Later he asked himself if he should have found more words. Should have said that he had always wanted to tell him that he loved him. Or that being so far away from his usual surroundings had made him think of what was important, and that when he did . . . But that wouldn't have made it any better.

They rode in four jeeps, the officer in the lead, then

the Canadian, then the German, and the *comandante* at the rear. They each sat in the back seat, up front were the driver and another soldier. The Canadian and the German would have liked to ride together. But the officer and the *comandante* wouldn't allow it. "No, *ingeniero*," they said to the Canadian, and "No, *profesor*," to the German. If there were any mines along the road through the mountains, they didn't want two observers blown up in one jeep.

They took off at breakneck speed. It was chilly, the jeep was open, the wind whistled, the German froze. After a while the asphalt gave out and they moved more slowly over gravel, dirt, and potholes, but still fast enough that he was tossed back and forth no matter how tight he held on. But that warmed him up.

The road wound its way up into the mountains. They were to rest at the pass at noon, put up for the night in a monastery halfway down into the valley, and arrive at the provincial capital by afternoon the next day.

"Can you tell me why they didn't take us over these stupid mountains in a helicopter?" The second jeep had blown a tire, and while the driver changed it the Canadian offered the German whiskey from a thin silver flask.

"Maybe it's a matter of protocol? In a helicopter we'd be in the hands of the military, but this way we're in the hands of both the rebels and the soldiers."

"They'd rather risk us being blown up than agree on protocol?" The Canadian shook his head and took another swig. "I think I'll ask."

But he let it be. The officer and the *comandante* were standing off to one side and talking excitedly. Then the *comandante* returned to his jeep, took the wheel, gunned past the other vehicles, sending up a spray of grass and soil from the embankment and forcing the Canadian and the German to leap out of the way, and stopped in the middle of the road in front of the officer's jeep. The Canadian handed the German his flask again without a word. "I've got more in my baggage."

4

THE HIGHER they went the slower their progress. The road got narrower, and worse. It had been hewn into crumbling rock that rose steeply on one side and fell steeply into the valley on the other. Sometimes they had to move a fallen boulder or fill a washout with stones and branches or secure the jeep behind with a rope whenever gravel had slid out from under the one ahead. The air was warm and damp, and steam was rising from the valley.

It was getting dark by the time they reached the pass. The *comandante* stopped. "We can't go any farther today."

The officer joined him. They exchanged low words that the German couldn't make out, until the officer shouted, "Climb out! We'll drive on again tomorrow."

To the left of the road was a large open square, at the

far end of which was a little church and a view to the faraway mountain chain turning gray in the dusk and wrapped in fog. The church was a burned-out shell. The frames of what had been doors and windows were blackened with soot, and the roof timbers were charred. But the tower had been left untouched—a squat cube, topped by a slender but likewise squared-off belfry that ended in a rounded crown with a large cross. As darkness swallowed the traces of fire, the church's silhouette loomed black and intact against the gray sky. It could almost have been a church in Bavaria or the lower Alps of Austria.

The scene came back to the German. It might have been twenty years before. He had been spending a two-week vacation with his son on a lake south of Munich. One evening at the beginning of the second week they had walked as they did every evening to the church at the far end of the village. It was on a little hill, with an open square leading from it down to the village; behind it meadows rose up to hills and mountains and finally the distant Alps. They were sitting on a stone bench in the square. It was autumn and already chilly, but the warmth of the day lingered in the stone. A convertible stopped at the edge of the square, and his ex-wife and her new young boyfriend got out, came over, and stood in front of the bench—his wife in a white dress with a gold belt, coquettish and self-conscious at the same time, her boyfriend in black leather pants and an open white shirt, standing with his feet well apart.

"Hello, Mama." The boy was the first to speak, sliding forward on the bench as if he were about to jump up and run, but he stayed seated.

"Hello."

Then her friend started talking. He insisted that they were taking the boy with them. The court had granted the boy's father just one week of fall vacation, the other belonged to his mother.

That was true, but they had agreed between them to do things differently this fall. His wife knew that, but said nothing. She was afraid. She was afraid of losing her boyfriend, although she realized how pompous he was and how pompously he was going on about how the boy belonged with his mother and with him, the man who now stood at her side. The boy's father saw her fear and, behind his pomposity, the fear of her boyfriend, who was aware of his inferiority when it came to achievements and a place in the world, leaving him unable to enjoy the advantage of being younger. He saw the fear in his son, who was acting as if all this had nothing to do with him.

The other man talked himself into a fury, shouting about kidnapping, a trial, and prison and barking at the boy to get into the car. His son shrugged, stood up, and waited. His father saw the question in his eyes and the demand that he fight and win—and then the disappointment that he was giving in. He could have yelled at the other man, punched him out, or run away with his son. Anything would have been better than to go along, to add a shrug of his own, and nod to his son with a smile of regret and encouragement.

Had he wanted to make things easier for his son? Or for the boy's mother? Or for himself? Was he secretly glad that his son was gone and he could get back to work?

The jeeps drove across the open square and parked in front of the church, with engines idling and headlights on. The officer and the *comandante* shouted orders, and the soldiers started busying themselves inside the church. The German walked across the square and past the tower, and discovered a two-room addition, also gutted, at the rear, and stairs leading from behind the chancel down the slope. It was too dark for him to see where they went. He stood there gazing at the stairs. Now and then a cry came up from below, like the cry of a bird in a dream. Then the officer called for him.

He turned around and started back. Only now did he notice someone crouching next to the top step. It startled him, and he felt as if he was being watched, spied on. He couldn't tell if the figure in a dark poncho was a man or a woman. Without looking up, the figure said something he didn't understand. He asked the figure to repeat what it had said, and it spoke again, but he couldn't even make out if what it said was a repetition or something else. The officer called for him again.

By the light of the headlights the soldiers were busy in the church, piling up charred wood from the roof, pews, and confessionals, and clearing an area around the altar in the chancel. The officer and *comandante* were nowhere in sight. The Canadian was sitting on the stone threshold to the tower, his thin silver flask in his hand.

"Come here," the Canadian called, waving the hand holding the flask.

The German sat down, took a swig, and rolled it around in his mouth till it burned.

"Can you tell me why they brought sleeping bags and food along if we were supposed to sleep at the monastery?" the Canadian asked. "What they're doing is building a fire to cook on and setting up camp in the chancel."

He swallowed the whiskey and took another swig. "For emergencies. They knew what the road is like and that we might run into an emergency."

"They knew what the road is like? And all the same they decided to take us over the mountains by jeep, instead of by helicopter?"

"I've never been in a helicopter."

"Ro-to-to-to," the Canadian went and waved the flask in circles around his head. He was drunk. Then they heard two shots and then, a heartbeat later, a third. "That was the *comandante*. At least it was his pistol. Do you have one with you?"

"A pistol?"

The *comandante* and the officer emerged out of the darkness. "What were you shooting at?" the Canadian called out to them as they approached.

"He thought he heard a rattlesnake." The *comandante* nodded his head toward the officer. "But there aren't any around here. No need to worry."

5

WHILE THEY ATE, the Canadian started in on the *coman-dante*. He had been the one who fired the gun, not the officer, so why was he denying it? After a while the officer began to make fun of the *ingeniero*. So, he had been able to tell that the shots were from a Tokarev. So, he knew what a Tokarev sounded like, and a Makarov and a Browning and a Beretta. Wasn't that amazing? That he of all people was so good at recognizing gunshots? That he knew so much about guns? He of all people.

The Canadian cast him a questioning look.

"After all, you left America for Canada back then, because you didn't want to have anything to do with guns, didn't you?"

"So?"

The officer laughed and slapped his thigh.

When the fire had burned down and they were lying in their sleeping bags, the German gazed up at the sky through what was left of the roof timbers. He was once again overwhelmed by the panoply of stars. He looked for some moving light that he could follow again with his eyes. But he found none.

A real father fights for his son. He battles for him. Or he flees with him. But he doesn't sit there and shrug. He doesn't watch with a stupid grin on his face while someone takes his son away from him.

Other similarly shameful scenes came back to him. A dinner with some older colleagues who rejected him and whom he despised but tried to win over all the same. That evening with his wife and her parents, when her father made it obvious that he would have preferred a different husband for his daughter, and he had sat there smiling politely. The dancing class where he had danced the last dance with the prettiest girl and was therefore entitled to walk her home, but could only grin and bear it when another boy, one of the bigger, stronger ones, snatched her away from him with a laugh.

His face was burning. He could barely stand the shame. Memories of his failures in life, of frustrated plans, of hopes now dead—nothing was as physical as shame. It was as if he wanted to get away from himself but couldn't, as if he were tugging and tearing himself apart. As if it were ripping him in two. Yes, he thought, that's what shame is. The physical sense of being torn in half, because you are or were only half-hearted. One half of me despised those colleagues, while the other was trying to win them over. I half hated my father-in-law and tore myself in half for my wife's sake, and I wanted that pretty girl, but not with my whole heart, not with all my courage. And I was only half a father to my son.

He fell asleep. When he awoke his mind was instantly totally clear. He sat up and listened into the darkness. He wanted to know what had awakened him. But the night was silent. He heard only the cry of a bird and a rustling sound, like wind through dead leaves. Suddenly the jeep parked outside the church door burst into flames with a loud pop. Before the German could creep out of his sleeping bag, the officer was dashing through the door, out onto the square, making for another jeep beside the one already burning. He released the brake and pushed. The German ran after him and helped. It was scorching hot beside the raging fire, he thought the flames would jump across at any moment. But together they managed it. The two other jeeps were parked at a safe distance.

"Didn't you . . ."

"Yes, I posted a guard at the door." The officer pulled the German back into the church. The chancel was empty. The others were standing to one side of the entrance, where the flames didn't illuminate the church's interior. No one said a word until the fire died out. Then the officer and the *comandante* whispered orders, and the men vanished into the darkness of night.

"We're climbing the tower. You go to the chancel. Here, *profesor,* take my pistol." The officer gave the German his gun. Then he and the *comandante* were gone, too.

The Canadian held the German back. "Tomorrow morning, as soon as it's light, we'll grab us a jeep and two of the boys and head back. If they don't want us to get to that stupid town, that's fine by me. I didn't go to Canada instead of Vietnam so that I could end up being killed here."

"But . . ."

"Where's your head? They don't want us. They

haven't killed us, although they could have, because they're being polite. But they're serious, and if we don't respond politely to their politeness, they'll stop being polite."

"Who are they?"

"How should I know? And I don't care, either."

The German hesitated. "But haven't we been assigned—"

"—the job of bringing peace to the country? Aren't we two of the twelve apostles of peace?" The Canadian laughed. "Don't you get it? It's like the president said: If the combatants are doing too well, there's no making peace with them. It's like with alcohol. Until an alcoholic has fallen so far, so deep that he can't go any deeper, he won't stop drinking." He pulled the flask from his pocket. "Cheers!"

6

EVEN THOUGH he was freezing, the German fell asleep. When he woke up, his arms and legs stiff, morning was breaking. He sat up and on his left he saw two jeeps parked nicely side by side and the other one stranded in the middle of the square. He hadn't realized they had pushed it so far last night. Fog was clinging to the trees on the slope beyond the square. The light was gray, but it still hurt his eyes.

He heard noises. Metal ringing against stone, over and over, and earth falling on earth with a plump smack. Were the drivers digging a grave? The sun rose, a pale yellow ball.

The ringing spades reminded him of a vacation at the shore and the sandcastle he had built with his son, because all fathers build sandcastles with their sons and his son wanted the father all sons have and to do the things with him that they all do with their fathers. At the same time his son had wanted a special sandcastle, one to brag about. But none of the schoolmates or playmates he could have bragged to were there, and despite all the work father and son put into it, it didn't accomplish its goal. They didn't accomplish their goal on a mountain hike a couple of years later, either. They didn't get as far as they had wanted—or that he had assumed they needed to get for him to show his son the joy of mastering a challenge. He thought of other situations where he had failed, demanded instead of praised, scolded instead of comforted, drawn away instead of getting involved. They moved through his memory like a distant train moving across his field of vision. A train he should have boarded, but that had long since left the station.

He felt weak, he leaned against the base of a column and looked at the sun. His teeth were chattering. As if the sun were just hanging up there, he thought. He was seized by the fear it might fall. Would it strike the earth, burn everything up or vaporize it with a hiss as it struck? Or would it fall into the void behind the earth?

He knew this was nonsense, and he knew that he was thinking nonsense because he was feverish. That there was no reason for the fear moving up through his body like the cold. It wasn't so cold, nor was there all that much reason for fear. He didn't need to worry about his son being born handicapped, ending up taking drugs, failing school, being chronically depressed, not graduating from college, not finding a wife. It had all gone well, even if none of it was his own doing. Even if he hadn't contributed what he ought to have contributed. Even if he still owed his contribution. Even if he had not paid his debt.

The sound of digging stopped. All the German heard was his own teeth chattering. He had to decide whether he wanted to go back with or even without the Canadian or drive on with the officer and *comandante*. He didn't want to risk his life. His son would soon need him to be a loving, kindly, generous grandfather. Soon—but out there the jeeps were being loaded, the officer and the *comandante* would presumably be taking their seats in the first jeep, assigning the second one to the Canadian and the third to him; maybe the Canadian would climb aboard, flask in hand, and they would all expect him not to gum up the works and make this difficult trip even more difficult. He had to decide. All the same, without bracing himself against the column, he would hardly be able to stand.

He had no idea where the Canadian, the officer, and

the *comandante* suddenly appeared from. They were standing at the entrance to the church.

"Our orders are to bring you to the town, and we're going to bring you to the town."

"Your orders are to bring us safely to the town. But whoever killed the guard last night and set the jeep on fire is going to blow us up somewhere down the road. Boom."

"What did you expect? That you were going to take a little drive in the country? For a picnic?" The *comandante* was furious.

The officer was more placating. "Whoever did that last night—that he came at night but didn't show himself yesterday means that he's too weak to show himself by day."

The German stood up and stepped outside the church. He was shivering, and his body ached. To the right of the church the drivers had dug a grave. To one side of it, the folding spades had been thrust into the mound of earth. On the other side lay two bodies. The German recognized the man who had been his driver yesterday, the throat gaping and bloody. Beside him lay a woman with several bullet holes in her chest. The German had never seen a corpse before. It didn't make him sick to his stomach, he wasn't shocked. Dead people simply looked dead. Was the woman the figure who had been sitting at the top of the stairs? Why had the officer or the *comandante* shot her? By mistake? Out of nervousness?

Two drivers appeared, laid the corpses into the grave, shoveled it full, and patted the earth with their spades. No cross, he thought, but then he saw one of the drivers tying two wooden sticks together to make one.

The others loaded baggage, sleeping bags, and supplies into the jeeps. The Canadian was trying to talk to the officer—who paid him no attention and kept walking around. The Canadian ran alongside trying to buttonhole him, but to no avail. The *comandante* was already sitting in the jeep.

Giving up on the officer, the Canadian glanced at the German and crossed over to him. "They won't drive us back." Then he noticed the German's jacket, heavy with the weight of the pistol the officer had given him during the night and that the German had tucked into his pocket. He grabbed it before the German realized what he was reaching for. He ran over to the officer, thrust out his chest, and waved the gun.

7

THEN EVERYTHING happened so quickly—the movements, the cries, the shots—that the German understood none of it. That was his first thought when he realized he had been hit: I'll never know what happened.

A book came to mind, a book in which a man described his heart attack, beads of sweat on his forehead and sweaty palms, a searing flash in his lungs, an ache in his left arm, pains in his chest, welling up and diminishing like a cramp, fear. Just like that, he had thought at the time, that's how the assault on his own life would be. But he felt no searing flash, no ache, no pain, no fear. His chest felt full, as if a bubble of warm liquid had burst in there and was running out inside him.

The shooting was over. The *comandante* shouted orders, a couple of men ran to the jeeps, others to the officer and the Canadian, who had sunk to the ground. The German couldn't tell how seriously the man was wounded. For a moment he thought he should do something about it, but was immediately aware of what an absurd idea that was. He wanted to be alone. He put one foot in front of the other and groped along, bracing himself against the wall of the church with his right hand. He wanted to make it to the stairs.

The pale yellow sun was still hanging there, but a little higher now. He saw that the slope that fell away behind the church was covered with chest-high brush and grass. That slope and the next and the next. Here and there a palm tree towered with its feather-dusty crown. The land was bleak, inhospitable, hostile. A cold breeze came up; it moved through the tall grass covering the hills. It looks like wind moving over water, he thought.

Then he thought of the debt he hadn't paid. Would his son have to make good on it for him? Would the bill be presented to him? Or was the meaning of his death that he was making good on his debt? That the bill wouldn't be presented to his son? That his son would not have to pay for his happiness?

He was cheerful for a brief moment. Ah, he said to himself, it's not too late, it's not too late to love my son. Maybe he's coming up those stairs right now? And even if it's only a vision—how beautiful it would be to see him coming up the stairs now, in his doctor's smock and stethoscope, dressed as I've never seen him, or in those same old jeans and that same old blue sweater, or as a little boy, running, laughing, out of breath.

Out of breath? Where had the warmth in his chest gone? Why were his legs, which had just been supporting him, no longer doing so? Before he could sit down on the stairs his legs buckled under him and he collapsed on the flagstones that connected with the top step. He was lying on his left side and saw dried blood, grass growing between the flagstones, and a beetle. He wanted to pull himself up, crawl to the stairs, and sit down on the top step. He wanted to sit there in such a way that if he died he would crumple up but stay sitting. He wanted to sit there so that if he died he would be looking out across the land and the land would be looking at him, sitting upright on the top step and dying.

He would never find out why he was being so vain in death—although no one was there, no one to see him, be impressed or disappointed by him. He could have found out if he had thought about it. But he would have had to think longer than he had time left. He didn't manage to pull himself up. He lay there on the ground, felt the cold wind, but could no longer see it moving through the grass. He would have liked to see those tousled, feather-dusty palms again, too. They reminded him of something; maybe he would think of it if he could see them again.

He realized he had only a few moments left. One moment to think about his mother, one moment for the women in his life, one moment for . . . His son did not come up the stairs. It had been too late after all. He was sad that at the last moment the movie of his life did not unreel before him. He would have liked to see it. He would have liked to do nothing, just relax and watch. Instead he had to think until the very last moment. The movie—why didn't death do what people promised it would? But then he was too tired to have wanted to see the movie anyway.

THE WOMAN
AT THE GAS STATION

1

HE NO LONGER knew if he had actually dreamt his dream at one time or had only been fantasizing about it from the start. He also didn't know what image, what story, or what film had triggered it. It must have been when he was fifteen or sixteen—the dream had stayed with him that long now. Back then, he would fantasize about it if a class in school or a day on vacation with his parents was too boring, later it might happen in a business meeting or on a train—when he was tired and had put his reports away, he would lay his head back and close his eyes.

He had told his dream a few times to one friend or another, and to a woman whom, years after their love affair and separation, he had encountered by chance in another city and idled the day away with, strolling and chatting. It wasn't that he would have wanted to keep his dream secret. There weren't many occasions to talk about

it. Besides, he didn't know why the dream had stayed
with him. He knew that it betrayed something about him,
but not what, and it was unpleasant to think that someone else might be able to see it.

2

IN HIS DREAM he is driving a car across a wide desert
plain. The road is straight; sometimes it vanishes into a
dip or behind a hill, but his eye can always follow it to the
mountains on the horizon. The sun is at its zenith, and
the air flickers above the asphalt.

He hasn't met an oncoming car for a long time, and
he hasn't passed one, either. The next town according to
a sign and his map is another sixty miles ahead, somewhere in the mountains or beyond them, and, as far as he
can see, there's not a house to the left or right. But then
beside the road on his left is a gas station. A large, sandy
area with two pumps in the middle, behind them a two-
story frame house with a roofed porch. He steps on the
brake, turns onto the sandy drive, and stops at one of the
pumps. The cloud of sand billowing up behind him
settles.

He waits. Just as he is about to get out and go knock
on the door, it opens and a woman steps out. She is still a
girl the first times he fantasizes his dream, but over the
years becomes a young woman, until somewhere between

thirty and forty she stops growing older. She remains that same young woman, even as he himself moves on past forty and fifty. She's usually wearing jeans and a checkered shirt, sometimes an ankle-length dress of bleached blue denim or a faded blue floral pattern that swings as she moves. She's of medium height, robust, but not fat, with a face and arms full of freckles, dark blond hair, grayish blue eyes, and a generous mouth. She approaches, striding purposefully, and with a purposeful gesture grabs the nozzle in her left hand, turns the crank with her right, and fills his tank.

Then the dream jumps ahead. How he greets her and she him, the way they look at each other, what they say to each other, whether she invites him in for coffee or a beer, or if he asks whether he can come in, how it is that they go upstairs together to her bedroom—he has never filled in the details. He sees her and himself lying in the rumpled bed after they have made love, sees the walls, the floor, the wardrobe, and the dresser, all painted a pastel greenish blue, sees the iron bed frame and sunlight falling through the venetian blind, its wooden slats painted greenish blue as well, and casting bright stripes across the walls, floor, furniture, sheets, and their bodies. It is only an image, not a scene with plot and words, only color, light, shadow, the white of sheets and the shapes of their bodies. The dream doesn't pick up the thread of the story until evening.

He has parked his car next to the house, beside her little pickup. There is a roofed porch at the back of the house as well, then a couple of beds of tomatoes and melons, and a hothouse that she's built to keep out the sand and in which she grows all sorts of berries. Beyond that is the desert with a little scrub growing here and there and a dry wash, which carries water in the winter and has eaten three or four yards into the gravelly soil over the decades or centuries. She showed it to him when she took him out to the pump that draws water from a deep well. He's sitting on the porch now and watching the sky grow dark. He hears her bustling around in the kitchen. If a car comes, he'll get up, walk through the house, and pump gas. And when she turns on the kitchen light and it casts its glow through the open door onto the floor of the porch, he'll get up; he'll go to the front entry and switch on the light that stands between the two gas pumps to illuminate the area out front. He asks himself whether the light will shine into the bedroom all night, tonight and the next night and all the nights yet to come.

3

OFTEN THE dreams that stay with us are in contrast to the life we lead. The adventurer dreams of homecoming, the stay-at-home of setting out for distant lands and great deeds.

The dreamer of this dream led a peaceful life. Not a dull, conventional life—besides his native German, he

English and French, had had a career both at home and abroad, had stuck to his convictions even when they met opposition, had overcome crises and conflicts, and in his late fifties now was vital, successful, and sophisticated. He was always a little intense, whether at work or at home or on vacation. Not that he was rash or volatile when doing what had to be done. He was calm. But there was always a tension vibrating beneath his listening, his answers, and his work, the result of his concentration on the task and his impatience because doing something in reality never kept pace with the doing of it in his imagination. Sometimes the tension was a source of distress; sometimes, however, it was also like an energy, a power that gave him wings.

He was a man of charm. Whether working with people or things, he had an engagingly clumsy, absent-minded way about him. Because he knew that his clumsy, absent-minded behavior wasn't fair to either people or things, he would court their indulgence with a smile that nicely suited his face. It emphasized a certain vulnerability about the mouth and a melancholy about the eyes, and because in his request for indulgence there was never a promise of improvement, but only the confession of an incompetence, his smile was abashed and full of self-mockery. His wife constantly asked herself just how natural his charm was, whether his absent-mindedness and clumsiness were a way of flirting with life, whether his smile was put on, whether he knew that his vulnerability and melancholy awakened in others a desire to console him. She never figured it out. The fact was that his charm won him sympathy from doctors, policemen, secretaries and salesgirls, children and dogs, without his ever seeming to notice.

His charm no longer worked on her. At first she thought it had worn out—the way anything wears out when it's been around too long. But one day she realized that she was sick and tired of his charm. Sick and tired. She was on vacation with her husband in Rome, sitting with him in the Piazza Navona, and he patted a begging stray dog on the head with the same engagingly absent-minded gesture with which he sometimes patted her head, while wearing the same engagingly abashed smile that accompanied the gesture when it was meant for her. His charm was only a way of holding back and keeping his distance. It was a ritual by which her husband covered over the fact that he felt inconvenienced.

If she had criticized him, he wouldn't have understood her criticism. Their marriage was full of rituals, and that was the very reason for its success. Don't all good marriages live by their rituals?

His wife was a physician. She had always worked, even when their three children were small, and as they grew older she had moved into research and become a professor. Neither his nor her work had ever stood between them; they had both divided up their days so that despite all the lack of time there was still sacred time, time for their children and time for themselves. Even when it came to vacations, there were two weeks every year when they left the children with their nanny—who was trusted to watch over them at other times too—and took a trip together. All of this demanded a disciplined, ritualized management of time, leaving little room for spontaneity—they knew that, but they also knew that their friends' spontaneity left them not with more, but less time for doing things together. No, their life was a series of rational and soothing rituals.

Only the ritual of making love had been lost. He didn't know when and why. He could remember a morning when he woke up and saw his wife's puffy face in bed, smelled the acrid scent of her sweat, heard her whistling breathing, and was repelled. He also remembered his own dismay. How could he be suddenly repelled, when until now he had found her puffy face nuzzleable, that acrid scent exciting, and the whistle of her breathing amusing? Sometimes he had used it as a *cantus firmus* for a melody that he would whistle to awaken her. It wasn't on that morning, but sometime afterward that their lovemaking faded away. At some point neither of them made the first move anymore, though each would have been aroused to follow the other's first move. A little aroused, just enough for a second move, but not for the first.

Neither of them had moved out of their shared bedroom, however. She could have slept in her study and he in one of the children's empty rooms. But neither of them was prepared for such a rupture in their rituals of undressing, falling asleep, awaking, and getting up together. Not even she, who was more austere, more matter-of-fact and enterprising, though there was something shy about her, too. She didn't want to lose what was left of their rituals, either. She didn't want to lose their life together.

And yet one day it was all over. One day they were making preparations for their silver wedding anniversary—the guest list, hotel rooms for the guests, the dinner at the restaurant, the boat excursion. They looked at one another and knew that what they were doing made no sense. They had nothing to celebrate. They could have celebrated their fifteenth anniversary, maybe even their twentieth. But at some point since then, their love had fled, had evaporated, and even if it wasn't a lie to go on living as if they belonged together, the celebration would be a lie.

She was the one to say it, and he agreed immediately. They would forget the celebration. And having come to that decision, they were so relieved that they drank champagne and talked as they hadn't talked in a long time.

4

CAN YOU FALL in love with someone a second time? Don't you know the person too well? Doesn't falling in love presume that you don't know the other person, that he or she still has blank spaces onto which you can project your own desires? Or if the need is that great, is the power of projection so strong that your idealizations not only fill up the other person's blank spaces, but also superimpose themselves on the finished, brightly colored map of their identity? Or is there love without projection?

He asked himself these questions, but they were more amusing than annoying. What happened to him over the next few weeks, whether projection or experience, was lovely, and he enjoyed it. He enjoyed talking with his wife, making a date to meet her for a movie or a concert, and taking walks together again in the evening. It was spring. Sometimes he would pick her up at the institute—waiting for her not at the entrance, but fifty yards away at the street corner, because he liked to watch her walk toward him. She took long strides, hurrying as she approached, because his direct look bothered her. In her embarrassment, she pushed her hair behind her ear with her left hand and managed a timid, wry smile. He recognized the embarrassment of the young girl he had once fallen in love with. The way she carried herself and the way she walked had not changed, either, and just as they had back then, her breasts jiggled under her sweater with every step. He asked himself why he hadn't noticed it all these years. What pleasures he had deprived himself of! And what a fine thing that he had eyes in his head again. And that she had remained so beautiful. And that she was his wife.

But they still didn't make love. At first their bodies were foreign to each other. But even after they had grown used to each other again, they did not go beyond tender touching when they awoke, taking walks together, sitting across from one another at meals or beside each other at the movies. At first he thought making love would surely follow, and it would truly be lovely. Then he asked himself if it really would follow, if it really would be lovely, and if he and she really still wanted it. Or was he no longer able to make love? In those years when their marriage was burned out, there had been two nights with other women, one an interpreter and the other a colleague at work, both after lots of alcohol and with a following morning full of awkward strangeness—plus occasional moments of joyless masturbation, usually in hotels on business trips. Had he forgotten how to make the natural connections between love, desire, and sex? Had he become impotent? When he tried to masturbate to prove his virility, he had no success.

Or did he and his wife simply have to leave that to time? He told himself there was no reason for haste and that it could just as easily be a year as a month, week, or day until they made love again. But his feelings told him something else. He wanted to get the lovemaking behind them; again he was impatient, since here too doing it in reality didn't keep pace with doing it in his imagination. The older he grew the stronger his impatience became in general. An unfinished task that lay ahead of him upset him, even when he knew there would be no difficulty taking care of it. There was something unfinished and upsetting about anything that lay ahead of him—in the coming week or in the upcoming summer, in the purchase of a new car or in their children's visit at Easter. Even in their trip to America.

The idea had been his wife's. A second honeymoon—wasn't what they were going through like being newlyweds a second time? When they were young they had often dreamed of taking the train across Canada, from Quebec to Vancouver, then on to Seattle, and then driving down the coast to Los Angeles or San Diego. At first the trip had been too expensive, later too long for two weeks of vacation without the children, and the train trip and all that driving too boring with the children in tow. But now that they had vacations to themselves, couldn't they take four weeks, or five or six, couldn't they afford any sleeping car, any limousine—wasn't it high time to make their old dream a reality?

5

THEY LEFT in May. It was April weather in Quebec; it rained often but briefly, and between showers the clouds parted and the wet roofs sparkled in the sun. On the Ontario plain the train passed through green fields that came to an end only where sky and earth met, a world of green and blue. In the Rocky Mountains the train got stuck in a snowdrift during a blizzard, and it took all night before the snowplow arrived.

They made love that night. The rolling and swaying of the train had prepared their bodies, as a hot day or a warm bath can. During their stop in the middle of nowhere the heating was only partly functional, the blizzard howled around the train car, and cold seeped through the windows and floor of their compartment. They crept into the same bunk, laughed, shivered, hugged, and held each other tight until they were wrapped in a cocoon of warmth. Desire suddenly began to overwhelm him, and for fear that it would pass again, he was hasty and actually happy only when it was over. She woke him in the middle of the night and their lovemaking was like quiet breathing. He was awakened in the morning by the whistle of the locomotive greeting the approaching snowplow. He looked out of the window at the snow and sky, a world of blue and white. He was happy.

They stayed for a few days in Seattle. Their bed-and-breakfast on Queen Anne Hill was on a slope with a wide view of the city and sound. Between high-rises they could see a multilane freeway with a chain of cars that seldom broke—a mix of color by day and a string of headlights upon headlights and taillights upon taillights by night. Like a river, he thought, whose current moves downstream on one side and upstream on the other. Sometimes the sound of a siren found its way up to them, as a police car or an ambulance shooed the other cars to the side, and that first night, when he couldn't sleep, he stood up each time and stepped to the window to watch a vehicle with a flashing red and blue light on its roof forge its way ahead. Sometimes the sound of a horn found its way up to them, too, as a ship offered its greeting entering or leaving the harbor. They were container ships, their colorful cargo stacked high, surrounded by sailboats big and small, with billowing colorful sails. There was always a strong wind blowing.

When he couldn't sleep he would watch his wife sleep. He saw her years, her wrinkles, the sagging skin under her chin, her ears and eyes. The puffy face, the acrid scent, and the whistle of her breath no longer repelled him. Their last morning on the train, he had awakened her just as in the old days with his whistling, happily taken her face between his hands and felt it, and after they had made love, happily taken in the scent of love and sweat under the blanket. To think that he could awaken her again like that, that he still commanded and enjoyed the rituals of their love, that she had not forgotten or lost any of it. To think that their world was whole again!

He realized that their love had created a world that was more than the feeling they had for each other. Even when they had lost the feeling for each other, that world had been there. Its colors had faded to black and white, but the world had remained their world. They had lived in and from its orderly arrangements. And now it was in color again.

They made plans. That was her idea as well. Should they remodel the house? Instead of three children's rooms, wouldn't one suffice for their visits, which were becoming more and more infrequent, or for visits by grandchildren someday? Hadn't they always wanted one large room where he could read and write the book that he planned to write years before and still occasionally gathered material for? Shouldn't they learn to play tennis together, even if neither of them could ever become a good player? What about that offer of a six-month job in Brussels he had told her about—was that still open? Should she take a half year's leave so they could live in Brussels together? He took pleasure in her ideas and in her eagerness. He planned along with her. But actually he didn't want to change anything in either of their lives; he just didn't want to say it.

He didn't want to talk about his fear of unfinished business. He didn't know where it came from, what it meant, and why it kept growing the older he became. It lay behind his rejection of change—with every change, whatever was still unfinished became an even greater burden. But why? Because changes cost time, and time was running past and away from him faster and faster? Why was it running faster? Is there some ratio between time as we actually experience it and the time still left to us? Does time pass ever more quickly as we age because there is less time left, the way the second half of a vacation, with the end looming ahead, passes more quickly than the first? Or does it lie in our goals? Does time seem too slow in our early years because we are waiting impatiently to be successful at last, to enjoy prestige, to be rich, and does it rush past in later years, because there's nothing more to expect? Or do the days hurry past as the years add up because we already know each day's agenda, much as a path gets shorter and shorter the more often we take it? But if that was so, he should actually want change. Had life really become too short to squander it in changes? But he wasn't all that old!

She never noticed that what lay behind all his objections was a general rejection. But once when he proved especially stubborn about holding fast to some foolish objection, she asked him with an annoyed laugh what it was he actually wanted. To go on living the life of the last few years?

6

THEY RENTED a large car, a convertible with air-conditioning, a CD player, and all sorts of electronic gadgetry. They bought a big stack of CD's, ones they loved and others just hit-or-miss. When they reached the cape from where they could see the Pacific for the first time, his wife put on a Schubert symphony. He would have preferred to listen to the American station that played music from his student years. He would also have rather stayed in the car instead of climbing out with her into the rain and just standing there. But the symphony matched the rain, the gray sky, and the gray rolling waves, and he had the feeling he had no right to disturb his wife's production. She had been driving and found the little road that led to the beach. She had remembered that there was a sheet of blue plastic in the trunk and wrapped him and herself in it. They stood on the beach, smelled the sea, listened to Schubert, gulls, and rain on the plastic, and gazed at a piece of bright evening sky behind the rain clouds in the west. The air was cool, but damp and heavy.

After a while he couldn't take it under the plastic any longer, stood there hesitating in the rain for a moment, then walked across the sand and into the water. The water was cold, his wet shoes were heavy, his wet pants clung to his legs and belly. There was not a trace of the lightness that the body usually has in water, but he felt light, and slapped at the water and let the waves knock him over. His wife was still thrilled by his spontaneity as they lay in bed that evening. He was more startled and embarrassed.

They found a rhythm for their journey, which brought them about a hundred miles farther south each day. They frittered away the mornings, made frequent stops, visited national parks and vineyards, and walked for hours along the beach. In the evenings they would take whatever they found, sometimes a shabby motel by the highway—with large rooms, the smell of disinfectant, and a TV bolted to the wall at eye level—and sometimes a bed-and-breakfast in a residential area. They would both be tired by early evening. At least that's what they told one another as they lay there in bed with a book and a bottle of wine, and his eyes would grow heavy and he would turn out the light on his nightstand. When he woke up again around midnight one evening, though, she was still reading.

Sometimes he arranged it so that he would wait and watch her come toward him. He would have her let him out at a restaurant and wait by the door until she had parked the car and then walked from the parking lot across the road. Or he would run ahead on the beach, turn around and watch her moving toward him. It was always beautiful, watching her figure and the way she walked, but it left him sad at the same time.

7

THE COAST and the roads in Oregon were fogbound. In the morning they hoped the weather would be better by noon, and in the evening they put their hope in the next day. But fog lay over the road again, hung low in the forests, and enveloped the farms. If the map had not put a name to the towns they drove through, often just a few houses, they would have missed them. Sometimes they drove for an hour or two through forests without seeing a single house or meeting an oncoming car or passing one, either. They got out at one point and the sound of the idling engine bounced off the mass of trees on both sides of the road, stayed close without fading, but was simultaneously muted by the fog. They turned off the engine and there was not a sound to be heard, no creaking branches, no birds, no cars, no ocean.

With the last town well behind them and the next one still thirty miles up the road, a sign announced a gas station ahead. Then they were there—a large graveled area, two pumps, a lamp, and beyond the gravel a house blurry in the fog. He braked, turned onto the gravel, and stopped at one of the pumps. They waited. When he got out to go knock at the door, it opened and a woman stepped out. She walked across the gravel, said hi, grabbed the nozzle, turned the crank, and started filling the tank. She stood beside the car, holding the nozzle in her right hand, her left propped on her hip. She noticed that he hadn't taken his eyes off her.

"The nozzle's broken, so I have to stay here. But I'll clean your windshield in a sec."

"Isn't it lonely here?"

She gave him a puzzled, cautious look. She was no longer young and her caution was the caution of a woman who had got involved too often and been too often disappointed.

"The last town was twenty miles back and the next one's not for another thirty—isn't it a little . . . I mean, don't you feel lonely out here? Do you live alone?"

She saw the seriousness, the concentration, and the tenderness in his eyes, and smiled. But because she was not about to be enchanted by his eyes, there was mockery in her smile. He smiled back, happy and embarrassed by what he would have to say next.

"You're beautiful."

She blushed a little, though it was barely noticeable under all her freckles, and stopped smiling. Now she was looking at him seriously too. Beautiful? Her beauty had faded, and she knew it, even if she could still attract men, still arouse their desire and pride—and still scare them, too. She scrutinized his face.

"Yes, it's lonely, but I've gotten used to it. Besides . . ." She hesitated, looked down at the nozzle, looked back up—directly at him—her face really red now, and stood tall, defiantly confessing her longing. "Besides, I won't be alone forever."

She stayed like that for a moment—standing tall, blushing, eye to eye with him. The tank was full, she screwed the cap back on, stepped away from the car, and hung the nozzle on the pump. She bent down, took a sponge from a bucket, flipped the washers back, and cleaned the windshield. He watched her curiously eyeing his wife, who was reading the map spread over her knees and glanced up briefly to nod at the woman and smile at him, but then went back to her map.

He found it disconcerting to stand there beside her doing nothing while she worked. At the same time he liked looking at her, liked watching her. She wasn't wearing jeans with a checkered shirt or a faded blue dress, but dark blue overalls, the same color as the logo of the gas station, with a white T-shirt underneath. She was robust, but had a lightness about her. There was a grace to her movements, as if she enjoyed both the robustness and lightness of her body. One strap of her overalls slipped off her shoulder, and she pushed it back up with one finger; taken together, both touched him like some shared intimacy.

When she had finished cleaning the windows, he gave her money, and as she started back to the house to get change he walked with her. After a few steps together across the crunching gravel, she laid her hand on his arm.

"You don't have to come along. I'll bring the change out."

8

So HE STOOD there out in the drive, halfway between his car and her house. She went inside, the door closed behind her.

How long, he asked himself, do I have to decide? One minute? Two? How long will it take her to get the change? How organized is she? Does she have a cash register with all the bills and coins separated, so that she only has to take out a couple of coins here and a couple of bills there? Is she hurrying, or does she know I'd be happy to have a few minutes more?

He looked down at the ground in front of him and

saw that the gravel was wet from the fog. He turned a piece over with the tip of his shoe; he wanted to know if the gravel was wet underneath, and it was. He had taught his staff that thinking and deciding are two different things, that thinking doesn't necessarily result in the right decision, or any decision at all, but instead can make a decision so complicated and difficult that it can paralyze decision making. Thinking requires time, deciding requires courage, that's what he used to say, and he knew that what he lacked now was not time to think but the courage to decide. He also knew that life keeps an account of both the decisions we don't make and those we do. If he were to decide not to remain here, then he would drive on, even if he had not made a decision to drive on. Stay here—what should I say to her? Should I ask if I can stay? What would she answer? Wouldn't she have to say no, even if she wanted to say yes, because she had to refuse the responsibility my question imposed on her? When she steps out the door again, I'll have to be standing here with my suitcase and my bag, and the car will have to be gone. But what if she won't have me? Or if she wants me now, but tires of me later? Or if later I don't want to stay any more? No, that's not how it'll be. If we want each other now, then we'll want each other forever.

He walked toward the car. He wanted to tell his wife that they had made a mistake, that they couldn't make their marriage whole again, even if they wanted. That there had always been a sadness in his joy these last weeks, and that he didn't want to live with that sadness any longer. That he knew he was crazy to risk every-thing for this woman he didn't know and who didn't know him. That he would rather be crazy than stay reasonable and sad.

When he was only a few steps away from the car, his wife looked up. She looked at him, leaned across the driver's seat, rolled down the window, and called out something to him. He didn't understand. She repeated that she had found the big dunes on the map. At breakfast they had remembered seeing pictures somewhere of big dunes, and had been looking for them on the map with no success. She had found them now. It wasn't that far, and they'd make it by evening. She was beaming.

The joy she took in little things—how often she had surprised him with that and made him happy. And the trust with which she had shared her joy – it was a child's trust, full of the expectation that other people are good, will be delighted by good things, and will respond with kindness. He hadn't seen his wife like this for years, only in the last few weeks had her trust come back.

He saw her joy. It welcomed and embraced him. Was he done? Could they drive off?

He nodded, half-walked, half-ran, climbed into the car, and turned on the engine. He drove off without looking back.

9

HIS WIFE told him about how she had found the dunes on the map, and why they hadn't found them that morning. Told him when they would arrive that evening and where they would be able to stay. How far they needed to travel the next day. How high the dunes were.

After a while she noticed that something was wrong. He was driving slowly, staring attentively into the fog, responding to what she said with an occasional grunt of agreement or encouragement—if he didn't want to speak, that was all right, but not those lips pressed tightly together and the tension in his cheeks. She asked him what was wrong. Was it something about the engine or the tires or the way the car was handling? Something about the fog or the road? Or something else? Her questions were casual at first, but when he didn't answer, they began to betray her worry. Wasn't he feeling well? Was he in pain? When he pulled over to the grassy shoulder and stopped, she was certain that it was his heart or some circulatory problem. He sat there frozen, his hands on the wheel, gazing straight ahead.

"I'll be fine," he said, and was about to go on to say that he just needed a moment, but the words had released the strain that had kept his lips tight, his cheek muscles tense, and the tears back. He hadn't wept for decades. He tried to choke back the sobs, but his choking turned into a whimper and the whimper into a howl. He made a motion with his arms that was meant as an apology, an attempt to explain that it had just come over him, that he didn't want to cry but couldn't help it. But then the urge to apologize and explain was washed away in a flood of tears, and he simply sat there, his hands in his lap, his head drooping, his body shaking, and howled. She took him in her arms, but he didn't yield to her embrace, just continued to sit there as before. When the weeping wouldn't stop, she decided to find a hotel in the nearest town and maybe call a doctor. She was about to try to lift him and push him across to the other seat, but he slid over on his own.

She drove off. He went on weeping. He wept for his dream, for what life had offered him and how he had resisted or failed it, for what was irretrievable and irreplaceable. Nothing returned, nothing could be repeated. He wept for not wanting what he wanted more passionately and for often not knowing what it was he wanted. He wept for what had been difficult and bad about his marriage, but also for what had been beautiful in it. He wept for the disappointments they had inflicted on themselves and for the hopes and expectations they had shared these last weeks. Not a thought crossed his mind that didn't have its sad, painful side, even if it was only the transience of all things beautiful and happy. Love, their marriage when it had been good, the good years with their children, the rewards of his job, his enthusiasm for books and music—it was all gone. His memory presented image after image to his inner eye, but before he could examine an image it was stamped in fat letters enclosed in a fat circle: Gone.

Gone? It was not simply gone, hadn't just slipped away behind his back without his doing anything. He himself was destroying the world that their love had created. And from now on that world would cease to exist— not even a black-and-white world instead of color, but simply no world at all.

He had no tears left. He was exhausted and empty. It dawned on him that he had been weeping for his marriage as if it were gone for good, for his wife as if he had lost her.

She looked across to him and smiled at him. "Well?"

They had passed a sign with the name of a town, its population, and height above sea level. A few hundred people, he thought, and already a little town. It lies only a few feet above the sea; the sea must be very near, even if you can't see it for the fog.

"Would you stop, please?"

She pulled over to the shoulder and stopped. Now, he thought, now. "I'm going to get out. I'm not going any farther. I know that I'm behaving impossibly. I should have known better. But I don't really know how I could have known any better. We're struggling to put things back together again. But we can't and I don't want to live with the shattered pieces. I just want to try one more time."

"What? What do you want to try?"

"Life, love, a new beginning, everything in fact." Under her startled, wounded gaze, it all sounded childish to him, too. What would he do, what would he do here, how would he live, what would become of his life back home—if she were to ask he would be unable to give her any answers.

"Let's drive to the dunes. You can still run away. I can't hold you. Let's talk, once you're out of your hole. Maybe you're right, maybe we haven't really got a good hold on what we did or didn't have together. Then we'll get it." She had her hand on his knee. "Okay?"

She was right. Couldn't they at least drive to the town by the dunes and talk it all through? Or couldn't he at least tell her just to leave him here and drive on, that he needed a couple of days to himself and would join her, for the flight back at the latest? And didn't he have to tell his wife about his dream and about the woman at the gas station? Wouldn't that be the honest thing to do?

"I can only run away." He got out. "Would you open the trunk?"

She shook her head.

He got out, walked around the car, opened the door on her side, and pulled the little lever between the door and the seat. The trunk lid sprang open. He took out his suitcase and his bag and set them on the ground. Then he slammed the trunk and walked back to her door. It was still open. His wife looked up at him. He gently, calmly closed the door, but it felt as if he were slamming it in her face. She went on looking up at him. He picked up his suitcase and his bag and started walking. He took a step and didn't know if he could take another, and once he had done it, if he could take another, and another. If he stopped, he would have to turn around, turn back, and get into the car. And if she didn't drive away soon, he could not go on. Drive, he begged, drive.

Then she turned on the ignition and drove away. He didn't turn around until he could no longer hear the car. By then, the fog had swallowed it up.

10

HE FOUND a motel and made a deal for a cheap rate for the next whole month. He found a restaurant with a counter, Formica tables, plastic benches, and a jukebox. He drank a lot, was absurdly cheerful at some moments, but could have started weeping again at others, if he hadn't told himself that he had wept enough for one day. It was the only restaurant in town, and he kept one ear cocked the whole evening, waiting for a car to pull up, for someone to get out—and for the footsteps on the gravel to be his wife's. His waiting was full of longing and full of fear.

The next morning he walked to the sea. Once again fog hung over the beach, the sky and sea were gray, and the air was warm, damp, and muffled. He had the feeling he had an infinite amount of time.

ABOUT THE TRANSLATOR

———

JOHN E. WOODS is the distinguished translator of many books——most notably Arno Schmidt's *Evening Edge in Gold*, for which he won both the American Book Award for translation and the PEN Translation Prize in 1981; Patrick Süskind's *Perfume*, for which he again won the PEN Translation Prize, in 1987; Christoph Ransmayr's *The Terrors of Ice and Darkness*, *The Last World* (for which he was awarded the Schlegel–Tieck Prize in 1991), and *The Dog King*; Thomas Mann's *Buddenbrooks*, *The Magic Mountain* (for which he was awarded the Helen and Kurt Wolff Prize in 1996), and *Doctor Faustus*; Ingo Schulze's *33 Moments of Happiness* and *Simple Stories*; Jan Philip Reemtsma's *More Than a Champion*; and *The Good Man of Nanking: The Diaries of John Rabe*. He lives in San Diego, California.